Promise in a Dream

by

Stella Jayne Phillips

Creekside Dreams, Book 2

Promise in a Dream

Cover Art by *Jennifer Greeff*

The Wild Rose Press, Inc.
PO Box 708
Adams Basin, NY 14410-0708
Visit us at www.thewildrosepress.com

Publishing History
First Fantasy Rose Edition, 2020
Trade Paperback ISBN 978-1-5092-3293-2
Digital ISBN 978-1-5092-3294-9

Creekside Dreams, Book 2
Published in the United States of America

Dedication

Dedicated to Christina, Sabrina, and Penny,
who read various versions of my works in progress,
and Melanie Billings, editor, for helping me every step.
Promise in a Dream was inspired by Cora and Annie,
great-grandmothers who chose love.

Chapter One

The Historic Palace Hotel combines the comfort of home with royal service. Palace guests begin the day with an excellent opportunity to plan the day's activities or make new friends while they enjoy complimentary breakfast items made on the premises and acquired from local businesses. Evening finds the lobby transformed into an intimate lounge serving wine and beer, many of the offered libations locally sourced. Built in 1917 by the original innkeeper, Mrs. Victoria Wyatt, The Palace Hotel enjoys a reputation for comfort and excellence. Oh, and did we forget to mention the ghost?

~from: Creekside Chamber of
Commerce.com/visitor information
****

Cold. Cold wind, cold cheeks, cold nose, cold knees. Cold, Andrea Hamilton leaned against her best friend's older brother James, grateful for their locked arms. His large body blocked some of the wind sneaking under her long, velvet maternity dress, freezing everything in its path. Who knew the temperature in Creekside could drop twenty degrees in the space of her best friend's morning wedding. With each step, her silver flats slipped on the icy sidewalk, James' strong arm, looped through hers, kept her upright. Using his free hand James unwrapped his scarf, loosely winding it around her neck. She nuzzled the warm wool, sniffed the hint of his aftershave. "Thanks," she mumbled through the scarf, her breath a white puff. The leather soles of her beautiful flats slid. James grabbed her with his free arm, locking her against his body. Andrea's heart raced. With James for stability, she straightened and planted both feet firmly on the sidewalk. "Thanks, again."

"No problem." His hold relaxed though he didn't let go.

Embarrassed, she struggled to stay upright on the short walk from Nikki's wedding reception to The Palace; Andrea watched her barely visible feet on the icy sidewalk. At seven months pregnant, her biggest fear was falling. Embarrassed, weird thought considering she'd grown up with James. Spent more of her childhood with his mother and sister than with her own parents. Too bad her feelings changed somewhere in the last few months, but his hadn't. She'd always be his baby sister's friend, not Andrea grown-up, not Andrea a woman he'd date. Anyway, her feelings were just hormones. Who would want a woman whose stomach arrived five minutes before her body, whose feet have disappeared?

"You all right?" he asked as they dodged a patch of ice on the sidewalk.

"Yep. Just cold." When they reached the sidewalk in front of The Palace, Andrea looked up at Room 15. The lace curtain shifted; Victoria, the hotel's resident spirit, stood at the window, her hand on the glass. Carefully, they climbed the steps to the hotel's front door. James pulled the door open; heat blasted and Bing Crosby admitted he was "Swinging on a Star." Andrea let warmth and Bing's mellow voice surround her. She unwrapped the scarf and handed it to James.

James motioned with one hand. "Turn around. I'll help you with your coat." She complied. He placed his hands on her shoulders, and when she released the button the heavy garment slid down her arms in a gentle caress.

"Thanks, I'll take it." She gazed into his hazel eyes. Hazel eyes filled with concern and compassion. No sign of desire, no sign of passion, no sign of attraction. Of course not. Hormones caused this sudden desire, the aching wanting, just her crazy pregnancy hormones. He ambled beside her to Room 11. "Great catch, by the way. Thanks for stopping my fall."

"Anytime. I'll walk you to the after party, okay?"

"Thanks." She stepped into her room and closed the door softly behind her. She heard his footsteps returning to the lobby, then the sound of his dash up the stair to the attic. In the shadowy room, she waited on the threshold. No sign of Victoria. She discovered her first few days Victoria's spirit haunted Room 11, usually appearing beside one of the two windows. If Andrea entered quietly and waited to turn on the lights, she sometimes caught a glimpse of The Palace's famous ghost. Not today. She kicked off the impractical silver flats and changed into fleece-lined leggings, knee-high socks, and a long, loose blue sweater. She glanced in the mirror; well, it used to be loose. A bottle of water in one hand and a granola bar without chocolate in the other, she snuggled into the wing back chair, pulled up the tiny ottoman, and settled, letting the room's warmth ease her tension. She missed chocolate, coffee, wine, and someone's arms around her in the night. Funny, she didn't miss Laurence. Snack finished, she lay down on the bed for a short nap. Curled on her left side, a pillow between her knees, she pulled a blanket over her shoulder and drifted off.

Knocking startled her from a familiar dream, and she yanked open the door.

"Hey, did I wake you?" James asked.

She silently groaned. "Sorry, I overslept. Can you wait ten minutes?"

"No problem. Take as long as you need. I'll be in the library."

With mumbled thanks, she closed the door. She glanced at her reflection in the mirror. "Ugh." Her curly hair stood up on one side and was flat on the other; a giant wrinkle marred her red cheek—a result of a fold in the pillowcase. This morning's carefully applied mascara now rimmed her dark eyes like a raccoon. Before pregnancy, she relished a reputation for being on time and always pulled together. The only meaningful time now was the countdown to her due date. Two months to go and her once stylish maternity clothes pulled tight. She was heartily bored with everything she could still wear except for the emerald dress she wore this morning to Nikki's wedding. Fifteen minutes later, she locked her door and met James in the library.

Early dark greeted them, and they strolled to Wellington's for the After Wedding Party. Last to arrive, they sat across from each other.

Wine glass in hand, Nikki rose from her chair and the room quieted. "Welcome to the after party. Thank you again for joining us. Your presence added so much to our joy. To friends and family." They lifted their glasses.

A black sky and drifting snowflakes greeted them when James and Andrea walked toward The Palace after the dinner party. "Ready to go in?" James' deep voice rumbled in her ear.

"Yep." He took her arm, guided her up the steps, and ushered her through the front door. Warmth surrounded her and James helped her with her coat. They strolled toward her room, and in the shadows Victoria stood at the door of Room 11, her hand raised to knock. Her arm dropped and the spirit glided silently through the closed door. Andrea glanced at James. He gave no indication he'd seen Victoria. "What's on your agenda tomorrow?"

"Moving Mitch and Colin's stuff to the basement," he admitted as he took her key and tapped it on the electronic lock. "Setting up their room in the hotel. "Good night, Andrea." James stepped back.

"Good night." Andrea stepped inside and closed the door. She waited in the shadowy room. No sign of Victoria. Whom did Victoria visit in Room 11?

****

James listened for the snick of the lock. He glanced toward the hotel's back door. Victoria's spirit hovered beside the door; a large dog stood alert beside her. Victoria gazed directly into James' eyes, lifted one eyebrow, and a dimple flashed in her cheek. Dog and woman disappeared. James strolled to the lobby. Nikki claimed Victoria pushed her toward marrying Alex. Reminded her life was more than running a business or parenting Sam. Every relationship mattered. What did their resident spirit want from him? He grabbed a glass of red wine from the bartender and ambled to the library. Settled in his favorite chair before the electric fire, he picked up a paperback and tried to focus on the mystery he started days ago. Instead, Andrea's smile, the feel of her body when he held her, steadied her, haunted him. He heard the patter of running feet, and four-year-old Sam dashed into the library. A few minutes later, Patrick plopped down on the loveseat in the library, a glass of red wine in his hand.

"What took you so long?" James asked.

"I walked Beth and company home. Colin's pretty excited about moving to the hotel."

"What about Mitch?"

"Not so much." Patrick shook his head, a slight frown on his face. "Nikki glowed all day today. I hope she can hang onto that after the honeymoon."

"She chose a tough road, running a hotel, raising three boys, marrying a cop. Where's Scott?"

"Casey's house." Patrick sipped his wine. "This summer seems to have changed things between Scott and Casey."

James lifted an eyebrow and gazed at his older brother. "Are you worried?"

"Yeah, but Scott keeps saying 'Don't worry, dad. We won't do anything stupid.' My definition of stupid and his may be different."

"Hey, you had the same girlfriend all through college. Scott starts college in the fall."

"Yeah, and look how my marriage turned out. Nikki married her high school boyfriend and their relationship ended in disaster."

"So, you don't plan to marry again?" James asked as he set his glass on the table.

"No plans either way but haven't found anyone

6

interesting enough yet."

"Do you think we're like Dad? Would one woman never be enough?"

"Absolutely not. No way would either of us try balancing two families at the same time."

"So why are neither of us married? I thought by now I would be."

"Don't know what your excuse is but I tried marriage. Took me awhile to figure out why I failed," Patrick admitted. "Too many assumptions."

"Assumptions? About Amy, or marriage?"

"Both. I assumed Amy and I agreed on the purpose of marriage. You know, build a family, grow old together."

"Our parents couldn't make grow old together work, but Amy's were married a long time when her mom died, right?"

"Yep. Twenty-five years. I assumed when Amy said she wanted to marry she'd be faithful."

"Ouch," James commented. "Sorry about that. Didn't realize she wasn't."

"Just one more way I failed as a husband." Patrick sipped his wine. "I assumed when she got pregnant she wanted to be a mother. Found out by the time Scott was a year old she wanted a child because her friends had children. The idea of caring for Scott scared her to death, and motherhood bored her." Patrick set his glass on the table. "What about you?"

"I assumed I'd meet someone, fall in love, and marry. Easy." James finished his wine. "I've met a number of special someones but no one I could live with forever. I'd hate myself if I disappointed a woman who loved me. Guess that's why I don't hang around long enough to find out if they could." He rose. "I'm hitting the sack."

Patrick stood. "Me too. After breakfast, we'll move." They climbed the stairs to the attic.

James flipped the light on in his room and tossed the key on the table inside the door. The room contained a small fridge, microwave, coffee maker, flat screen TV, two comfortable chairs, and a king size bed. No spirits tonight. Victoria, RJ, and Smokey must be somewhere else in the hotel, or wherever spirits go when they're not haunting. Patrick at least tried marriage, and today Nikki married for the second time. James pulled away before things got serious or chose women not interested in forever. How could he trust love would last? His father claimed to love mom but had a second family in Tucson almost from the beginning. Not love. Love didn't cause the hurt his mom felt when she found out. He was barely six, but he remembered her tears. When he and Patrick hit adolescence, she not only explained the facts of life but described exactly how women should be treated, everything from the importance of honesty to asking politely and accepting a no.

Wearing sweatpants, he slid into bed, tumbled into sleep. Just before dawn, he woke to the sound of a child's laughter. Early winter light peeked through the curtain. In a shadowy corner stood Victoria, beside her a man, his arm around her shoulder. They smiled as a young boy and a large dog tumbled across the floor; the boy's laughter warmed the room. James pushed himself up. The vision disappeared. The faint sound of laughter and the familiar scent of lavender drifted through the room. Victoria created a happy home for her child in a hotel. Why didn't Arthur Welles mention RJ's father in the book about Victoria and the hotel? Was he a part-time love, like James' father?

****

Winter sun glinted through the windows, and the familiar scents of coffee and cinnamon surrounded James when he ambled into a lobby buzzing with conversation. Andrea's abundant curls, pulled away from her face with a headband, framed her bright eyes. A peach color stained her lips. He shook himself away from thoughts of her lips. Where had those thoughts come from? Full plate and mug of coffee in hand, James plopped into a chair beside Andrea. "Morning." The others chorused a response. "What's our plan?"

"Fill Nikki's truck with Colin and Mitch's stuff. Haul everything to the basement apartment, repeat if necessary," answered Patrick.

"Let's do it." He pulled Nikki's truck key out of his pocket.

Two hours and what felt like at least a hundred trips down the stairs, James, Patrick, and Scott stood in the basement apartment surrounded by furniture and clothes.

"What now?" asked Scott. "We can't leave their room like this."

"No," Patrick answered. "You remember what their room looked like at Beth's?"

"Not really; they'd already taken the beds apart when we got there."

"Let's arrange the beds and stuff over there, away from the kitchen. We can probably find a little table in the storage room and a couple of chairs," James suggested. Finished, they admired their work. "Looks good, just needs a TV, a couple of comfortable chairs and it's a man cave."

"Except they're boys and we don't dare give them a TV," answered Patrick.

"Yeah. Just like you wouldn't put a TV in my room," Scott commented and dashed upstairs. Patrick stopped at the owner's suite and offered Megan and Sam lunch. James knocked on Andrea's door. Sam walked between Patrick and Megan, James took Andrea's arm, and they headed toward Rosa's. They strolled the sidewalks, expertly dodging clumps of tourists and wet patches. Yesterday's bitter cold and wind gave way to today's blue sky, the winter wind replaced by a gentle chill breeze. Laughter and the hum of conversation surrounded them.

"Did you get everything put away in the basement?" Andrea asked as they walked away from the busy square toward Rosa's.

"We did. What were you up to this morning?"

"Working. Exactly what I'll be doing this afternoon, after a nap."

"Nap? So you nap every day?"

"Pretty much. The doctor says I have to put my feet up at least thirty minutes a day, and I always fall asleep."

"That's what happened yesterday? Baby put you to sleep?"

"Yeah, and I overslept." Andrea grimaced remembering what she looked like when he knocked on the door. "What are your plans for the rest of the week now you've moved Mitch and Colin?"

"I'm running The Palace with a little help from Scott, Patrick, and Eric."

"Well, if you need my help just let me know. I don't haul bags up and down the stairs but I'm excellent at front desk and bartending."

"Might take you up on that." Seated at a round table at Rosa's, Sam regaled them with stories of baby Zoe. Every time he left the room, Kassie and Neil's daughter shouted his name, "Sam, Sam, Sam." The minute he returned she'd laugh. When he sat down, she climbed all over him. James watched Andrea's face light up at Sam's stories of the demanding baby Zoe. He didn't remember her laughing when he'd seen her with Laurence. No surprise. Laurence had a high opinion of himself and a low opinion of everyone else. He'd dated a few women like Laurence but none of them lasted. Too high maintenance. Maybe Laurence was different in private, but he doubted it.

****

Nikki and Alex returned to The Palace after retrieving Mitch and Colin from Windsong Ranch on New Year's Eve. Nikki wrapped James then Patrick in a bear hug. She knelt and Sam rushed into her arms. "Whoa, did you grow while I was gone?"

"Aunt Nikki, you always say that."

"Let's check out Mitch and Colin's room." They trooped down the basement steps. Nikki opened the door and backed up. "You two go first. It's now officially your space."

Holding Sam's hand, Alex's arm around her shoulder, Nikki watched her stepsons examine their new room. The basement included a full bath, small kitchen, wood floor, and door separating the apartment from the laundry area and the storage room. Mitch said nothing; a frown marred his handsome, young face.

Colin stood in the empty space, originally intended as a sitting area. "Cool, all we need is a couple of chairs and a TV. So Dad, when do we get them?"

Alex lifted an eyebrow. "You buying?" Colin shrugged. James, Scott, and Patrick laughed.

****

Snuggled beneath warm blankets, Nikki curled against Alex, using his shoulder for a pillow. "Alex, Mitch is unhappy. He didn't like their room," she whispered against his chest.

"Angry more than unhappy." Alex pulled her tight against him, finding comfort in her warmth.

"Did we do the right thing? Should we have moved in with Beth?"

"No. I'm forty. Don't you think it was time to leave Mom?"

"Time for you? Definitely. Maybe not for Mitch. Did you talk to him about the move? Was he okay with it?"

"I tried. Mitch doesn't do change, but I do. Come on, sweet wife." He reached under her and settled her across his chest. "See, this is a good change." He placed his lips against hers, slowly deepening the kiss. His hands roamed her body. She moaned. They came together, lovers familiar and new. Later, Nikki curled against her husband and drifted into sleep.

Alex felt her body totally relax, her even breathing against his skin. Sleep eluded him; instead, his conversation with Mitch when the wedding date was chosen haunted him. When he explained the wedding would take place on Boxing Day, Mitch asked "Why?"

"Why Boxing Day?"

"Why marry her? You're sleeping with her. You're

at the hotel all the time."

"We're engaged, but you sound surprised we're marrying."

"I don't get it. She's got a kid. You have us. We don't need any more kids."

"It's not about more kids, Mitch. Nikki and I want to be together, build a future together. Getting married is just the beginning."

"It's stupid." Mitch stomped out the kitchen door and pounded up the steps to his bedroom.

Married one week, Alex held his beautiful young wife in his arms and worried. Parenting didn't come with a manual and neither did marriage. How could he fix this? No answers appeared, and he drifted into sleep.

****

Just before dawn, Nikki woke to the shushing sound of a rocker on a wood floor. In the shadowy corner of the room, Victoria rocked, a baby wrapped in a yellow blanket held in her arms. The shadow of a man stood in the corner. Victoria hummed a quiet lullaby, made eye contact with Nikki, and then disappeared, leaving behind the echo of a lullaby and the drifting scent of lavender. Nikki closed her eyes. Victoria's appearance reminded her the time had come to share her news with Alex. She touched her still flat belly. They were barely pulling together their blended family, and now there loomed the possibility of adding one more. Would Mitch and Colin accept another child? Another change? In his sleep, Alex pulled her against his warm body. His even breathing and steady heartbeat comforted her. She drifted back to sleep, her last thought, whatever happened next they'd face together.

Chapter Two

****

From her perch behind the front desk, Andrea hummed along with the Beach Boys "Warmth of the Sun" and admired the sun's reflection on the sparkling lobby windows. The buzz of conversation and aroma of coffee surrounded her. A mug of peppermint tea, its scent settling her indigestion, sat cooling beside the open laptop as she checked reservations and scheduled checkouts. Andrea clicked print for the list of checkouts, and the hotel's cell phone rang. "Good morning, Palace Hotel. How may I help you?"

"Good morning, Andrea," James replied. "You're on phones this morning?"

Andrea wondered if Nikki turned her personal cell phone off when she lay down. James rarely called on the hotel's phone. "I'm filling in for Nik. Eric's handling breakfast, so I offered to take the phone and desk so Nik could sleep in."

"Nik sleeping in. Is she okay?" James asked, concern clear in his voice.

Andrea regretted mentioning the sleeping in. "She's okay, just really tired. Should I have her call you back?"

"No, just tell her I'm coming up Friday night."

"I'll see you Friday, then." She should be happy to see James, but Andrea knew Nikki wasn't going to be happy when she realized he was checking on her, again.

Distracted by a steady stream of checkouts and phone reservations, Eric's announcement he was leaving caught Andrea by surprise. With the lobby finally empty, she grabbed the hotel cell phone and, to Garth Brooks' declaration of "Friends in Low Places," sauntered down the hallway toward Nikki's suite. Andrea raised her hand to knock and Nikki pulled open the door. "Feeling better?"

"Much, thanks," Nikki answered. "Didn't mean to startle you. Thanks for helping this morning."

"No problem." *Might as well let her know.* "James is coming up Friday."

"Why?"

"He didn't say. I put him in the attic, okay?" Andrea handed Nikki the hotel phone.

"Yeah. The attic is his favorite room." She slipped the phone in her pocket. "I'm headed to the basement. Let me know if you need anything."

Andrea watched her friend walk away.

15

At the end of the hallway, Victoria held the hand of a young boy. Victoria focused first on Nikki then on Andrea. The ghost winked and then vanished. *Yeah, Victoria, I think you're right. Both of us are pregnant, but only one of us is admitting it.*

****

Settled at the desk in Room 11, her feet propped on a tiny footstool, Andrea focused on her laptop and puzzled her way through a client's confusing email. Thoughts of James tried to sneak in, but she pushed them away. Soon enough she'd deal with her ridiculous attraction. Finished for the day, she closed her laptop, grabbed her coat, and headed toward the lobby. A walk in the winter sunshine sounded good. "Hey, Nik. You okay?" Andrea asked. Nikki sat behind her desk. An open laptop rested on the desk but Nikki stared off into space.

"Fine." Nikki shook her head and asked, "Where are you off to?"

"My daily walk. Want me to take Georgie?" Andrea glanced around the office looking for the tiny white dog.

"Georgie has too much social life. She's at Catherine's on a playdate with Belle and Ariel."

"I'm sure a playdate is more fun than a pregnant lady walk," Andrea admitted. "Is Catherine using well-trained Georgie to improve the puppies' behavior?"

Nikki shut down the laptop. "That's the theory anyway. Georgie is the pack leader because she's an adult. The puppies are supposed to mimic her good behavior."

"Is it working? Last time I saw Belle and Ariel they were jumping all over Hope and Lily."

Nikki shrugged. "Too soon to tell. If nothing else, being with Georgie will socialize them." Nikki came around the desk and pulled a leather jacket off the coat rack. "If you'll wait a few minutes, I'll walk with you."

Across the veranda, down the steps they walked, turning left onto Beatrice Street under a crystal blue sky. "Do you suppose Chance spends as much time with Catherine as his puppy does?" Andrea asked.

"Probably more. The first time he spotted Catherine in the lobby, he looked like he'd been hit by lightning." They dodged clumps of tourists on the sidewalk. "Before we could blink, he bought Sanders House, right next door to Catherine. If he wasn't such a sweetheart, I'd be worried about him as a stalker." Tourists strolled the sidewalks around the square, stopping in small clumps to window shop. "Let's go to Serendipity. Casey framed some of her drawings yesterday."

"Good idea. At least we know we'll be surrounded by love." Would James ever look at her the way Chance looked at Catherine? It was too late for love at first sight; they'd seen each other for the first time when she was five and James eleven. "Plus Chance painted the Valentine's window for Serendipity a couple of days ago."

They crossed the street and stopped in front of Serendipity. Lit by winter sunshine the Hickory Building's front window glowed with hearts in every shade of red and pink. The barest of outlines suggested some hearts hidden within people hurrying across the square while other hearts rode proudly on sleeves belonging to laughing men and women. In one corner, beside the gazebo, Matthew and Georgia Lea, the

Hickory Building's resident ghosts, held each other in a passionate embrace. Lounging on a cloud, Cupid, his bow at the ready, took aim, a smirk on his face.

"Young love. You probably remember the feeling," Andrea quipped.

"Very well," Nikki agreed and gestured toward a drawing of a family sitting on a blanket on the grass. The man bore a striking resemblance to Chance Pagent, the woman, shown in profile, could be Catherine. "I only hope they find a happier ending than I did."

"Nik, this time you'll find a happy ending. Right?" Barely visible at one side of the window, a couple stood on The Palace's front veranda. His arm rested on her shoulder, her arm circled his waist. Though their features were indistinct, Andrea recognized Alex and Nikki.

"Oh, I'm happy."

"But scared. When's the baby due?"

"How did you know?" Nikki asked.

"Clues. At the wedding, you toasted with a wine glass but never drank the wine. Same thing with the after party. You're exhausted and a little gray in the morning but fine by noon. Plus, I've known you since kindergarten. Does Alex know?"

"I haven't said anything." She pulled open the door. "You're right, I'm afraid."

They entered Serendipity. Standing at the loft railing, Georgia and Matthew embraced. The lovers stepped back, still holding hands. Their lips met; they dissolved. Nikki commented, "Someone's having a lovely day."

"Sad when spirits have a better love life than I do," Andrea admitted.

"Good afternoon, ladies." Ainsley strolled toward them. "How may I help you today?"

"We're here to see Casey's new drawings," Andrea answered. "Scott claims they're the best yet."

"Excellent. They're throughout the store so I'll let you wander." Ainsley stepped back. "Did you also come for the blanket?"

"Blanket?" Nikki asked. "So my secret's no longer a secret. How did you know?"

"Would you believe a spirit told me?" Ainsley quipped.

"Ainsley, after two years living in a haunted hotel, I'd believe anything."

Andrea and Nikki wandered through the shop and admired Casey's drawings. When they returned to the front of store, Ainsley sat in the rocking chair embroidering a yellow blanket. "What did you think?" she asked.

"If I had unlimited funds I'd buy one for every guest room. Instead, I'll think about buying two, one for each attic room. Unfortunately I already spent my decorating budget for this month on your brother's painting," Nikki answered.

"The Palace needed Chance's painting. Are you ready to look at blankets?" Ainsley moved to another chair, offering Nikki the rocker. An hour later Andrea and Nikki left Serendipity. Nikki held a Serendipity gift bag in one hand, her other arm looped with Andrea's. Folded inside the bag was the pale green blanket, edges adorned with dancing baby tigers. In the center, a momma tiger stood guard over her baby, her mate standing beside her.

"Your secret's no longer a secret. When will you

tell Alex?" Andrea asked as they ambled toward the hotel.

They crossed the street. "Since I'd rather he heard the news from me, tonight. He probably won't be home until late."

"You could leave the blanket out." They crossed the square. "Although, I don't know if he's any good at taking hints."

"No, I can do this. I'm just going to give it to him straight. We're still sorting out combining our families. The boys haven't really adjusted to having a stepmother, and before the year is out, they'll have another sibling."

"Nikki, you want this baby, right?"

"Absolutely!"

"So what's the problem? You and Alex love each other, and you're married. You own a hotel, so there's always room for one more." She gently knocked shoulders with Nikki. "You were engaged for six months, so it's not like you agreed to marry because of the pregnancy."

Nikki pulled open the hotel's front door. The hum of conversation blended with Gordon Lightfoot crooning "Sundown," and warmth surrounded them. They waved to Eric at the front desk and strolled to Nikki's sitting room. Returning her jacket to the coat rack, Nikki turned to Andrea. "But what if it happens again? What if I lose this baby too? If I fall apart, will Alex leave?"

"Oh Nik, you and Aaron were barely twenty-one." Andrea wrapped her best friend in a hug. "You're thirty-three, older, wiser, and so much stronger. Not only did you come back stronger from your loss and the divorce, you built yourself a new life, and then put your life on hold to care for your mom. Now, here you are the successful innkeeper, Sam's guardian, stepmother, and Alex's wife. You'll manage whatever happens."

****

The hotel's back door latched with an audible click when Alex entered at eleven o'clock. The hallway lights cast shadows between the doors; he heard a door close on the second floor and idly wondered how full they were tonight. Placing his key against the electronic lock, he opened the door to the basement stairs and descended. At the door to his sons' room, he paused. How many times in their young lives had he opened their door and watched them sleep? He'd spent so much of their childhood working nights and weekends, he'd missed their days. Now those days filled with activities that excluded him, sports, school, the ranch, and their friends.

Mitch stretched diagonally across his bed, pillows on the floor. Curled in a tight ball, Colin slept in the center of his bed, nothing showing above the blankets but the top of his brown head. Colin was angling for a TV plus a couple of comfortable chairs. He dreamed of turning their basement room into a man cave fit for a teenager. Mitch wanted to move to the ranch full-time. He wanted out of this blended family or at least as far away as he could get. Alex picked up Mitch's pillows, laying them carefully on the bed. Marrying Nikki, pulling his blended family under one roof warmed him, but Mitch's stubborn anger saddened him. With a last look at his sleeping sons, Alex closed the door and climbed the basement stairs.

"All quiet in Creekside, Chief?" Nikki, ensconced

in her favorite rocker, asked as Alex entered the sitting room a few minutes later.

Alex sat on a chair beside the door and pulled off his boots. "Winter quiet, wife." He admired the picture she made, wrapped in a quilt, her feet, encased in heavy socks, rested on a small ottoman. He pulled his gun from the back of his waistband and walked to the safe hidden on the top shelf of the closet. Gun locked safely inside, he strolled to Nikki, leaned down, and buzzed her cheek. "I'm getting a beer; do you want anything?"

"I'm good." Nikki's sigh was audible in the quiet room. "Alex, we need to talk."

Alex opened his beer and dropped into the wingback chair. "Figured that when you were still awake. It's way past my favorite innkeeper's bedtime." Alex watched her worry her lower lip with her teeth, a sure sign of anxiety.

"Alex, I'm pregnant."

"I know, Sweetheart." Alex set the beer on the table and took her hand, twining their fingers together. "I wondered how long you'd wait to tell me."

"How? How did you know?"

"Lots of clues, Nik. You can barely drag yourself out of bed in the morning but are bouncing around as usual by noon. You carefully chose the wine for the wedding but lifted your glass to your lips without taking a sip. On our honeymoon you cried when the hero blew up the plane he was flying in order to save the world." He touched her chin with one finger and brought her gaze to his. "Why, love, why didn't you tell me?"

"According to Andrea, superstitious nonsense."

Alex stood, picked Nikki up, and sat down,

nestling her in his lap. "Explain. What superstitious nonsense?"

"I told you I miscarried when I was young. The doctor confirmed the pregnancy on a Tuesday afternoon, and I told Aaron after dinner. We were thrilled. I woke up Wednesday morning to cramping and blood. By noon, the baby was gone."

Alex tightened his arms around her. "Oh, Nikki. That must have hurt." He placed a gentle kiss on her lips, and his hand caressed her arm, offering comfort. "Barely time to go from celebration to grief. Have you seen the doctor yet?"

"Last week." Nikki yawned. "I'm already farther along. You're happy, Alex, about the baby?"

The warm bundle of his wife nestled on his lap, Alex answered, "More than happy, Nikki. I can hardly wait."

****

Georgie's whine woke Alex. Her breathing even in sleep, Nikki's head still rested against his shoulder. In the center of the room, Georgie sat up, her focus on a shadowy corner. Alex concentrated, listening for Sam's monitor, no sound from him. Trying not to disturb Nikki, Alex propped himself up and looked around the shadowy room.

Victoria stood beside the window, a baby held in her arms. A man stood beside her, his arm around her shoulder, his head bent toward the bundle in her arms. Victoria lifted her head. Her gaze met Alex's. A tender smile crossed her face. The vision disappeared. Alex pulled Nikki tighter against his body. The beat of her heart, the soft sighs of her even breathing comforted him. His love, a woman of courage.

So many losses in her young life yet she found the courage to let grief go and love again.

Chapter Three

Eckie-Taylor Wedding

George Wyatt Eckie and Faith Elizabeth Taylor united in marriage on March 1, in Phoenix, Arizona. Friends and family members of both the bride and groom attended the ceremony and reception held at the home of the bride's parents, Owen and Lucille Taylor. The new Mr. and Mrs. Eckie will make their home at Eckie House on Spruce Street. Welcome to Creekside, George and Faith Eckie.

~The Creekside Reporter, March 10, 1905

****

James hopped out of his SUV, a black duffle bag in his hand, and climbed the front steps of The Palace Hotel two at a time. He yanked open the front door and ambled to the front desk. "Hey, Andrea." James dropped the duffle on the floor. "You taking up inn keeping as your new profession?"

"I'm a woman of many talents." Andrea handed him the room key. "How was your drive?"

"Good, easy." James took the key. "Where's my baby sister?"

"Laundry. I'll text her you're here." Andrea glanced at the phone. "She'll meet you in the sitting room in thirty minutes."

James grabbed his duffle and climbed the steps two at a time. In the attic, he dropped the duffle on the bed and glanced at the mirror. Cringing at his tousled hair, James grabbed his brush and forced his hair into a semblance of order. As usual, when he worried, he pushed his fingers through the heavy locks making a mess. He could use a shave, but hell, he wasn't going on a date, and the scruffy look was still in. Twice a day most days he scraped the black stubble from his face. Tonight no date, no work, great. He tossed the razor back in his shaving kit. A few months ago, he realized dating, like shaving twice a day, was something he did, more chore than pleasure. The drinks, coffees, first dates, flirting couldn't hold his interest. He had a few good friends, a tight knit family, a business he'd built from nothing, and too many acquaintances. Something was missing.

His father had two families by the time he was James' age. One in Tucson, the other in Scottsdale. He spent every other week with each family. Two wives and five children when James' mother discovered the second family. With his father as a role model, could James create a single family, a forever family? Or was he flawed in some way like his father, unable to commit to one woman? He'd stay single before he'd insult a woman he loved and hurt his children the way his father had. He pushed the past behind a mental door marked Do Not Enter, pasted a winning smile on his face, and entered Nikki's sitting room. She looked up from her place in the rocking chair, her eyes twinkling. His baby sister. "You're drinking tea?"

"Yeah, it's cold, and the tea helps," Nikki answered quickly. "I'll share the tea or I've beer and wine."

James leaned over and buzzed her cheek. "Beer,

I'll get it." Walking to the refrigerator, he noticed Nikki chewed her bottom lip. A nervous habit left over from childhood. "You're looking good, little sis. What's different? New haircut?"

"New haircut."

"Cute. You look like an elf."

"Cute? Elf? Thanks, I think. I'm not sure women in their thirties are supposed to be cute or elfin, though."

"But you can pull it off." He plopped on the sofa. "You're frowning, what's up?"

"James, I'm pregnant." For the space of two heartbeats, the room held its breath. Perfect silence reigned.

James stood and pulled Nikki into his arms, holding her tight. "Congratulations, baby sis. Another Benton on the way." He swayed, rocking them back and forth. His baby sister having a baby, amazing. His heart sent a prayer for a healthy baby and a safe delivery. No grief this time, only joy. Nikki relaxed into his embrace.

"Stark, James. This baby is another Stark."

"Maybe in name, but in heart? A Benton." He released her. She returned to the rocking chair and he plopped into the wing chair. "Does Patrick know?"

"No, I'll tell him tomorrow. Don't you tell him, and remember the only reason you know first is your sudden visit today."

"Doesn't matter the reason, I still know first." He sipped the beer. "Be sure you tell him I already know. He'll hate it."

"No matter how old you get, no matter what you know or do first, you'll always be the second son. You get that, right?" Nikki commented.

"Yep," James admitted. "It's exactly why I love knowing anything first."

"Why did you visit today?"

"I was worried. Wednesday, Andrea said you were too tired to work. Was it the baby?"

"Yeah, not sick just pregnant. Let's both try not to worry, okay?"

"Sure, I'll try." James looked around the sitting room and noticed the unusual quiet. "Where are the boys and Alex?"

"At Windsong Ranch. Becca had a baby boy last night, came home this morning. Beth was already out there, and Alex took the boys to meet their cousin. I stayed home because I knew you were coming."

"Do you want to go now?"

"No, Alex and Sam will be back soon. Alex works tonight. I'll go tomorrow and spend the night. You can help Andrea cover for me tomorrow and Sunday."

"On that thought, I'm out of here. What time is dinner?"

"Alex and Sam will eat at the ranch so whenever you want."

"Did you already cook or can I pick something up? How about Rosa's? I'll invite Andrea, okay?"

"Sounds good."

James sauntered from the sitting room. In the shadowy corner beside the hotel's back door, Smokey lay at Victoria's feet. Victoria tilted her head, smiled, looked him directly in the eye, and disappeared. The spirit probably already knew about the baby. She drifted through the hotel, appearing randomly. She'd raised a child in The Palace, infant to grown man. Now another newborn would begin childhood living in the hotel. Brave women, Victoria, his sister Nikki, and Andrea.

At the front desk, he heard Andrea explain she'd be happy to send luggage to the second floor via the dumbwaiter, but The Palace did not have an elevator. Andrea glanced up and met his eyes. An evil grin crossed her face. "However, James is free now and will be happy to show you to your rooms and deliver your luggage."

"Welcome to The Palace." James shoved the luggage into the dumbwaiter, gently clasped Andrea's wrist, removed the room key from her hand, and led the middle-aged couple up the steps. On the second floor, he tapped in the dumbwaiter code and pulled out their luggage.

"Pretty clever, looks old," the man commented.

"The Palace was built in 1917; the dumbwaiter is original though the locking system is new."

At the door to Room 30, the man asked, "Aren't you James Benton?"

"Yes, and you are?"

"Winston Ames, we met at Orange Tree Country Club. Thought you were an accountant or something?"

"I am, Benton and Associates." James set the luggage beside the door to Room 30.

"Don't mean to be rude, but why are you carrying luggage in this little hotel?"

"Favor for a relative. Enjoy your stay, Mr. Ames." James smiled all the way back to the front desk. Winston Ames, arrogant Ames, friend of Laurence's. Bet he didn't realize the desk clerk was Laurence's former girlfriend, the baby she carried Laurence's youngest child. "You recognized him?" he asked

Andrea.

"Of course. Business and golfing buddy of Laurence. Arrogant and not much of a golfer. Poor loser and he cheats."

"Yep. He didn't recognize you?" James asked as he leaned an elbow on the front desk.

"No reason he should. I never played with Laurence's friends because I refused to let them win or cheat and Laurence knew it." Andrea shook her head. "Stupid me."

"Why stupid? No reason you should allow cheating or throw a game to pacify a bunch of idiots."

"True." Andrea pushed herself back onto the stool behind the desk. "But knowing he allowed cheating should have been a red flag. How stupid I didn't see allowing cheating as a character flaw? What kind of man cheats to lose or win?"

"You're better off without him."

"I know. I dodged a bullet because he didn't want the baby. Wasn't because I was smart, just lucky." A young couple walked in and ended their conversation.

James meandered over to Catherine's and played with his goddaughters, Lily and Hope. Chance Pagent, Catherine's next-door neighbor, dropped by. Catherine offered to let him stay for dinner. Their easy way with each other in the kitchen told James the shared meals were a regular occurrence. He hoped a relationship with Chance worked out for Catherine. He'd caught the proprietary way Chance touched her shoulder and took her hand. The little girls were crazy about Chance, climbed all over him, and peppered him with a constant stream of questions and demands. James declined the dinner invitation. He walked the residential streets on the way to the hotel. He'd promised Craig, his best friend and Catherine's deceased husband, no matter what happened he'd take care of Catherine and the girls. Looked like Catherine had everything under control, and Chance was angling to help. Good, she and the girls deserved all the happiness they could find. James missed his best friend Craig. Was the loss of a relationship built on shared memories since middle school the reason he felt restless and alone even in a room full of people?

Scents of oregano and basil filled the air when James picked up takeout from Rosa's. Music and conversation competed with sounds of cutlery against glass dishes. He paid the tab and stepped outside into a quiet night. After he shared the take-out with Nikki, he took Georgie for a walk. James climbed two flights of stairs to his attic room. He tossed his room key on the table by the door; before he flicked on the light, he scanned his room. There she was, Victoria, standing in a shadowy corner by the window. A boy about ten years old dressed in a miniature suit stood beside her. A light flashed and the vision disappeared. Must be family picture day for spirits. He remembered those, especially after Nikki was born. Single mothers weren't unusual when his sister was born. Many of his friends lived in households like theirs led by a mom. In Victoria's day, the early 1900s, single motherhood was unusual. He wondered how difficult Victoria found managing alone in a world full of traditional families.

****

At midnight, Andrea heard the hotel's backdoor open and then softly close. Familiar footsteps walked quietly to the basement door, the snick of the electronic lock, the soft whoosh of the closing door. Alex, returning from work, checking on his sons. Did her parents complete the same ritual when she was young? Did they return from social events and check on their children? She'd never ask, but she doubted it.

In high school, she shared Nikki's midnight curfew, claiming Nikki's family rules as her own. Drew, her younger brother, followed no rules. Eventually, his lack of rules landed him in a military boarding school for middle and high school, ROTC in college, and a career in the Army. She found structure and security in Nikki's family. Drew found them in the military. She worried about being a parent. She wanted more for her child. More than parents who paid little attention, expecting the nanny, then the teacher, to raise their children. Baby Ella moved, kicking her. Andrea whispered, "I'll do better for you. I learned parenting from Nikki's momma, so I'll do better for you." She drifted back to sleep.

Alex slipped off his boots at the sitting room door, locked his gun in the closet, and quietly entered Sam's room. At the foot of the bed, Georgie lifted her head and watched him. Sam slept in a tumble of blankets, curled against his pillow. Alex left the room, softly closing the door. Dressed in old sweat pants, he tumbled into bed beside his sleeping wife. Carefully he curled his long body around her, moving her slightly so her head rested on his shoulder. Nikki snuggled tighter against him and whispered, "Welcome home, Chief."

"Thought you were asleep. How's my innkeeper?" He buzzed her cheek, nuzzled the back of her neck, and lay his hand on her still flat abs.

"Sleepy, but just drowsing, waiting for you."

"Boys okay? Hotel okay?"

"Boys are fine. Hotel's fine." Nikki sighed.

"But?"

"We probably need to tell them about the baby. So many people already know, I'd rather we told them before they heard somewhere else."

"Not looking forward to telling the boys?" Nikki shook her head. "I can tell them, at least Mitch and Colin."

"No, I want to tell them at the same time. They're brothers now and the baby is their sibling"

"But Mitch is going to find a way to let us know he's not happy," Alex stated, confirming why Nikki hesitated.

"Exactly. And his unhappiness is going to rub off on the other two."

"But you're happy, right? Happy about the baby?" He caressed her lithe body with long strokes, offering comfort.

"Happy and terrified," Nikki admitted. "Unhappy if Mitch won't be happy. Worried about how Colin will feel. And Sam, first he lost his place as only child, next he'll go from youngest to older brother. So many changes in such a young life."

"Hmm. Let me think. Let's hold off a couple of days, okay?"

"Okay. I'm about to fall asleep anyway." Nikki's body relaxed against him and her breathing evened.

Alex let memories wash over him. Twenty-four years old, recently promoted to detective, he and his very pregnant wife Vanessa held hands and meandered through a baby store. Vanessa carried her list, all the best baby products, everything they needed for Mitch, due in just a few weeks. Gifts for Mitch filled the second bedroom in their apartment, gifts from a shower thrown by Vanessa's friend Lindsey. The crib, still in its box, waited until they had time to assemble it. Alex pushed the cart through the store. Vanessa chose which car seat, which stroller, which port-a-crib and Alex added them to the cart. As he handed over a credit card, Vanessa leaned against his shoulder. "Did you know the cost to raise a child is over two hundred thousand from birth to eighteen?" Typical Vanessa, always curious about everything, her brain stuffed with random facts.

"Then why do I feel I've spent at least two hundred thousand just getting ready for Mitch?" he asked as he signed the receipt.

"It's just an average. Our child is definitely special." He stuffed the receipt in his pocket and grabbed her in a bear hug. Her head fit just below his chin, her big belly pushed against him and he felt Mitch kick.

"Soccer player or maybe football," he predicted.

"Not a cowboy like his daddy?" she teased.

"Doubtful, since his daddy's a city cop."

Happy and innocent they believed the future stretched before them, plenty of time to raise their child together. They were wrong. By the time Mitch was three and Colin eighteen months Vanessa was gone, stolen from them by an aneurism.

He pulled Nikki tighter against him. In a shadowy corner of the room, he saw Victoria sitting in a rocking chair, her hands protectively caressing her obviously pregnant belly. Beside her, his back to Alex, stood a tall man dressed in a long coat, a small leather bag in his hand. On a whisper of air Alex heard, "You'll let me know. As soon as the baby comes, you'll let me know?"

Victoria grasped his hand. "Of course." He touched her cheek with his lips, stepped into a shadow, and disappeared. Victoria rocked once more, looked directly at Alex, and dissolved. Alex closed his eyes. Unlike Victoria's lover, he'd be at the birth of his child. Nothing would keep him away. He promised his unborn child the best father he could be and drifted into sleep.

Chapter Four

Dear Momma,

Thank you again and again for the lovely wedding. I'm thrilled with my new home. George did an excellent job. The house sits on a huge property and has an orchard and a creek. We can hardly wait to fill the rooms with children. First, we'll need furniture, cooking equipment, and linens. When we walked in the door, the empty rooms echoed. I remember wishing for a quiet place to study away from the little kids when I lived at home. Now I miss their noise and laughter. We'd love to have you visit. Give my love to everyone.

Love, Faith.

~from *Beloved Wife, Mother, Sister, and Friend, A Biography of Faith Taylor Eckie* by Emaline Eckie Benson

****

"Morning, little sis," James greeted Nikki when he plopped down beside her at breakfast. Guests filled the lobby tables. The low hum of conversation and click of flatware against glass plates competed with Etta James' "At Last." "Where are Alex and Sam?"

"Good morning, James. They're at the station," Nikki answered and lifted her mug to her lips. "Alex needed to check in and Sam tagged along."

James lifted his coffee mug. The scent of cinnamon from the bread pudding competed with the alluring aroma of coffee. "So what job did you assign me today? I know there's a schedule already arranged."

Nikki handed him a list of instructions. "You're on laundry duty. At five you can open the bar."

James nodded hello at Eric. "So, Eric's on this morning. What's Andrea doing?"

"She's in her room. When Eric leaves, she'll take over the front desk."

Her gaze drifted toward the front door, and James followed her gaze. Sam and Alex climbed the steps to the veranda. Dressed in jeans, boots, and heavy jackets, they looked like characters from a western movie, only things missing were Stetsons and horses. Sam mimicked Alex's walk until they reached the veranda. He yanked open the door and dashed inside, sliding to a halt beside Nikki.

"Aunt Nikki, Uncle Alex let me turn on his computer and we looked stuff up together. Then he gave me a bunch of papers to sort. Officer Corbin gave me money for the pop machine so I could buy his soda."

"Soda at nine in the morning?" Nikki grimaced.

"Yeah, he says the coffee at the station is yucky. Hi, Uncle James. Are you going to the ranch with us?"

James tousled Sam's hair. "Nope. I'm taking care of The Palace."

"Well, see ya later. I gotta get Georgie ready to go." Sam dashed out of the lobby.

Alex leaned down and kissed Nikki's cheek. "Ready, innkeeper?"

"Ready." Alex pulled out her chair. "Enjoy your day, brother dear. Call if you need anything."

James gathered the dishes, set them in the bus cart,

and watched Alex and Nikki stroll the hallway to the suite. Alex's arm rested across her shoulders. Just as they reached the door, Andrea came out of Room 11. Nikki greeted her; Alex made a comment. Andrea laughed and waved them off. Wearing black jeans, flats, and a giant Palace polo shirt, she walked toward him, looking like a strong wind would topple her forward. Tendrils already escaped from the knot of curls on the top of her head. His heart warmed, his blood heated. No. Not Andrea. He couldn't be attracted to Nikki's pregnant friend. He dated tall, slender blondes, sometimes redheads, or brunettes, but all of them were mysterious. He enjoyed solving the puzzle of who they were and what they dreamed. Nikki's childhood friend, Andrea, wasn't a mystery. "Morning, Andi."

"Morning." Her eyes twinkled, and her smile turned sly. "I hear you drew laundry duty." Andrea dropped a tea bag in a mug and filled it with hot water. "Hotel's nearly full; bet there's a huge pile of towels waiting down there just for you." She moved behind the front desk and greeted a couple ready to check out, the mug left sitting on the desk. Accepting the obvious dismissal, James headed to the basement and huge stacks of towels.

Hours later, his growling stomach reminded James he needed lunch. He meant to raid Nikki's fridge. When he reached the kitchen, Andrea leaned against the counter, a glass of water in her hand. He asked, "Hey, did you have lunch?"

"Nope, I've been too busy."

"How about a sandwich from the deli?"

A wistful expression crossed her face. "Hmm,

turkey on toasted marbled rye, baby spinach and tomato, plus bacon. A sprinkle of Italian dressing." Her eyes drifted shut. "On the side a dill spear and homemade potato chips."

"So, guess you mean yes. Write down your order and I'll go."

Andrea blushed. "Please. I'll buy if you'll go. I'm craving turkey and there's none in my fridge or Nikki's."

James handed her a pen and paper from the counter. "Write your order down. I'll get my jacket." He bounded up the stairs. The desire on her face while she described lunch nearly turned him on. What was wrong with him? Sweet, funny, straightforward Andrea? How could Andrea turn him on? She looked like a kid, dressed in jeans and the polo shirt. A kid with a watermelon under her shirt. Didn't seem to matter, suddenly she turned him on. Maybe he should forget the jacket and let the frigid air cool him.

Seated across from each other at a table beside the lobby window they shared lunch. Sun glinted through the window; a breeze pushed a few dried leaves across the veranda. Andrea entertained him with anecdotes involving hotel guests with unusual requests. James hoped he smiled at all the right times. Watching Andrea eat lunch distracted him. Her face assumed a satisfied expression with every bite of the sandwich. After each homemade chip, her pink tongue darted out and licked the salt from her peachy lips. Thoughts totally inappropriate for lunch in an open lobby raced through his mind. So wrong his thoughts about a young, pregnant woman carrying another man's baby. A woman he'd known as a child.

****

When James disappeared, heading back to the basement, Andrea cleaned off the table and loaded the plates in the dishwasher. She enjoyed their time together but James seemed distracted. Maybe he found her boring. She hummed along with The Rascals "A Beautiful Morning" and dust mopped the lobby's wood floor. Ella kicked. "Hmm, is that your opinion? You don't think I'm boring, right?" she whispered to baby Ella.

A few minutes after nine, Andrea checked the peephole at the sound of a knock on her door. James stood on the other side. "What's up?" she greeted him as she pulled open the door.

"Did you have dinner?" James asked. On cue, his stomach rumbled.

"Yeah, Nikki left shredded chicken chili," Andrea answered. "Want some?"

"Yes. Where will I find it?"

"Kitchen behind the bar. I'll get the chili and heat it up." Andrea stepped into the hallway and pulled the door shut behind her.

"Thanks. I'll meet you in the kitchen after I lock the upstairs veranda." James sprinted up the stairs, taking them two at a time.

Andrea ambled to the kitchen. The container of chili waited on the refrigerator's top shelf, clearly marked. She didn't mind serving James because each time reminded her of the good times at Nikki's house when they were kids. Pulling the leftovers out, serving family style so they could share. When she graduated from high school, Nikki's mom gave her a photo album, every picture a shared memory with the

Bentons. Her favorite was on the cover, taken the first day Nikki brought her home from kindergarten. Andrea missed her stop and was too scared to tell the bus driver. Nikki whispered, "Don't worry. You can come home with me. When Patrick gets home, he'll call your mom. Maybe she'll let you stay for dinner."

"You sure it's okay?" It was better than okay. Mrs. Benton called Andrea's dad and asked if Andrea could come over on the bus every day. Nikki would have a playmate after school. In the first picture, Nikki and Andrea were holding hands and laughing. Behind them, Patrick and James used their fingers to give the girls horns. Andrea discovered what a family could be like, full of laughter and love.

Her eyes misty, Andrea set the heated chili in front of James. "Want company while you eat?" she asked.

"Sure. You okay?" He used a thumb to flick a tear from her cheek.

She dropped into the chair across from him. "Yeah. Pregnancy hormones, just feeling a little sentimental."

"About what?"

"I was thinking about your mom, the chili's her recipe."

"Yeah, I recognized it." He looked into her eyes. "I miss her too."

Later he walked her back to her room. "Thanks for finding my dinner. Nikki's instructions included the comment she'd left me something but no clue where or what."

"No problem." She pulled the room key from her pocket. "Guess she had too many other things on her mind."

"Yeah the instructions for the laundry were very

detailed. Guess the laundry was more important than dinner."

"Night, James. See you in the morning."

James nodded in reply. He waited while she opened the door and stepped inside, closing it quietly behind her. At the sound of the deadbolt locking, he turned toward the back door. Victoria glided toward him; he felt her presence next to him though she appeared transparent. She disappeared through the closed door of Room 11. James listened, wondering if he'd hear a scream from Andrea. Nothing. Did Andrea know Victoria visited Room 11? Did she realize she wasn't alone?

****

On Sunday night, Nikki, Alex, Sam, Mitch, Colin, and Georgie piled out of Alex's truck. Before they reached the hotel's back door, Alex stopped Mitch and Colin. "Go take your showers and clean up. Family meeting in your room in an hour."

Colin asked, "About what?"

"Get cleaned up and we'll talk," Alex replied.

"Me too, Aunt Nikki?" Sam asked.

"You too." She tousled his already windblown hair. "Go take your shower." Sam grabbed Georgie's leash and coaxed her toward the back door. Alex moved beside Nikki, taking her hand.

"It'll be okay, love," Alex whispered just before he pecked her cheek.

"Hope so. He used to like me a little, I thought."

"He still likes you, me he's not so crazy about right now." An hour later, they entered the boys' cave. Alex and Nikki pulled a small leather sofa on a dolly. "Boys, give us a hand. Where do you want this thing?"

Colin answered, "Right here. Now all we need is the TV."

Three boys lounged on the sofa, in order by age with Sam at one end next to Colin and Mitch at the other. Alex looked directly into the eyes of his oldest son. "We're having a baby. Sometime in July, we're adding one more member to the family." Dead silence.

"Aunt Nikki." Sam hopped off the couch and hugged Nikki. "Please don't have a baby like Zoe." The tension broke amid laughter, except for Mitch.

"Congrats, Dad, Nikki," Colin added. "But don't think the baby's joining us in guy cave."

Mitch stared at Alex. "That it? Family meeting over?"

"Yeah, except you guys need to help Nikki as much as possible," Alex added.

"Sure, Dad," Colin chimed in.

"You two get some sleep. School tomorrow." Alex took Nikki's hand and walked toward the door. Sam rushed ahead, bouncing out the door and running up the steps.

"I'm ready, Aunt Nikki," Sam called from his bedroom.

Nikki strolled to his door. Georgie lay curled at the foot of Sam's bed, her bed abandoned. She raised her head, smiled her doggie smile, lay down, and closed her eyes. "Checklist completed?" Nikki asked Sam.

"Completed. I don't think I need the list anymore, Aunt Nikki."

"Okay. Don't use it anymore."

"Good. Aunt Nikki, are you my mom?"

Nikki sat on the edge of the bed. She wasn't surprised the question popped up tonight. "I'm like your mom, I'm your guardian. Sheri Larson is your mom."

"I know, but she's in heaven. What about Mitch and Colin, are you their mom?"

"Stepmom. Their mom's in heaven too."

"Is Kassie Zoe's mom?"

"Yes, Kassie adopted Zoe so she's her mom."

"So, if you adopt me, you'd be my mom. Then I'd have two, like Mitch, Colin, and Zoe."

"Is that what you want?" Nikki held back tears.

"Yeah." Sam finally gave into exhaustion, his eyes closed. "Be my mom."

Nikki listened to his even breathing, leaned over, and kissed his cheek. In her heart, she was already his mom, a second mom filling in for a best friend. She joined Alex in the bedroom.

He glanced up from the book on his lap. "What's wrong?"

"Sam wants me to adopt him."

Alex rose and pulled Nikki into his arms. "It's about time."

****

Monday. Nikki sat at her desk, laptop open to her personal email. Beside her, the cup of peppermint tea grew cold; at her feet, Georgie slept. She stared at an email addressed to Sam's Uncle Max. What words should she use to tell Sheri's brother she was adopting Sheri's son? He'd accepted her guardianship because Sheri warned him when she made her will. Now she hoped he understood Sam wanted the adoption. She started typing.

Dear Max,

Hope you are safe and well. I'm attaching a few

photos from our Boxing Day wedding. Sam looks handsome in his suit. While he could hardly wait to take it off, especially the tie, he enjoyed dressing like Mitch, Colin, and Alex. We are all living in The Palace so Sam's life didn't change much except he wants a horse since Mitch and Colin each have one.

Last night, Sam asked me to adopt him. This is the first time he's brought adoption up. I can't get in Sam's head, but I think marrying Alex brought this on. Sam asked about Mitch and Colin's mom. She died years ago. He wanted to know if I was their new mom or their aunt. He figured out if I adopt him, he will have parents on earth. I know I can't replace Sheri. She was a wonderful friend and loving mother and I'll make certain Sam knows she loved him best. I'm filing for adoption. Sam's right, parents on earth are a good idea.

Max, you will always be Sam's uncle, Sheri's brother, and I encourage you to make as much of that relationship as your profession allows. The door's always open, your room ready.

Be safe,
Nikki

"You finished it?" Andrea asked as she dropped onto the chair beside Nikki's desk.

"Finished, pressed send. I hope he understands."

"Can he do anything to stop the adoption?" Andrea took Nikki's hand in both of hers.

"I don't think so. I don't want to hurt him, though. He's a good guy, and Sheri maintained he was the best of big brothers. It's his profession and lifestyle she objected to."

"Yeah. She claimed he'd never grow roots, and the

only way he'd leave the military was if his next stop was the cemetery." Andrea released Nikki's hand.

"Gruesome thought, but probably true." Nikki signed off and shut down the laptop. "So, on to happier thoughts. Catherine and Ainsley will be here in a few minutes."

"Tea and coffee already set up in the library. You're sure Catherine's okay with having a reception at her house after Ella's baptism?"

"Catherine survived a dual four-year-old birthday party for Sam and Lily at her house. Mostly adults for a baptism? Should be easy."

They settled in the library and a few moments later Catherine and Ainsley joined them, Catherine humming "Rock-a-bye-baby."

"Funny," Andrea admitted. "Will you be around in a couple weeks when she refuses to sleep?"

"Nope. Been there, done that. Twice." Arrangements finalized, checklist completed, Ainsley and Catherine rose to leave.

At the doorway, Catherine turned back toward Andrea and Nikki. "Andrea, we need to plan your shower too."

"Not until after the baby, okay? I appreciate the thought but I'm living in a hotel room."

Ainsley interjected, "But you could still have a shower."

"Nowhere to put the gifts."

As they returned the tea and coffee service to the kitchen, Nikki commented, "I feel like a terrible friend. I should have moved you to a double room weeks ago. I'm sorry."

"No, you're the best friend. I didn't want to move.

I ordered a cradle for Ella; we'll be fine in Room 11."

"You're sure?"

"Yes, absolutely. Let me bring my baby home to Room 11, okay?" Andrea wrapped the leftover snacks and placed them inside the refrigerator.

Nikki closed the dishwasher door. "Okay. You'll let me know if you change your mind?"

"I promise."

Andrea stopped just inside Room 11 and looked around. Lace curtains filtered the winter sun streaming through the two windows. The muted colors of a wedding ring quilt covered a four-poster bed, its plain white bed skirt disguised pullout drawers. A small TV hid behind the doors of an armoire whose top drawer folded down into a desk. A soft blue throw lay across a wingback chair. Andrea visited The Palace a few times by herself while she was still with Laurence and stayed in different rooms. The day she showed up pregnant and sad, Nikki convinced her to stay at least until the baby came. Nikki showed her every empty room. When they walked into Room 11, suddenly Andrea felt better, a little more at peace. Room 11 was like a favorite blanket. The room wrapped her in comfort, protected her. She wanted Ella to have the same comfort. Her baby needed Room 11.

Andrea joined Nikki's family in the sitting room for dinner, everyone except Alex. Sam chattered happily, explaining all the school happenings. When Sam paused for breath, Colin asked, "Can I sign up for flag football, Nikki?"

"Did you play last year?"

"No. But I want to this year."

"Let me check with your dad. I've no objection,

but we'll see. Do you have paperwork we need to sign?"

"Yeah."

"What about you?" Nikki asked Mitch. "Are you trying out for something?"

"Yeah, basketball. I'll talk to my dad. What time will he be home?"

"Ten."

"May I be excused?" Mitch asked.

"Yes."

After dinner, Nikki and Andrea loaded the dishwasher in the hotel kitchen. "Do you remember how you felt when Drew was born?" Nikki asked.

Andrea thought back to the first time the nanny handed her Drew. "I remember holding him for the first time. He was so small."

"Not any more though, huh? You're six years older, right?"

"Yeah. I thought when Drew was born we would be a family, like your family."

"Were you jealous of Drew?" Nikki asked.

"There was nothing to be jealous of. I had very little of my parents' attention before his birth and they ignored us equally. Do you think James was jealous when you were born? You're about the same distance apart."

"I never felt any negative emotion from either of my brothers other than their attempts to protect me, to take the place of my father."

"Are you afraid Sam will be jealous? He went from only child to youngest child. Not exactly the usual progression."

"Not really. Sam's so much like Sherri, his heart so

big he welcomes everyone."

"True. Then you're thinking of Mitch and Colin?" Andrea tried to remember if she was ever jealous of Drew. Mostly she remembered worry. Drew barreled toward self-destruction even as a kid. "They're so much older. I think it's too early for Mitch and Colin to be jealous. The baby's not real to them yet."

"Yeah. I'm probably rushing the worry about jealousy." She latched the dishwasher. "Everything just feels difficult. Mitch isn't happy, but he doesn't seem to pass his unhappiness onto Sam."

Andrea pulled Nikki into a bear hug. "But in a few months, you'll hold your baby."

"True, and she'll already have a best friend in Ella."

****

By ten, Sam slept soundly. His nanny, Megan, was in her room working ahead on her preschool lesson plans. Today, Megan told Nikki with the full-time job at the preschool she hoped to move into her own apartment by September. Then what? How would Nikki manage Sam, a new baby, and still run The Palace? A problem for another day. She curled up in her favorite chair and waited. The lock on the back door clicked. She heard the whisper of Alex's footsteps, the little creak the door to the basement made, then silence. She closed her eyes, picturing her husband with his sons. Ten minutes passed, again the little creak, whisper of footsteps. The sitting room door opened.

"Hello, my lovely innkeeper." Alex dropped on the bench beside the door.

"Welcome home, Chief."

Alex took his boots off then locked his gun in the

safe. He slowly opened Sam's door. Finally, he came to Nikki; his lips met hers in a gentle kiss.

"Everyone present and accounted for?" she asked when he ended the kiss.

"Yep." He took her hand, pulling her up. "Let's you and I hit the bed."

Nikki woke to the tinny sound of an old radio playing a slow waltz. Alex slept curled around her, one large hand covering her belly. Nikki searched the room for the music's source. In a shadowy corner, Victoria danced in the arms of a tall man. They twirled. Laughter filled the room. The waltz drifted to a close, the vision dissolved, the scent of lavender remained. Nikki closed her eyes and placed her hand over Alex's. The rhythm of his breathing and the familiar scent of lavender lulled her to sleep. Her last thought, Victoria had her lover only part-time yet the moments they appeared together filled the room with love.

Chapter Five

Dear Little Sister Violet,

Happy Happy Birthday! I hope you love your gifts especially the ones from George and me. We'd love you to come for a visit, but you know it's up to Momma and Daddy.

~from Beloved Wife, Mother, Sister, and Friend, A Biography of Faith Taylor Eckie by Emaline Eckie Benson

****

Tissue in hand, Nikki wiped at the tears streaming down her cheeks. Max's email swam before her eyes. Pulling herself together, she straightened her shoulders and started again.

Hi Nikki,

Thank you for the photos. You made a beautiful bride. Though you asked for neither my permission nor blessing with regard to Sam's adoption, you have both. One request. When Sam's older, I'd like to tell him about his father and give him the few things I have of Derek's. I'm not sure what Sheri told you, but they met when Derek came home with me on leave. If he'd known about Sam, nothing would have kept him away. Hard telling my baby sister the man she loved couldn't come back. Sam should know his father was a hero who loved his mom.

Let me know how I can help with the adoption.

Thank you, Nikki, for pulling my nephew into your family. Sam's right, parents on earth are a good idea.
Max Larson

Nikki remembered Sheri's anguish when she learned Derek died before she could tell him about Sam. Sheri meant to find someone who shared her need for roots. Instead, she fell hard for Derek, career military just like Max.

"Nikki?" The sound of Andrea's voice brought her back to the present. "You okay?"

"Yep. What's up?"

Andrea dropped into a chair in the office and watched Nikki wipe away a few tears. "You sure you're okay?"

"Just remembering. Good timing. James reserved the attic again this weekend. I bet I hear from Patrick before the end of today."

"It's your birthday this weekend."

"Exactly."

"On that thought, I'm going on my pregnancy walk." Andrea levered herself up from the chair. "Do you need me for anything before I go?"

"Nope. Just watch your step."

"Hard to do when I can't see my feet."

Winter sunshine greeted Andrea as she strolled through the hotel's front doors, across the veranda, and carefully navigated the three stairs to the sidewalk. Couples and families crowded the sidewalk. Sometimes the world seemed populated solely by families and couples. Soon she'd stroll through town carrying Ella in a sling or pushing her in a stroller. She smiled at the thought and a young couple coming her way smiled in return. She checked out the movies scheduled for

Twenty-four Hours of Love at the movie house. How did the owner find so many different movies with Love in the title? This year's selection included *Zombie Love; Eat, Pray, Love; Love Bug; and Can't Buy Me Love.* Humming the Beatles' "Can't Buy Me Love," she walked on. Sunlight glinted on the window of Serendipity making the hearts dance.

"Good morning," Ainsley greeted her as she stepped through the door. "What brings you to Serendipity? What fabulous find are you searching for?"

Teasing, Andrea asked, "You don't know?"

"I'm not a mind reader, I just feel emotions," Ainsley admitted. "All I'm getting from you is happiness."

"Good read. I'm happy because Nikki's birthday is Saturday."

"Ahh." Ainsley grinned. "And her family will be here to celebrate, including James? No wonder you're happy."

"What are you trying to say, exactly?"

"I might be wrong, but it looked to me like you and James had a connection."

"Of course we do," Andrea admitted and felt a slight flush warm her cheeks. "I've known James for nearly thirty years."

"But now it's different?" Ainsley asked, her eyebrows raised.

"How did you know?"

"Can't read minds but emotions? Different story," Ainsley admitted.

"It's probably just hormones." Andrea glanced around the shop filled with art. "So where will I find

Casey's drawings? Nikki commented she'd buy them all if she could."

"All over the store. After all, everything in Serendipity is a fabulous find."

Andrea meandered down aisles of shelves filled with elegant displays of art glass, framed drawings, candles, one of a kind bowls and vases. She hoped only Ainsley could read her feelings for James. At twelve, she'd confided her adolescent crush on James to Nikki and she could still see Nikki's initial look of horror. "James? My brother James? No." When Andrea started to cry, shocked her best friend thought she wasn't good enough for James, Nikki pulled her into a hug. "Ick, he's too old, and he's my brother. I don't see the attraction. But someday, if you married him you'd be my real sister. Now that would be cool." Andrea turned a corner and there it hung, Nikki's gift. About the size of a poster, framed in plain wood stained dark, Victoria and her lover waltzed. Shadows hid the room, delicate lace curtains shifted in an invisible breeze, the lovers' eyes locked, and they danced.

Ainsley joined her in front of the drawing. "Ahh. You found Nikki's gift." Ainsley lifted the drawing from the wall. "Let me send the drawing over."

Andrea looked down at her belly. "Yeah, I'd probably drop it."

"You'll have it by Thursday, okay?"

****

Saturday. Behind the front desk Andrea sat on the stool, laptop open, and verified the room number for Jason Smith. "Room 30?" At his nod, she continued, "It's free through Wednesday. Same credit card?"

"Thanks. Do you need the card again?"

"No. We're good." She glanced down and completed the transaction, Jason Smith walked away as Tracey Lawrence promised you'll "Find Out Who Your Friends Are."

"Hello, Andrea." An unfortunately familiar voice.

Andrea closed her eyes, recognizing the voice she hoped never to hear again. Schooling her face to show no expression, she opened her eyes. "Laurence." She looked directly into cold blue eyes.

"So, Winston was right, your new profession is innkeeper." Laurence looked around the lobby furnished with antiques; a smirk marred his classic good looks. "Not much of an inn."

Andrea took three deep breaths, calming her temper. Laurence loved to put others down, his favorite form of entertainment. She took a fourth breath and heard heavy footsteps on the stairs. From the corner of her eye, she spotted James and Patrick almost at the final stair. Focused once more on Laurence, in a calm voice Andrea asked, "Why are you here?"

Laurence stared at her belly, distaste crossing his face. "I see you stupidly didn't change your mind."

James stepped beside Laurence, leaned casually against the front desk. "Laurence."

Annoyance crossed Laurence's face. "Ames was right; you work here too. Bellhop, right?" He laughed at his own joke.

"Sometimes," James admitted. "Today I'm the bouncer."

Patrick ambled to Laurence's other side and winked at Andrea. "And I'm his assistant."

Laurence looked from one brother to the other then at Andrea. "What is this? I want talk to you."

Andrea looked directly in Laurence's eyes. "Not interested."

"Well, you can listen anyway." Laurence's cheeks flushed.

James shook his head. "See, that's where you're wrong, Larry. Andrea doesn't have to listen to you."

Patrick chimed in, "Because you're leaving."

"Not without talking to Andrea."

Patrick looked at James and smiled. James grinned and Alex walked in the front door. "What's up, gentlemen?"

"Hey, Alex," James answered. "We're just escorting Laurence out."

"Need help?" Alex offered.

"Who are you?" Laurence asked belligerently.

Alex pulled his shield from his pocket. "The police chief."

"Good, I want these guys arrested for threatening me."

Alex shook his head. "Sir, these gentlemen own the property you're standing on. If you stay when they've asked you to leave, it's trespassing." Alex lifted a brow at Patrick. "I'll walk you out."

"All right, but Andrea, this isn't over." Laurence turned and stormed out the front door, Alex right beside him.

Alex returned to the lobby where Patrick and James still leaned on the front desk, grinning at each other. "Threatened him?" he asked the brothers.

"No way. We hadn't gotten to threats yet," James answered.

"No threats," Patrick agreed. "We were just going to pick him up and take him outside, like the trash."

"Sorry you guys got involved. Really, I could have just talked to him," Andrea admitted.

In unison, James and Patrick shook their heads. "You're one of us, so if you don't want to talk to him, you don't." James shrugged. "Simple."

Patrick added, "Looked to me he wanted to lecture, not discuss. Anyway, he was disrespectful. No disrespect allowed in our palace."

"Agreed. I'm going downstairs and visit my wife. You okay, Andrea?" Alex asked.

"Yeah. I'm good."

Patrick started down the hall beside Alex, their low voices an indistinct rumble.

"Sure you're okay?" James asked.

"Of course. I knew someday he'd return to annoy me," she admitted.

"But after the baby was born would be better?"

Andrea shook her head. "Never would be best. How well do you know Laurence?"

"Not well. Didn't like him so spent little time with him, just at stuff we were both invited to. Why?"

"He'll be back. I know him well. He needs to bury me under his superior wisdom and remind me how stupid I am. How dumb I was to choose a baby over him. He won't give up until he's sure I've heard him."

"Andrea, you don't have to listen to him anymore."

"But it may be the only way to get him to go away for good."

"If you decide listening is what you need to do then Patrick, Alex, and I can be with you when you meet." James took her hand. "You're not alone. Make the meeting on your terms in a place you feel safe."

"Laurence isn't violent."

"Andrea, there's all kinds of hurt. He may not physically touch you, but he's disrespectful. You deserve better." He leaned over the counter and buzzed her cheek. "You deserve the best." He disappeared down the hallway toward his sister's suite.

Then can I have you? Andrea looked at her hands clasped on the shelf made by her belly. *Probably not.*

****

"Happy birthday. Happy, happy birthday," they chanted as Nikki took a deep breath and blew out the candles. They clapped. Conversations filled the sitting room, Nikki served cake, and Alex dipped ice cream. James refilled drinks. After final hugs and good wishes, the room was quiet, food put away, guests gone.

"Alone at last. Now I can wish you a proper happy birthday," Alex said as he climbed into bed, pulled Nikki into his arms, and gave her a smacking kiss.

"Hmmm. What would be a proper happy birthday, dear chief?" Nikki wrapped her arms around him.

"Why one that makes you very, very happy." His hands slid under her nightgown, caressing bare skin. They drifted down her spine, caressed her bottom, wandered up her sides, gently kneading her breasts. "Are you happy?" Alex whispered.

Nikki caressed his shoulders, arms, and back. "Oh yeah." She took his face in her hands, brought his lips back to hers. "And I'm going to get happier."

Just before dawn, Nikki woke to the sound of a whispered lullaby. In a shadowy corner Victoria rocked, a baby wrapped in a yellow blanket nestled on her shoulder. Nikki's cell rang with the chorus of "What's Love Got To Do With It?" The vision disappeared. "Andrea?"

"Nikki, it hurts. It's time," Andrea said between panting breaths.

At six in the evening, Ella Nicole Hamilton joined the family. Nikki sat beside the hospital bed, watching Andrea nurse her daughter. "She looks like you. Same shape eyes and nose."

Andrea grasped Nikki's hand. "Thank you, Nik. You're a real pro as a labor coach."

"Not my first time." Nikki gently squeezed her hand. "You've a crowd of visitors out there wanting a peek. Let me know when you're ready."

Andrea lifted Ella to her shoulder, closed her gown, and gently patted Ella's back. Cradling a now sleeping Ella in her arms, she took a deep breath and released it. "Ready."

They came bearing gifts, Patrick, Scott, Casey, James, and Alex. They admired Ella and congratulated Andrea. The room filled with flowers, balloons, teddy bears. Finally, only Nikki remained.

"I'm going home now. You and Ella wore me out," she admitted. "Even though you did all the work."

"You'll pick us up tomorrow?" Andrea placed Ella in the bassinet.

"I'll be here early." Andrea's eyes drifted shut. "Rest now." Nikki pushed a wayward tendril of curly hair off Andrea's cheek and tiptoed out the door directly into Alex's arms.

Leaning against the wall, James watched Nikki and Alex walk away. He should follow, get in his car, and return to The Palace. He wanted to see Andrea and Ella one time without distractions, without others around. He quietly opened her door. She slept; her brown curly hair covered the pillow, a sharp contrast to the snow-white linens. He tiptoed around the bed to the bassinet. Ella's fist rested against her tiny pink lips. Dark lashes lay on her red cheeks and blonde fuzz covered her head. He stepped quietly to the head of the bed, bent over Andrea's sleeping form, and placed a soft kiss on her forehead. He turned and disappeared from the room as quietly as he entered.

Early dark greeted James outside the hospital. Driving through the night, he smiled at a memory of Craig holding Lily. His best friend, a father. Craig and Catherine posed in front of the church; sleeping Lily dressed in a white dress ready for her christening. After Craig died, he'd put the photo away. What he remembered best wasn't Lily's gown or her cry of surprise when Craig handed her to the pastor. What stayed with him was the look the photographer caught on Craig's face as he gazed at Catherine and Lily. A look so full of tenderness and love James felt like a voyeur watching something so private. How could Laurence throw away his daughter and her mother? Yet James' father did exactly the same thing. He disappeared before Nikki was old enough to have any memories.

Catching Eric about to close Victoria's, James grabbed a glass of wine and strolled to the library. Plopped down in his favorite chair, he asked Patrick, "You going home tomorrow?"

"Yep. Thoughtful of Ella to join us when we're already here."

"Maybe she just wanted a big audience for her entrance."

"She got an audience." Patrick sipped his drink. "Pretty baby as babies go."

"Definitely doesn't look like Laurence." He sipped his drink. "How does a man walk away from his child? How did our father walk away from us, from Nikki?"

"Don't know." Patrick shook his head and clasped the now empty glass in both hands. "Man, I hung onto Scott like a barnacle when Amy left, so afraid she'd change her mind and want shared custody."

"Barnacle?"

Patrick shrugged. "Hey I've spent the last eighteen years living by the ocean."

"So where is Scott?" Patrick raised an eyebrow. "Forget I asked. He's with Casey." James finished his wine. "See ya tomorrow." He loaded the glass in the dishwasher and climbed the stairs to the attic.

James paused on the threshold of his room. No sign of Victoria. Changed into sweatpants, he stretched out on the king-size bed, surprised he wasn't anxious to go home. No one waited at his condo. Women's names populated his contacts list, but he knew he wouldn't call one of them. His last relationship ended months ago due to lack of interest, at least on his part. He drifted into sleep, already missing his siblings and friends.

The sound of a squeaky rocking chair woke James just before dawn. In the shadows, Victoria rocked and gazed with wonder at her nursing child. A male voice whispered from the shadows, "Vicky, if only…"

"Shhhh," Victoria answered quietly. "Things are as they are, and this precious moment is enough. No regrets, our child is perfect."

The man moved from the shadows and took a seat on a straight chair beside Victoria. Victoria swaddled the infant. "May I?" the man asked. Victoria laid the baby in his arms. They disappeared.

James drifted back to sleep, his last thought why did RJ's father not marry Victoria and live in The Palace? Warmth and love surrounded the small family whenever they appeared. What kept them apart? Although the man appeared only a part-time resident in the hotel, the tenderness in his expression, the gentleness in his voice indicated he loved both Victoria and RJ. Whatever made him leave, his heart lived at The Palace.

Chapter Six

Dear Momma,

Thank you so much for the box of baby things. All the tiny gowns are so pretty trimmed with embroidered farm animals. There's a Lutheran church here now so George agreed we'd have the baby baptized and the white gown trimmed with lace will be perfect. I wish you were here but know you can't leave Daddy and the other children.

~from *Beloved Wife, Mother, Sister, and Friend, A Biography of Faith Taylor Eckie* by Emaline Eckie Benson

****

The March sun through the stained glass windows turned Ella's white gown into a rainbow. On Andrea's left, Nikki held the candle, Patrick stood on her right acting for Drew in Absentia. Ella, her tiny forehead marked with the sign of the cross, slept in Andrea's arms. Her cries during the baptism wore her out. As Pastor Tim intoned the final words of the liturgy, Ella frowned and her tiny fist found her rosebud mouth. "Peace be with you."

"And also with you."

As one, they turned to face the congregation. "Welcome, Ella Nicole Hamilton. Welcome to our family," intoned Pastor Tim. The congregation clapped. Ella slept on.

Diaper bag slung on his shoulder, James walked beside Andrea. Bright sun, blue sky, chirping birds, and the scent of new growth surrounded them. "Drew couldn't make it?" he asked.

"Army doesn't consider baby baptism a family emergency." Her eyes lit, her lips turned up. "But he's plotting a trip to Creekside in his near future."

"Nikki says you're going back to Scottsdale?" James asked as they crossed the street.

Andrea felt the warmth of his hand on her back as he guided them around a clump of tourists "Yeah, in a couple of weeks. Just overnight. Now it's safe for me to travel, I have to attend a quarterly meeting at work."

"Will you stay at your townhouse?"

"Can't, it's leased. I might drive down and back in one day so I don't have to leave Ella overnight."

"You're welcome to stay with me." He guided her up the walk to Catherine's. "The guest room is yours if you want it."

"Thank you. Let me think about it." Really, how much rest would she get with him down the hall? She already spent too much time thinking about him, too many nights dreaming about him. Not so innocent dreams either.

"Whatever you decide let me know when you're in town, and we'll go out to dinner," James offered.

Catherine met them at her door. "Come in. You're the last to arrive. Everyone's ready to celebrate Miss Ella." She reached for Ella, nestled her against her shoulder.

They walked through the house to the backyard. A cacophony of sound greeted them. Children ran through the yard, chased by the puppies, Belle and Ariel. Hope rode on Chance's shoulders, her little hands grasping his red hair. Mitch and Colin threw a football in Chance's yard next door. Nikki tugged her toward lawn chairs set under a tree; James joined Patrick and Alex at the buffet table. Andrea plopped in a lawn chair beside Nikki and stilled. Celebration of life, celebration of hope all in honor of Ella Nicole. Creekside surrounded by family and friends, exactly what Ella needed. She and Ella would make their permanent home in Creekside. She turned toward Nikki.

The party started breaking up, and suddenly James stood beside her. "Walk you home, little girl? Carry your books?"

She handed him the diaper bag. Good-byes, thank yous, and hugs exchanged, they strolled through the warm afternoon.

Andrea unlocked her door, pushed it open, and faced James.

"Text me when you decide, and I'll send you an electronic key." He handed her the bag. "I'll see you tomorrow at breakfast?"

Ella fussed. Andrea nodded. "Night, James." She stepped inside and closed the door.

James heard the door latch and deadbolt click into place. Thinking about a glass of wine, he glanced toward the lobby. Victoria stood at the end of the hallway. Their eyes met, she nodded her head once and disappeared. Hmm, she seemed to approve his asking Andrea out to dinner, giving her his guest room. Was The Palace's resident spirit playing matchmaker?

Whispering words of comfort, Andrea bathed Ella and dressed her for bed. Standing beside the bassinet, she softly patted her daughter's back, crooning a lullaby. Ella slept. Andrea scrolled through the pictures on her phone and the ones Nikki texted her. Choosing the best, she downloaded them to her laptop and created a slide show for Drew.

Dear new Godfather, yep you! Sorry you couldn't join us but I know you wanted to. Not sure Ella really enjoyed the day but everyone else did. Except maybe Pastor Tim when he put water on Ella's head and she screamed. Attached are pictures of the day. Let me know when you can visit. Love and hugs, your big sister and little niece. PS. Take note of the look on Ella's face in the first picture. Can't you just hear the scream?

Andrea crawled between the sheets and imagined herself at dinner with James. The lights were low, the conversation in the restaurant muted, the music a romantic instrumental. A blend of love and passion shone in James' eyes. Perfect fantasy. A grownup version of her schoolgirl dreams. Andrea drifted into sleep.

In the darkest hour of the night, the nightmare began. She opened the townhouse door to Laurence. He smiled, desire shining in his eyes. Determined to tell him now, no more procrastination, she invited him to sit in the living room. He looked surprised and she realized he expected an invitation to her bed, why else would she ask him to meet her here? A sad testament to the state of their relationship—casual dates and meaningless sex. He lounged on the sofa, tension coiled in her belly, and she sat poker stiff on a chair facing him. Looking him straight in the eye, she admitted, "I'm pregnant."

His face flushed. "Get rid of it." Charming, witty Laurence was gone, replaced by an angry stranger.

Without a word, Andrea stood and walked to the front door. "Get out." She wasn't at all surprised by his response.

"No. Get rid of it. I don't want more children. You knew that." He followed her to the door. "You'll never get a penny from me."

Andrea gazed into his ice blue eyes. "Get out."

"Let me know when it's gone." The door slammed.

Andrea woke to Ella's cry. After cleaning her up, Andrea cuddled Ella in the wing chair, nursing her. Settling a satisfied Ella in her bassinet, Andrea climbed between the sheets. It would have been so much better if the slamming door had been the end. Instead, he called and left angry voice mails. She blocked his calls. She contacted an attorney. Against the attorney's advice, she set up the paperwork allowing Laurence to forfeit parental rights in exchange for avoiding child support. The day after Ella's birth, her attorney delivered them, Laurence signed. She'd hoped the signing would be the end. Of course not. He still didn't want Ella, his harassment wasn't about a change of heart. No, bruised pride because she chose her unborn child over him. Smartest thing she'd done so far. Andrea pushed thoughts of Laurence away and counted her breaths. Eventually she drifted back to sleep.

****

"Morning, Andrea and Ella," Nikki greeted and joined them at a table for breakfast. "So what day works for your baby shower?"

Andrea raised her hand in a stop motion. "Wait, I've still no room for anything else." She handed Ella to Nikki. "Tell you what I am ready for."

"What?"

"Ready to pass on the maternity clothes. All cleaned and packed in a box."

"I don't need them yet but I'll be glad to hang them in my closet." Patrick, Scott, and James joined them at the table. "Morning. Who wants to show off their muscles before you head home?"

"Morning. What's up?" James asked looking from Nikki to Andrea. "Who's moving?"

"No one. There's a box of clothes in Andrea's room you can move to mine."

"Sure, let me eat first." James nodded toward Ella sleeping in Nikki's arms. "Want me to hold her while you finish breakfast?"

Nikki handed Ella to James and he settled her against his chest. "We'll just keep passing her around." Nikki caught a look on Andrea's face as James patted the baby's fuzzy head and stroked her back. Longing? Couldn't be. She turned her attention to Patrick. "So, what's this I hear about you selling your house?"

"Where did you hear that?" Patrick asked as he sipped his coffee.

"Scott."

Scott looked up from his breakfast. "You didn't say it was a secret, Dad."

"It's not. Scott's starting at NAU in September. Figure I'll look for something smaller. Maybe a townhouse or condo." He shrugged. "Or maybe a shack on the beach."

"I can just picture you," James commented, "dressed in a three-piece suit leaving a shack on the beach. The lawyer beach bum.'

"Hey, you never know."

Nikki gazed into the blue eyes of her oldest

brother. The conservative one, the smart one, the hardworking one, the responsible one, and lately, the one with weary eyes. "You could always move in to The Palace."

Patrick teased, "At the rate we're taking over the rooms there won't be any left to rent." Dishes stacked in the bus tray, James carried the box from Andrea's room to Nikki's, and they were gone.

Eric headed downstairs to wash towels, Nikki planted herself behind the front desk, checking out departing guests, Andrea and Ella grabbed the stroller and left via the back door for a walk. The Palace quieted in the spring sun, the sound of the vacuum cleaner as Patricia cleaned the rooms, the quiet whir of the dumbwaiter as she sent the linens to the basement. When spring break hit in a couple of weeks, every room would fill. This morning she'd caught Mitch's expression when Alex kissed her goodbye. So angry, her stepson. After two months, he was still so angry. All her men were at Windsong Ranch today. Becca had a full day of paying riders and she wasn't quite ready to handle them herself. Plus, mucking stalls and grooming horses were still out of the question. Tonight, she'd pin Alex down; they needed counseling. If he didn't agree, she'd go alone.

****

Pushing the stroller one handed, Andrea called the deli for takeout. As she ordered her favorite turkey sandwich, she pictured James' face the day they shared a deli lunch. If she didn't know for sure it was impossible, she'd swear he was being turned on. After one turn around the Square, she pushed Ella up to the deli counter and collected lunch. Blanket spread on the grass, Ella asleep on the blanket, Andrea leaned against a tree and pulled a romance novel borrowed from The Palace library from the diaper bag. Two hours later, she was startled from the imaginary world by Ella's cry. A glance at her phone and, "Ella, it's time to go home. I bet you're hungry and wet." A few minutes later, she cruised through the hotel's back door.

At the door of Room 11, Victoria raised her hand to knock. Andrea waited silently, Ella stopped mid cry. Victoria glided through the closed door. Looks like company for the evening. Why had she ever considered raising her baby alone in her Scottsdale condo? With Ella's arrival and all the baby paraphernalia, a little more space than the hotel room would be helpful. But, living in The Palace she never felt lonely. Her best friend, her new friends, and a resident ghost more than made up for a lack of space.

Bathed, fed, rocked, read to, and cuddled, Ella slept in the bassinet. Andrea sat at the pulldown desk and opened her laptop. Work related emails she responded to first. Opening her personal account, she deleted without opening Laurence's five emails. Drew's email she opened.

Hey older sis,

Thanks for the pics of baby Ella. So pretty. Can't wait to see her. Will you still live in the hotel in a few weeks? Can you get me a room there for the first weekend in April? Room for two. Yeah, I'm bringing my girl. I want her to meet you and Ella. Let me know. Love, Drew.

Andrea answered assuring him she'd still be living in the hotel in April. Bringing his girl to meet the older sister, was it the same as bringing her home to meet mom? Home. She doubted Drew thought of Phoenix as home. By twelve, he was totally out of control, skipping school, disappearing sometimes for days with no explanation. Already nearly six feet, he passed for older and used that to find trouble and run with older kids. Right after graduation, she and Nikki moved into an apartment near ASU. Before school started, her mother called. They were sending Drew to a Waynesboro, Virginia boarding school. Could she fly out there with him? They didn't have time. Difficult flight with a surly teen. The worst part, pulling him into a hug he refused to return, watching her little brother pick up his bags, turn his back, and walk away alone.

She and Nikki saved their money and flew out to see him at every holiday. She sent him little gifts for no reason. Her parents paid his bills and showed up for graduation. Drew rarely returned to Phoenix, moved directly from Waynesboro to a university in Texas, and then into the military. Occasionally, he would show up at her townhouse on leave for a few days. They emailed a lot. Curled under the covers, she prayed his girl loved him. He deserved love.

Andrea woke to quiet conversation, the words indistinguishable, the tones tender, gentle. In a shadowy corner, Victoria faced a young man in military uniform, their hands clasped. They dropped hands, conversation stopped; he reached out and pulled her into his arms. "Ahh, Mom." They rocked back and forth slightly. He let go. She stepped back. They disappeared. The room filled with sadness and a drifting scent of lavender.

Andrea felt Victoria's sadness and her fear. While Drew didn't go off to war at twelve, he left Andrea and home for a new place. A place where Andrea couldn't protect him, couldn't check on him last thing to make sure he slept in his own bed. Sending him to boarding school probably saved his life but knowing the move was best for Drew didn't change how much she'd missed her little brother.

****

Quiet hour, breakfast over, check out done. In the hours between check out and check in, The Palace dozed in the spring sunlight and Nikki worked in her office, Georgie asleep beside her. The distant whir of the vacuum meant Patricia cleaned the attic. Her niece, Thalia, handled the laundry, a concession to Alex's insistence Nikki worked too hard. A banging on the front desk bell broke Nikki's concentration. As she walked to investigate the impatient guest, Nikki recognized the woman standing at the desk, her hand ready to bang again. "Good afternoon Mrs. Hamilton. Welcome to The Palace." Andrea's mother.

"Of course. She ran to you," Mrs. Hamilton answered, disdain dripping from her voice. "You probably convinced her to have the baby."

Ignoring the accusation, Nikki asked, "What brings you to The Palace?"

"I'm here for my daughter. Where is she?"

Nikki schooled her features into a helpful expression. "I suggest you call her cell."

Mrs. Hamilton pulled out her cell. "Andrea, where are you?" She paused. "I'm at the front desk of this no star hotel." Mrs. Hamilton shoved the phone back in her bag.

Nikki stood behind the front desk. She might have to wait until Mrs. Hamilton gave up and left if Andrea decided not to see her. She could plan meals in her head while she stood at the front desk staring at Andrea's mother. Mrs. Hamilton sported a new hair color, a subdued blonde with darker low lights. Smooth skin covered high cheekbones, no crow's feet at the corner of her eyes, no laugh lines. Amazing for a woman pushing sixty. No doubt an excellent cosmetic surgeon. The front door opened and Andrea, Ella carried in a sling, strolled in. Andrea was protecting her privacy, not letting her mother know where she lived.

"Mother." Andrea looked into her mother's face and nodded in greeting.

"There you are. I thought you lived here." Mrs. Hamilton frowned. "Laurence said you did."

"What brings you to Creekside?"

"I came to talk some sense into you."

"Of course." Andrea indicated a table in the corner of the lobby. "Coffee?"

"No. What are you doing? You've given up everything for a baby."

Andrea looked curiously at her mother. "Did you feel you gave up everything when I was born?"

"No, of course not. I was married; we hired a nanny as soon as you were born. I didn't give up anything. Our friends were having kids so we did. You gave up everything, your townhouse, your job, Laurence, your social life. Just for a baby." She grimaced.

Andrea felt Ella's heat against her body, her heartbeat against her chest. She looked into her mother's eyes. Her mother didn't understand. The moment she saw Ella's heartbeat on the ultrasound, only Ella mattered. Instead of her usual anger and frustration, Andrea suddenly pitied her mother. How sad, a heart so small there was no room to love her children or grandchild. "Is that all you wanted to say?" she asked.

"Isn't that enough? You know I'm right. Hire a nanny, come back to Scottsdale, apologize to Laurence, and take your life back."

Andrea rose, meeting over. No reason to hang around for another lecture. "Are you driving back tonight?"

"Of course. I've a dinner reservation with friends."

She fit me in between social engagements as usual. "I'll walk you to your car." When they reached the pale blue BMW parked across the street, Andrea opened the driver's door. "Thanks for the visit."

"So you'll be coming back?" her mother asked as she slid gracefully into her car.

"Have a safe drive." Andrea closed her mother's door and turned away. In the window of Room 15, she saw Victoria, her hand on the glass and a smile on her face. Maybe she appreciated Andrea's handling of an unwelcome guest. After all, Victoria spent her adult life as an innkeeper. Surely not every guest was welcome. Andrea crossed the street, climbed the steps to the veranda, and entered the lobby. Nikki stood behind the front desk.

"Your conversation was interesting. I've always admired how you manage to talk to her without saying anything, without answering her questions," Nikki commented.

"Practice," Andrea admitted. "She only hears herself anyway. As long as I look like I'm answering and keep my voice calm she doesn't know the difference."

"I remember trying non-answers with my mom, only one time, though."

"Yeah. I remember too, the time Doug took us on a scenic tour of South Mountain in the middle of the night, off road in his dad's sedan."

"And we got stuck and a cop helped us push the car back on the road."

"And you tried not really explaining what happened to your mom."

"Yeah. Didn't work. Boy, was I grounded." Nikki grinned. "But it was worth it."

"She didn't even ask to see Ella."

"Be grateful Ella slept through the visit. Your mom's loss. Ella's perfect." Nikki came from behind the desk and smoothed Ella's fuzzy hair. "Perfectly beautiful, Ella."

In the darkest hours of the night, Andrea woke to the sound of a whispered lullaby. Clothed in shadows, Victoria rocked a bundle wrapped in a yellow blanket. Victoria looked up from her baby and directly into Andrea's eyes. Victoria smiled, one eye closed in a slow wink, she hummed the lullaby's refrain, and dissolved. Only the fading music of a quiet lullaby and the lingering scent of lavender remained.

Andrea drifted off to sleep. Her last thought Victoria understood about putting your child first, choosing to support a new life.

Chapter Seven

June 16, 1907
Dear Momma and Daddy,
You have a granddaughter. Emaline Elizabeth Eckie joined us at six this morning. Baby and I are both doing fine. George claims he's exhausted. Emaline's so pretty, momma. She looks like you and a little like Violet.
~from Beloved Wife, Mother, Sister, and Friend, A Biography of Faith Taylor Eckie by Emaline Eckie Benson

****

"Drew!" Nikki hurried around the front desk and wrapped her arms around Andrea's brother. "It's been way too long." She stepped back, grabbing both his hands. "Let me look at you." In his brown eyes, she saw a new sadness and new knowledge. During the last three years he'd gone to war, been wounded, spent time in a hospital. Still almost too beautiful for a man, a new hardness firmed his jaw, and new lines bracketed his eyes.

Drew let go of her hand and took the hand of a slender woman with light brown hair. "Nikki, this is Jodi. Jodi Williams, meet Nikki Stark, owner of The Palace." Nikki offered her hand, looking into twinkling hazel eyes. "Nik, where's Andrea?"

"Taking Ella for a stroll. Let me check you in." She

moved behind the desk. "Ahh, there they are."

Drew turned and dashed toward the front steps and Andrea. He wrapped his sister and niece in a bear hug. Nikki glanced toward Jodi.

"He's happy to be home," Jodi commented.

Nikki took the other woman's hand. "Welcome to the family."

****

The next day, Jodi claimed a need to shop for a gift for her mother and Nikki offered to tag along to Serendipity, leaving Andrea and Drew time to catch up. Ella rode in the stroller and the siblings walked around the square, finally plopping down on a blanket under a tree. "Mom came to see Ella?" Drew asked.

"Not exactly. She wanted me to return to Scottsdale and Laurence."

"Why am I not surprised?" He lifted Ella from the stroller, nestling her against his shoulder. "What about Ella?"

"I just need a nanny, and I can have my life back, according to Mom."

"Well it worked for her," Drew commented. "She and Dad both abdicated responsibility for us right from the beginning. What did you say?"

"Nothing really. No point discussing anything with her, she doesn't hear me, so I just thanked her for the visit. Has Jodi met our parents?"

"No, and I'm not going to Scottsdale this trip. From here, we're off to Lake Havasu City to visit Jodi's parents."

"Is this the official meet the parents visit?" Andrea handed him a bottle of water and pulled another for herself. "Have you met them before?"

"Already passed the meet the parents test. They visit Jodi a lot in Colorado Springs. She's the baby, and they keep threatening to move close by as soon as they retire."

"You like them."

"I do." Drew tipped the bottle back and downed half. "They're a close-knit family. They remind me of Nikki's family."

"Not like our parents, huh?"

"Not at all." He absently patted Ella's back. "Andrea, I'm going to propose." Her warrior brother blushed.

"Good. I'll cross my fingers she says yes." She wrapped her arms around Drew. "I'm so happy for you, little bro."

"Thanks, sis." He returned the hug. A moment later, Nikki and Jodi joined them and talk turned to the gifts Jodi bought.

Jodi looked first at Andrea then Nikki. "Did you know Serendipity is haunted?"

Nikki asked, "What did you see?"

"Lovers at the loft's railing."

"Georgia and Mathew," Andrea and Nikki chorused and laughed.

"So it's not some kind of trick?" Jodie asked.

"No, just business as usual in Creekside."

****

From behind the front desk Andrea and Nikki watched Drew toss bags into the trunk of the rental car, open the passenger door for Jodi, and climb behind the wheel. "He looks good, Andi. He seems happy."

"Yeah. He's in love, and she loves him back. He's happy." She sighed.

"Jodi's lovely."

"She is and he's going to propose. She comes from a loving family. Maybe Drew will finally find a loving family of his own."

Nikki squeezed Andi's hand. "He's always had a loving family. You love him, I love him, and we always let him know. When he rushed out to hug you and Ella, Jodi commented he was happy to be home."

"Ahh. She's perfect for him."

Tuesday morning dawned bright and clear. Nikki, Ella held in her arms, stood beside Andrea's SUV. Andrea, seated behind the wheel, admitted, "This is harder than I thought it would be."

"Yeah, I can see your tears. Thank you for trusting me to care for Ella."

"I'll see you both tomorrow night." She rolled up the window and drove away. Ella would be fine. She finally understood her friends who claimed the hardest day was the day they returned to work after maternity leave. Andrea focused on the scenery and singing along with the radio. Might as well enjoy this break from her regular life. Meetings scheduled all day, working lunch with her supervisor, afternoon training session, and dinner with James. Tomorrow a meeting with her attorney, then her realtor about the townhouse tenants, lunch with her father at Orange Tree Country Club, a little retail therapy, finally home to Ella. No surprise her father offered lunch when she texted him about returning to Scottsdale. As soon as she moved into the college apartment with Nikki, he started offering her lunches, frequently including Nikki in the invitation.

First day in six months in the office and the time flew by. She stole away twice to call Nikki and check on Ella. Nikki texted her pictures of Ella sleeping and kicking her legs while lying on a blanket. The best one, a selfie, Ella sleeping in her swing, Nikki sitting beside her a book open on her lap. The caption read Tough duty?

Suddenly, it was five-thirty. Andrea drove through rush hour traffic to James' condo. Overnight bag in hand, she climbed the flight of stairs. At his front door, she hesitated. Ring the bell or let herself in? She rang the bell. The door opened, and James greeted her with, "Welcome home."

Andrea laughed, recognizing the take on Nikki's greeting to hotel guests. "Thank you," she answered with a regal nod of her head. James grabbed her bag and carried it toward the guest room. "Thanks for letting me stay."

"Hey, no problem. Reservations seven o'clock at Grassroots, okay?"

"Perfect. Gives me enough time to clean up."

Seven o'clock, Andrea sat across from James on the patio of Grassroots. Music pounded from hidden speakers, diners laughed and talked. Not a romantic ambience, a young casual one. But perfect. Her first date with James without first date nerves. She imagined what he would think if he knew she considered this a date.

"How is working remote working for you?" he asked.

"Love it." She sipped the wine. "Only wish I'd asked for remote sooner."

"Do you miss the office at all? Your co-workers and coffee breaks?"

"Not at all. I still talk with them frequently." She

popped a cherry tomato with blue cheese crumble in her mouth, relishing the combination of juicy, sweet tomato and tangy cheese. "I might miss them more if I worked from my townhouse. The Palace is full of people and my best friend is across the hall so I'm only alone if I want to be."

"And I'll bet Victoria visits you."

"Of course. I'm living in her home." Did James see Victoria? Or was he just teasing? Did he know Room 11 was favored by Victoria and her lover?

When they returned to the condo, Andrea pulled her cell phone out and shared the last text from Nikki.

—We moved the bassinet to our room, she's all tucked in. Great practice for when her best friend is born!— Attached, a picture of Ella sleeping.

"Will you be able to sleep without her in the room?" James asked.

Andrea gazed at James. Missing Ella may not be the only thing keeping her awake. "I'll probably wake every few hours since she doesn't sleep through the night. Nikki and Alex may be in for a long night with her in their room." For a moment, they stood awkwardly in the hall between the bedrooms. "Thanks for dinner and the guest room. I'll see you in the morning." Andrea lifted up on her toes, intending a peck on his cheek. He turned his head, their lips met. James pulled her closer, wrapping her in his arms. She lifted her arms, placing them on his shoulders, allowing the kiss to deepen. She pressed her body tight against his, opened her mouth slightly in invitation. Surrounded, she felt surrounded by his warmth. Months since a man's arms embraced her, she felt her blood heat, her body respond. James gentled the kiss. His arms still wrapped her in warmth, her head rested against his shoulder. She found comfort in the beating of his heart.

James took a step back, releasing her slowly. Holding only her hands, he gazed into her eyes. He released her. "Good night, Andrea." He stepped back.

"Good night," she mumbled and opened the guest room door. As she changed for bed, her thoughts ran in tangled circles. What did the kiss mean? Why did he stop? She only meant to kiss his cheek, something she did often. How did they go from a friendly cheek buzz to heated passion? What next? There were so many reasons the kiss wasn't a good idea. She was a single mom now, Ella her first priority. Nikki was her best friend. How awkward would it be if she had an affair with James? Worse, when their affair ended, and James' reputation almost guaranteed it would, could she lose her best friend? Wait, it was just a kiss. An excellent kiss, which warmed her down to her toes, but that was her take. Probably just a nice kiss for James. Mentally, she stuffed her awakened feelings in a bag and zipped it tight. No, tomorrow they'd probably ignore the whole thing. She didn't see James often anyway. Confident they could go on being friends and relegate the kiss to a slight stumble in judgement, she closed her eyes and focused on slowing her breathing. Her last thought, before darkness claimed her—after all, it was just a kiss.

A buzzing alarm and the smell of coffee woke her. Disoriented, she looked around the unfamiliar room. James' guest room. So not a dream, reality. The dinner, the laughter, the passionate embrace. Now breakfast. Andrea dressed, straightened the room and its connecting bath, and packed her bag. Accepting she'd delayed as long as possible, she walked into the light-filled kitchen. James stood at the stove, cooking pancakes. Crispy bacon waited on a paper towel beside the stove. Andrea grabbed a mug and poured her coffee. "Morning. How can I help?"

"Your timing's perfect. Have a seat." James stacked pancakes on two plates, added bacon, refilled his mug with coffee, and carried everything to the table. She dropped into a chair and he joined her, asking immediately about her plans for the day.

Obviously, we're not going to talk about last night. What did she expect? He was a guy. Anyway, conversations beginning with 'about last night' rarely ended well. She relaxed, responded to his questions, and threw in a few of her own. An hour later, the kitchen was clean, and they were ready for the day. They left the condo together; he loaded her bag in the back of the SUV. Her final view was of him standing in the parking lot, sun glinting on his brown hair as she drove away.

By the time she arrived at Orange Tree Country Club to meet her father for lunch, Andrea felt smart, productive, and organized. Her attorney held a copy of her will making Drew and Nikki joint guardians of Ella Nicolle Hamilton. All Andrea's assets would be held in trust for Ella's support with the guardians as trustees. Her realtor promised to offer another year's lease to her current tenants. Head held high, to do list finished for the morning, Andrea strolled into the restaurant. He slid from the booth and stood when he spotted her, always courteous her father. She crossed the room and for the first time noticed what a handsome man he was, not just distinguished but handsome. Would Drew look like Dad at sixty-eight, tall, perfect posture, full head of snow-white hair?

He took her hands and kissed her cheek. "Thank you for joining me."

As they slid into the booth, she answered, "I appreciate the invitation." The server arrived, stopping conversation. Orders placed, Andrea picked up the conversation. "You look great, Dad.

"So do you. Motherhood agrees with you. How is Ella?"

Surprised by the inquiry, Andrea took a moment to respond. "Great. Growing fast, not sleeping through the night, but getting better." She gazed into her father's eyes and found genuine interest, surprising. "Would you like to see her picture?" He nodded and Andrea pulled out her phone showing him how to flip from picture to picture.

"She's beautiful. Looks like you did as a newborn. Nikki's holding her, right?"

"Yeah. Nikki was my labor coach. She held Ella before I did. Nikki's why I could leave Ella behind this trip. She's babysitting." Andrea flipped to Nikki's text and the picture of a sleeping Ella.

"Thank God for Nikki." Spencer Hamilton paused and sipped the iced tea. "I mean that, Andrea. Please tell Nikki I thank God her family gave you what I couldn't."

"What do you mean, Dad?"

"From the first day you stayed at Nikki's after school, you changed. You blossomed, from shy and sad, to laughing and outgoing. Best thing I ever did for you was convince your mother to let you stay at the

Bentons' after school."

"Aunt Jane and Ms. Effie taught me to cook, to clean, to make mud pies, stand on the swing, and dip chocolate cookies in milk." Andrea remembered her mother's horror the first time she tried dipping a cookie in milk at home.

"They taught you to laugh, to play, to stand up for yourself," he added. "Things we didn't teach you."

"Okay, Dad, I'm starting to worry here. What's going on? You and I don't have deep conversations, especially not about Nikki." Conversation stopped when the server arrived, took their order for a dessert to share, and coffee, and departed.

"We're divorcing. Your mother's filed for divorce," Spencer blurted. "She found someone else, thank God."

Puzzled, Andrea asked, "You're happy about the divorce?"

"Relieved. I promised I'd never leave. I promised when I convinced her to marry me. I was obsessed with her. Temporary insanity or something. I kept my promise; I lived the life she wanted. Finally, it's over and I'm free."

Andrea's eyes grew wide; her father wanted a different life? How could that be? "You convinced her to let me go to the Bentons' after school. You sent Drew to military school and made sure I took him." Looking into hazel eyes exactly like her own, she said, "You made sure I had money to visit him at holidays."

"From the first time I held you, the first time I held Drew, I fell in love. But I promised her the life she wanted, the life she seemed to need. She needed to come first, but it didn't mean I didn't love. Please, let me know my granddaughter."

Suddenly a few snippets of memory arranged themselves into a pattern. Brief flashes of her father in the pool, tossing six-year-old Drew in the air, Drew's laughter as he hit the water in a cannonball. Her father, sitting on the bed in her room, talking her through long division. Her father, sitting on the kitchen floor, rolling a ball back and forth with toddler Drew. Each memory ended the same—her mother arrived demanding Dad get ready for something now, or they'd be late. Her head filled with long buried memories, Andrea gazed at her father.

"Spencer, Andrea," an unfortunately familiar voice interrupted. "I'd heard you were back."

"Really," Andrea responded. If possible, she'd avoid a scene, but James and Patrick were right, no reason for her to deal with Laurence, ever. Then, silence.

Laurence looked from father to daughter and frowned. "Andrea, I'll meet you at Village Tavern at four. We need to talk."

"No." Andrea sighed in pleasure. She felt great. No qualifier, no argument, just no. Silence.

Spencer slowly stood, facing Laurence. "Go away," he demanded in a quiet, calm voice. "Go away now."

Laurence's expression clouded with anger. The server appeared with dessert. Laurence stomped away. Andrea gazed into her father's eyes, narrowed with concern. The server walked away. Spencer asked, "Has he been giving you much trouble?"

"Today's the third time I've seen him since I told him I was pregnant. He signed the papers forfeiting his parental rights. He thinks I should listen to his greater wisdom, and I won't."

"He's always been an arrogant ass."

Surprised, Andrea laughed. "Exactly."

Spencer walked her to her SUV and held open the driver door. Andrea placed the key in the ignition and lowered the window. He leaned in and kissed her cheek; the scent of his aftershave triggered a memory. "Dad, when you and Mom came home from social events did you come in my room and check on me?"

"I wondered if you even knew."

"Dad, anytime you want to meet your granddaughter, give me a call." Andrea squeezed his hand where it rested on the window ledge. "I can get you a deal on a hotel room." He took her hand and squeezed in return. She closed the window, waved a final goodbye, and drove away. In her rearview mirror, she noticed he stayed in the parking lot watching her. Her interest in retail therapy disappeared. Instead, she visited her rented storage unit, removed a box labeled spring and summer, and drove away from Scottsdale. Her playlist provided a cheerful backdrop to her wandering thoughts as she cruised the highway. The conversation with her father pushed her to examine her childhood from a different perspective. She understood loyalty and keeping promises, but putting the needs and wants of another adult over those of your children, nope.

****

Andrea paused on the sidewalk in front of The Palace. Guests occupied the front porch rocking chairs, a couple sat at a small round table drinking wine, sunlight glinted off the windows, an older gentleman occupied an Adirondack chair on the upstairs veranda, his eyes closed, a book face down on his belly. Home, she was finally home. Up the steps, across the veranda, she yanked open the door. Nikki stood behind the front desk, Ella asleep in a front pack. Beside her, barely perceptible in the staircase shadow, Victoria appeared, a smile lighting her face, her hands on her hips. Handing a key to a young man, Nikki directed him upstairs. When he turned toward the stairs, Nikki's eyes met Andrea's and a grin split her face. Victoria disappeared.

"You're finally home. We've been waiting."

Andrea lifted Ella from the pack, lay her against her shoulder, and sighed. Home, yes, she was finally home.

After she closed the bar and checked on Mitch, Colin, and Sam, Nikki knocked on the door to Room 11. "I just had to come over and say goodnight to our girl," she admitted when Andrea answered.

"Of course," Andrea agreed as Nikki stood beside the bassinet, reached out a hand, and softly patted Ella's tiny back. "Thank you for taking such good care of her."

"I loved every minute. How was your trip?"

"Good but weird. Have a seat and I'll tell you about it," Andrea answered as she perched on the edge of the bed.

"Everything at work okay, your boss is satisfied with you working remotely?" Nikki asked as she plopped into the wingback chair.

"It's all good. It's amazing what can be accomplished in one day because that's all the time you have."

"So work's good. What else is good?"

"Tenants want to renew the lease on my townhouse for another year. I signed my will and gave my attorney a copy. Assets go into a trust for Ella. You and Drew are joint guardians. Dinner with James at Grassroots was awesome. Love the food and the place, and your brother's good company."

"Good, so what was weird?"

"Lunch with Dad at Orange Tree. My parents are divorcing."

Nikki's jaw dropped, her eyes widened. "No way."

"I probably looked just like you do when Dad told me. Even weirder than the divorce is Mother found someone new and Dad sounds relieved."

"So how do you feel?" Nikki asked. "Doesn't seem to matter how old the children are, divorce is tough. It changes the family dynamics and can mess up the loyalties."

"Mostly I'm surprised she found someone else. Mother's not exactly an easy person to like, much less love. Plus, Dad gave into her about almost everything. Will the new man be as accommodating?"

"Who knows? Maybe she was tired of being in charge. Were you surprised your dad is happy with the divorce?"

"Shocked. But the divorce is not the weirdest part. He wants me to thank you and your family for giving me what I needed to thrive. And he wanted me to thank you for helping me support Drew."

"Hmm. Solves the mystery of the money always available for us to visit Drew. It's like seeing the past from a totally different perspective. An alternate reality."

"Yeah. It changes everything and nothing. Your mom and Ms. Effie raised me, made me the person I am. Still, it feels good knowing he loves us, he just felt helpless to show it."

"Well, I'm glad you missed your stop the first day of kindergarten. I'm grateful you're my best friend." They hugged goodnight.

Hand on the doorknob to her sitting room, Nikki glanced toward the hotel's back door. Beside the door stood Victoria, a large gray dog, ears perked, posed at attention beside her. Victoria drifted toward the door of Room 11, Smokey on her heels. They disappeared, leaving behind the scent of lavender. Consummate innkeeper, Victoria seemed to be keeping a special watch on Andrea and Ella. No wonder Andrea was hesitant to move to another room.

****

Exhausted from two emotional days, Andrea slipped into bed. The hour before dawn, she woke to whispered voices. In a shadowy corner, a tall man held a toddler in his arms. Victoria stood beside him. In a deep voice, gruff with emotion, he said, "Take care of your mother, son."

Victoria's higher voice whispered, "We'll be fine. You be safe." He set the boy on a wooden rocking horse and reached for Victoria, wrapping her in his arms. They disappeared, leaving behind an intense sadness and the shushing sound of a wooden rocking horse. Andrea closed her eyes. Was her father unhappy each time her mother pulled him away from his children? Did he feel overwhelming sadness when he sent Drew across the country to boarding school? She drifted into sleep.

****

Sunlight filtered through lace curtains warmed Nikki's back. Ice melted in the glass of herbal tea sitting on the desk. Mid-afternoon, The Palace dozed in the spring sun. The quiet hours between check out and check in. The quiet hours when Sam, Mitch, and Colin attended school, Alex worked keeping Creekside safe, and Andrea worked from her room. Nikki hummed along with Blue Suede's "Hooked on a Feeling" and updated the receipts from Victoria's, saved the spreadsheet, and closed her laptop. What happened between James and Andrea two weeks ago was none of her business, but she meant to find out anyway.

Nikki knocked on the door to Room 11, Victoria appeared and glided through the closed door. Victoria wanted answers too.

Andrea pulled open the door and invited her in. "You waited longer than I expected."

"What are you talking about?"

"Oh, am I wrong? You're not here to find out what's going on with James?"

"You're right. You're my best friend and he's my brother." She drifted over to the bassinet and caressed Ella's fuzzy head. "But you don't have to tell me. I want you to, but you don't have to. And I don't want details because it would be weird. He's my brother. I'm babbling. Ugh, are we back in high school?" She plopped on the corner of the bed.

Andrea pulled out the desk chair and sat. "Nikki, I don't know what's going on. He took me to dinner." Nikki nodded. "And at the condo, he kissed me. Not like a sister or a friend."

Nikki grimaced. "I get it, no details please."

"Next morning, he made breakfast. He didn't mention the kiss and neither did I. No 'about last night' conversation."

"That's it, just a kiss?"

"Yeah. I'm not sure which of us was more surprised. But he does call me sometimes, which is new."

"What do you talk about?" Nikki held up her hand in a stop signal. "No, wait, don't tell me. No details. But tell me, it's good he calls, right?"

"Yeah, it's good."

Nikki gazed into familiar hazel eyes, hazel eyes belonging to the woman she thought of as a sister, but better. A best friend with a shared childhood. If two people she loved made a life together, made each other happy it was a good thing. A little weird because James was her brother and Andrea like a sister, but still good if they could be happy together. "I always knew you'd be the perfect sister." She strolled to the door. With her hand on the knob, she turned back. "Let me know if I can do anything to encourage this romance, like babysitting or anything." She sauntered through the door to the sound of Andrea's laughter.

Chapter Eight

1907

Dear Momma,

It was so hard to watch you and Daddy leave yesterday. Baby Emaline and I both miss you. Thank you again for letting Violet stay with us for a few months. Mrs. Hunter can use the help with the house, and George promises he'll help Violet catch up in mathematics. The scarlet fever messed up her schooling, but we'll be sure she's ready for next year. We've found her an art teacher, too. He teaches at Arizona Normal School in Flagstaff.

~from Beloved Wife, Mother, Sister, and Friend, A Biography of Faith Taylor Eckie by Emaline Eckie Benson

****

Family dinner, Sam, Alex, Mitch, Colin, and Nikki settled around the dining table in the sitting room. Alex gazed at his very pregnant wife. She glowed, her skin, her eyes, her pink cheeks. The therapist helped, she was more relaxed, less worried. Mitch commented about the pork sliders, a positive comment. The counselor was making progress, or Mitch finally decided to accept his life as is. The learner's permit probably helped and the driving lessons. Plus, Nikki found time to take Mitch out practicing. Colin laughed at Sam's anecdote about the trials of kindergarten and the weirdness of girls. Sam was more like Nikki than she knew. Steel surrounded by velvet. Determined to force Mitch and Colin to accept him, using charm and warmth to bludgeon them into submission.

Alex interrupted the conversation. "I have an announcement." Silence. He read surprise on Nikki's face. "Road trip on Friday to Prescott. Sam's adoption will be finalized on Friday."

"And we're all going?" Colin asked.

"All of us, yes."

"Yea! Mom Nikki, on Friday you'll be Mom Nikki." Sam jumped up and grabbed Nikki and a few tears slid down her cheeks.

Sam, this child who wormed his way into his heart. "And I'll be Dad Alex since I'm married to Mom Nikki."

Sam frowned. "I've never had a Dad before."

"Sure you did. You just never met him. He died before you were born. He was a soldier like your Uncle Max," Nikki assured him.

Wearing a quizzical look, Sam asked, "Is he in heaven like Mom, since he was a soldier?"

"Of course," Nikki answered. "He's probably keeping your mom company."

After dinner, when the dishes stood like soldiers in the dishwasher, Nikki and Alex checked on Mitch and Colin, then Sam.

"You surprised me," Nikki commented as she climbed into bed. "I didn't know we were doing a family road trip to Prescott." She nestled against Alex's chest.

"Nik, it's important. Something affecting you and

Sam affects us all. Mitch and Colin need to understand Sam is your son, their brother, my son."

"I agree. But Mitch is better, happier. I was afraid to rock the boat."

"God, I wish I could save you worrying about anything but especially about Mitch."

"You can't. Accept it. I love Mitch and Colin. How could I not love them? They're your sons. Now my sons. Soon to be older brothers of our daughter."

"Yeah, who could have guessed a girl after three boys?"

"Sam will probably be just as overprotective as James and Patrick. James was six when I was born."

"Yeah, but your father wasn't around. They felt responsible." Alex rubbed her back in gentle circles. "Why wasn't your father around?"

Her body relaxed at his tender caress. "When Mom told my father she was pregnant after a six-year break he was livid. They started shouting at each other; at least, that's what Patrick told me. My father blurted out he already had five kids and he couldn't afford six."

"Five kids?"

"Yeah. Seems during the weeks he spent in Tucson he set up a second family. Three kids, all girls, one younger than Patrick, two younger than James. Mom filed for divorce the next day. He came home to find his personal stuff piled on the front lawn."

"Did he visit James and Patrick?"

"At first, he showed up on his court-appointed days. He claimed between the court-ordered child support and his other family he couldn't afford to take them anywhere, and Mom refused him entrance into the house. He gave up."

Alex pulled her closer, distracting her with tender kisses and passionate caresses. She moaned. He touched her everywhere, loving the softness of her skin, her round belly, swollen breasts. He rubbed her gently at the junction of her thighs, and her sudden orgasm surprised him. Her breath evened out, her heartbeat settled, and her eyes drifted closed. Her story explained so much about her relationship with Patrick and James. When Nikki announced their engagement, James and Patrick each took him aside. The message, he'd better take excellent care of their little sister. They were watching. They wouldn't sit idly by if he hurt her, if he allowed anyone else to hurt her. Alex drifted into sleep, the beat of Nikki's heart a comforting rhythm. His wife, his love, and soon the mother of his daughter.

Just before dawn, Alex woke to the sound of childish giggles. He searched the room. In a shadowy corner, Victoria sat on the floor in front of a checkerboard. RJ, looking about seven years old, sat across from her. Victoria frowned and RJ giggled. "I've got you, Mom." Another giggle, the vision disappeared leaving only the fading sound of childish laughter. One of the best sounds in the world—the sound of happy children. Alex whispered a prayer for the safety and happiness of all children and drifted back to sleep.

****

Friday, adoption day. Quiet broken only by the yearning voice of Tim McGraw singing "My Old Friend" surrounded Andrea. From the front desk, she watched cars drive slowly by and tourists strolling toward the Square. Thirty minutes ago the hotel rang with laughing, talking Bentons and Starks. Sam's adoption road trip turned into a family celebration.

Patrick and James surprised Nikki, arranging a banquet room at Prescott's Hassayampa Inn for dinner after the official signing of the adoption papers. Nikki promised pictures the moment Sheri's son Sam officially became Samuel Nicolas Larson Stark. Across the street, a tall man with a full head of white hair opened the door of a silver luxury car, pulled a small duffle from the back seat, and paced toward The Palace. Her father yanked open the front door and hesitated on the threshold. "Welcome to The Palace, Dad." Andrea came around the front desk and hugged him.

Spencer Ridgeway Hamilton dropped his bag and wrapped his arms around Andrea. "Thank you, Andi. I'm so glad to be here."

Forcing control, Andrea slowly stepped back, and then scooted behind the desk. "Your room's ready. I've put you next door to me." She grabbed the keys and led her father down the hall.

"Where's Ella? Where's Nikki?"

"Ella's with Nikki's nanny, Megan. They took a walk toward the Square. Nikki and a crowd of Bentons and Starks are in Prescott at Sam's adoption hearing. They'll be home very late." At the door of Room 9, she handed her dad the key. "I'm manning the desk until five. You're welcome to keep me company or chill in your room or the library or whatever suits you."

"I'll clean up and meet you in the lobby."

At least Ella had one interested grandparent. One parent, one grandparent, one uncle and a herd of Bentons and Starks.

Between check-ins, they talked, about Drew, about Nikki's family, about Creekside, about famous ghosts. No conversation about Andrea's mom, no mention of

97

Laurence. Eventually Megan and Ella returned. Andrea lifted Ella from the stroller and nestled her against her shoulder. "Dad, meet your granddaughter, Ella Nicole Hamilton." She placed Ella in her father's open arms. "Ella, meet your grandpa." Ella opened her eyes. Spencer's smile lit the lobby as he stroked Ella's fuzzy head, cradled her against his chest.

****

Saturday morning Andrea, Ella nestled in a front pack, shared a table with Nikki, James, and Patrick, surrounded by the smell of coffee and sound of conversation. Andrea rose when she spotted Spencer strolling into the lobby. Dragging another chair toward the table, she greeted him. "Grab coffee and breakfast, Dad."

Spencer stopped first at the table, buzzed Andrea on the cheek, and placed a soft kiss on the top of Ella's head.

"Good morning, Mr. Hamilton," Nikki greeted him. "Do you remember my brothers, Patrick and James?"

"It's good to see you." Spencer held out his hand. "Please call me Spencer."

Seated with breakfast before him and a mug of coffee in his hand, Spencer asked, "Nikki, where's the rest of your family? Andrea said something about a herd of Bentons and Starks?"

"Yesterday, herd was a good description. Alex and the boys are at Windsong Ranch working with the horses. Sam finally rides well enough to join them for the weekend. The young man handling check outs is my nephew, Scott."

In his classy way, Spencer asked questions about

Alex, his sons, Sam, Scott, Patrick, and James. Andrea admired her father's charm, encouraging everyone else to talk. His interest was genuine; it's why he was successful. He honestly cared about others, about their hopes and dreams, their successes and their struggles. Sad, he hadn't been able to transfer his concern and interest into parenting, especially for Drew who spent his childhood angling for attention.

After breakfast, Andrea, Ella, and Spencer toured Creekside, discussing historic buildings and ghost stories.

****

On Sunday morning, from his perch at the front desk James watched Andrea, Ella in her arms, walk her father to the car. They hugged and Spencer drove away. When Andrea pulled open the hotel's front door, James greeted her from behind the front desk. "Welcome to The Palace."

"Very funny since I live here. Speaking of living here, I'm surprised you're still here."

"I have connections with the owner. Free late check out."

"Enjoy your stay." She ambled toward the hallway.

"Hey, Andi," James called. She turned back, her eyebrows lifted in question. "You enjoyed his visit?"

"Yeah, I did." She leaned against the end of the desk. "He really is a nice man, something I occasionally forget."

"You've had a rocky relationship. He seems ready to change that if he can."

"I want it too. Especially for Ella and hopefully for Drew."

James felt his cell vibrate. Alex? He stepped away

from the desk. "Alex, what's up?"

"James, you still at the hotel?"

"Yeah."

"Good. Sam broke his arm; we're on our way to the clinic in Ellsworth. Can you and Nikki meet us there? Have Scott pick up Georgie from Windsong, too."

James dropped the phone in his pocket. "I'm taking Nikki to Ellsworth. Sam broke his arm. Please call Scott and have him pick up Georgie at Windsong." James dashed down the hallway. At the sitting room door, he stopped, took a deep breath, and let himself in. Book face down on her lap, legs resting on the ottoman, Nikki slept. James touched her cheek.

Her eyes opened. "What's up, brother?" She tossed the book aside.

"Sam broke his arm. I'm driving you to Ellsworth to meet Alex." He grimaced as the color drained from her face. "Where's your bag?"

Nikki pushed herself from the chair. "I'll get it. Go get the car. I'll meet you out back."

****

At seven o'clock, Andrea heard the slamming of the back door and a mixture of voices. She finished Ella's bath, dressed her in pjs, and settled in the chair to nurse. All the time wanting to rush across the hall and comfort Nikki and Sam. But Ella needed to come first.

Ella's tummy full, Andrea texted Nikki. —*Ur home?*—

Nikki's response, —*Oh yeah, come quick. Sam wants you to see his cast and he's almost asleep.*—

Andrea picked up a dozing Ella and stepped across the hall. Nikki answered the door, her eyes drooping.

"Come in. Sam's wound tighter than a clock but exhausted. James just helped him with a bath. He says he's too old for me to help him and Alex is in the guy cave with Mitch and Colin."

"Okay if I go in?"

"Yeah. He's in bed; James and Georgie are trying to settle him down. He'll be grateful for more of an audience. Be prepared to sign the cast."

"You're exhausted." Andrea pulled Nikki into a one-armed hug.

"Honestly, having my own arm broken would have been easier than watching the doctor set Sam's."

Andrea released Nikki. "Yeah, I'll bet. Let me visit Sam before he crashes."

An unfamiliar scene greeted Andrea in Sam's room. Sam's head rested on a pillow, his arm on another pillow above his head. His favorite pajamas lacked the left sleeve, replaced by a bright blue cast extending from wrist to bicep. Georgie lay on the end of the bed, her head up, alert. Sam's eyes glittered with mirth, his laugh almost manic. James sat on the edge of the bed, his voice low and soothing.

"Aunt Andrea, look at my cool cast. I broke two bones."

Andrea sat on the edge of the bed. "Way cool. Two, huh? Nice cast."

"Yeah, can you sign it?" Sam held his broken arm toward Andrea.

James stood to get out of the way.

Andrea handed a now sleeping Ella to James. "While I sign, can I tell you a story about my brother Drew? He had a cast just like yours."

James handed her a permanent marker and moved

away.

"Tell me, was it as cool as mine?" Sam asked. "How did he get it? Did he cry when he broke his arm?"

"Yeah, he probably did but I didn't ask." Andrea signed "Aunt Andi" with a flourish and a small heart at the end. "Drew was a little older than you, eleven."

"Did you see him break it?"

Andrea remembered every curse word out of her younger brother's mouth when she found him on the grass, stunned he'd fallen. "No. I didn't see the break, but I did see him fall off the roof."

"Was he chasing bad guys?" Sam asked, his brows drawn down in a frown. "Why else would Drew be on the roof? He's cool."

"Yeah, he's cool and smart now. But at eleven he was silly." Andrea considered sugarcoating Drew's reason for being on the roof. But honesty was usually best. "Drew was sneaking out to meet some friends. Drew was strong and big for eleven. He stood on the balcony outside his room, pulled himself onto the roof, jumped to the garage roof, and used a nearby tree to the ground. This time something went wrong. The roof was slippery. He slid off the roof and landed hard."

"Was your mom mad? Did she drive him to the hospital?"

"Mom wasn't home," Andrea answered as she carefully set Sam's casted arm on the pillow. "I drove Drew to the hospital. I was seventeen."

"Good. I'm glad you drove Drew." Sam's eyes started to close. "My stepdad drove me. My brothers supported my arm on the way." His voice faded. "Now I have a cool cast." His eyes closed and he drifted off.

Andrea joined Nikki in the sitting room. Curled on the couch, her hair wet from a recent shower, Nikki was dressed in a giant sweat suit to accommodate her growing belly. Ella slept in her arms. "Did he finally give up?" she asked.

"Yeah. I bored him with the story of Drew's broken arm."

"I remember. You couldn't reach your parents so you called my mom," Nikki commented. "We showed up in the hospital and claimed he was one of ours. Mom signed the treatment forms. Stupid Drew escaping across the roof. You couldn't have stopped him if he just walked out the door."

"Yeah. Getting out wasn't the appeal; it was the danger in his method of exit." She transferred Ella from Nikki's arms to her own. "So how did Sam break his arm?"

"Teenage girls, Mitch and Colin showing off, little brother trying to keep up. Disaster. Sam tried to jump a small, dry wash. His trusty steed was not impressed. Sam went over the wash without his horse. Lucky he wore a riding helmet, lucky only his arm broke."

"Mitch and Colin?" Andrea asked.

"Alex is still in the guy cave. Mitch stayed with Sam and Colin rode for Alex. When I got to the clinic, Sam sat on Mitch's lap, Mitch supporting his arm. So tender."

"They bonded, finally."

"Oh, I think they bonded a long time ago. Mitch has such a good heart. He just didn't like his life changing or sharing his father with another brother and a stepmother."

"Mitch watches you, Nikki. The bigger your belly,

the more he watches."

"Yeah. He worries. He was pretty little when Vanessa died but somewhere in his memory I wonder if he associates pregnancy or a new baby with the loss."

"Families are the very devil."

Ella finally asleep in her bed, Andrea crawled between the sheets and stretched. The warm presence inhabiting her room wrapped around her like a familiar blanket. She drifted off. In the dream, angry voices filtered up the stairs. Her parents fought, again. She recognized the sound though the words were unclear. Another sound reached her. Drew. She watched her seventeen-year-old self walk through the connecting bath to Drew's room. He thrashed around in his sleep; his broken arm complete with cast banged against the wall. Andrea knelt beside his bed, tried to wake him from the dream without startling him. She whispered his name, stroked his cheek. Drew's eyes opened. "Andi?"

"Nightmare?"

"Yeah." Sadness clouded his eyes, tinged with a trace of fear. "They're sending me away."

"What? Where?"

"Military boarding school somewhere in Virginia. They're throwing me away."

"No, Drew. I'm moving to an apartment for college. You're eleven; they can't leave you home alone once I move out." And they won't stay home with you, she didn't add.

"Yeah, I might break another arm." Andrea straightened his blankets, adjusted the cast on the pillow, and watched his eyes close.

She woke to dawn filtered through lace curtains. In

a shadowy corner Victoria and young RJ danced, his feet on hers, their hands clasped. The dancers drifted around the room to silent music, stopped beside her bed. RJ executed a charming bow and Victoria answered with a graceful curtsey. Smokey bounded into the room with a wagging tail and a bark. The spirits disappeared.

Andrea drifted to sleep; her last thought was Victoria set an excellent example of the joy of parenting, teachable moments turned into fun.

Chapter Nine

Dear Momma and Daddy,

Thanks for your letter and advice about handling Baby Emaline's late night crying. Just as you said, there was no way I could let her cry. The rocking chair's a big help and rubbing her gums gives some relief. I'm enclosing a separate letter from Violet addressed to you both. She wants to go to school in Creekside rather than going home. You said Lila and Jacob might stop on their honeymoon trip and pick her up. They are welcome to stay with us. Violet is also welcome to live here as long as she wants, if you'll allow it. She's been a big help, made some friends, and she can attend the Creekside School when it opens next month. George will make sure she gets back to you in time for school if that's what you decide. We'd love to keep her here, though, if that's okay.

~from Beloved Wife, Mother, Sister, and Friend, A Biography of Faith Taylor Eckie by Emaline Eckie Benson

****

Warm breeze, bright sun, tourists strolling around The Square, perfect day to hang out with Ella on the patio at Cuppa Joes. Ella dozed in the stroller. Something about even a short walk knocked her out. Andrea flipped through a magazine and sipped her coffee. A shadow fell over the table.

"Hello, Andrea."

Ugh, not again. Laurence. She ignored him and stared at the magazine. A chair scraped the concrete patio, the shadow moved. He wasn't going away, he sat down. "Laurence," she responded in a flat voice. She lifted her head and stared into his eyes.

"This time you're going to listen."

"Then will you leave me alone? No visits, no calls? Pretend you don't know me?" *What did I ever see in you?*

Laurence stared at her, surprise on his face. "You can't want me gone."

"It's exactly what I want. No more harassment," Andrea said.

"You're mine. You belong with me."

She slowly shook her head and let one corner of her lips lift. "Never yours. I always belonged only to myself."

"Your mother said you were getting a nanny and moving back to Scottsdale. Coming back to me."

"You believed my mother?" Of course he did, he believed whatever he wanted to believe regardless of the truth. "As if she'd know anything about me." *As if you know me at all.*

"Why would you give up everything we had for a baby? I've got kids and they're nothing but expensive trouble," he said.

"You wouldn't understand. Are you done now? Will you go away?"

"If you don't come back now, you've missed your chance." He pressed his arms on the table and leaned toward Andrea, scowling. Color stained his checks, his fists clenched.

"Not gonna happen." Rising, she accidently tapped her nearly full cup of coffee, sending the hot liquid running across the table, where it stained Laurence's white sleeves. Before he could scoot back, the coffee dripped off the table's edge onto his lap. She grabbed the stroller handles and walked away, her mirth floating on the breeze.

"Hey, what's so funny?" Nikki asked when she joined Andrea and Scott at the hotel's front desk.

Andrea struggled getting the words out around her giggles. "Nikki, you should have seen him. The look on his face as the hot coffee hit his lap."

"Who? Who drowned in coffee?"

"Laurence."

"You saw Laurence, and you're laughing?"

Andrea, her laughter under control, answered, "Amazing, huh. He showed up at Cuppa Joes, I accidently knocked over my coffee and it landed on his lap."

"And you didn't get pictures?"

Andrea's grin turned to laughter. "Oh, I should have."

"So, is he gone for good this time? Was drowning him in coffee enough of a hint?" Nikki asked. "Was it an expensive shirt?"

"Oh yeah. This was my last chance. If I didn't return to Scottsdale this minute, we're done," Andrea answered. "All his shirts are expensive, custom fitted."

"Dumb ass just didn't get it you were done the minute you threw him out of your townhouse."

"Shame, Aunt Nikki, you said ass," Scott commented. "Good thing Dad's not here."

"Not afraid of Patrick. Good thing Sam's not here,

he'd repeat it." She frowned at Scott. "Don't mention it to Alex either. What happens at the front desk stays at the front desk." She turned with Andrea toward the hallway. "Unbelievable," Nikki commented as she and Andrea strolled down the hall. "Unbelievable you had a last run in with Laurence, no Bentons around to back you up, and you walked away laughing."

"Couldn't have worked out better if I'd planned it."

****

Hours later Andrea settled Ella for the night in her bassinet. Dressed in a black nightgown created from T-shirt material, Andrea climbed into bed, Laurence's expression as the coffee dripped off the table a happy memory. Over, her affair with Laurence was finally, truly over and all she felt was relief. No hurt, no anger, no sadness, just a giant sigh of relief. Her eyes drifted shut. She slept.

Ping, the cell phone's notice of a text woke Andrea just as Ella let out a tiny cry. Rolling out of bed, she set the phone beside the rocking chair, lifted Ella. "Yuck, stinky diaper on a pretty girl." Entertaining Ella with silly sounds, she cleaned her up and stripped off the soggy pjs. Five minutes later, they were ensconced in the rocker, Ella nursing, her tiny fist wrapped around Andrea's nightgown. "Let's see who texted so early."

From Drew: —*We're engaged. It's official. Ring and everything.*— Attached was a photo of a white gold engagement ring, a large center stone surrounded by tiny diamonds.

Andrea moved Ella to the other side. "Just a minute and I'll catch your satisfied smile and send congratulations to your Uncle Drew."

Andrea attached Ella's photo to a text.

—Congratulations to you both. We're so happy!—

After breakfast, Jackson called. "I've a listing you may like. Not for lease but for sale."

"I'm interested. When can I see it?"

"Today, if you want. It's vacant and just came on the market."

Andrea's heart raced with excitement. "Today."

Jackson lounged against the veranda's front railing. He dashed to the front door and held it open as Andrea pushed the stroller. Jackson picked the stroller up and carried it down the three steps to the sidewalk. "Hey, ready to tour Eckie House?"

"We're ready," Andrea answered as she grabbed the stroller handles and they ambled away from the hotel. "I can hardly wait."

"You know it's haunted, right?"

"Any building more than a few years old in Creekside claims a ghost. It's all good. What do you know about Eckie House?"

"The original building is older than The Palace, The Hickory Building, or The Movie House," Jackson answered. "The kitchen was totally remodeled and modernized a couple of years ago. The original owner stayed until 1953. Since Faith Eckie died, it's had two owners with vacancy between. It's been vacant this time for about a year."

"This is Creekside; the building has a name. It's old, so there's a story."

They meandered away from the business district. "When George Eckie arrived in Creekside the town was tiny. Immediately, he built Eckie House on twenty acres. As soon as the house was finished, he left town. He returned one month later married to Faith Taylor.

He was forty; she was eighteen. Faith gave birth first to Emaline then to George Jr. George Sr. died during a bank robbery, leaving Faith a wealthy twenty-five-year-old widow with two small children and a very large property. That much of the story is verifiable."

"And then?" Andrea prompted.

"Legend claims one day a woman with a young child arrived, asking for work. Her husband was dead; she had nothing, nowhere to go. Faith took her in. Next, a former lady of the evening big with child. Faith took her in, too. Soon, women heard of Eckie House, a place of safety for themselves and their children."

"Eckie House must be big if Faith sheltered several families." Jackson handed Andrea the official listing. "Seven bedrooms?"

"Plus housekeeper quarters and an apartment over the garage."

"Did Faith sell the twenty acres?"

"Over time, she built small homes surrounding the main house, parcels of land she sold. Each parcel was bought by a woman who arrived in Creekside with nothing but her children and hope."

"So Faith built a neighborhood of women and children."

"Exactly. Eventually George Jr. and Emaline grew up, created their own families, and moved away. But until Faith's death in 1953, Eckie House was a refuge for women and children."

"Why are you so familiar with Faith's story?"

"I could claim I'm an excellent realtor who extensively researches each piece of property."

"I'm sure you are an excellent realtor...I hear a but." Andrea smiled.

"But Emaline Eckie wrote a short biography of her mother," Jackson admitted. "There's a copy in the historical society library."

Four blocks from The Palace, Eckie House stood three stories tall, a white porch wrapped around the building, a driveway stretched from the street, curling around the house, a lady with beautiful bones. Towering blue spruce trees stood sentinel beside the front walkway. Climbing roses wrapped around front porch pillars in an explosion of color, their perfume drifting on the summer air. There were four stairs to the porch, then it was about ten feet from the last step to an ancient wood door with stained glass decorating its top. Andrea crossed the threshold. Home, Eckie House was home. Logically, what would she do with four acres of land, seven bedrooms, a housekeeper apartment, a garage apartment, and nine and a half baths plus a living room, dining room, parlor, kitchen, breakfast room, and a sunroom stretched across one side of the house?

"It's zoned for a bed and breakfast; that's what the last owner intended and why the house has a commercial kitchen. Or you could remodel it into a triplex or quadruplex and the council would probably support the change since there's a precedent for multiple family units in the neighborhood."

Standing in the empty parlor, Andrea felt the hope, warmth, and comfort. They wandered through the house. Outside, Jackson pointed out a stand of fruit trees partially screening the second garage from the house.

After they walked back to The Palace, Andrea turned to Jackson. "I'll make an offer."

****

Just before dawn, Andrea woke to the sound of childish laughter. In a shadowy corner, RJ and another boy tumbled in a pile of gangly arms and legs. Smokey barked and then whined. Both boys, in sock feet, stood, looked at each other with big grins, took three quick steps, slid across a wooden floor, and tumbled, laughter filling the room. Smokey barked. The vision disappeared. Would she miss the usually happy spirits in The Palace when she moved? Or would the spirits of Eckie House appear? Would they keep her company, the way Victoria did?

Dancing into Nikki's office, Ella held in her arms, Andrea announced, "Eckie House is mine. They accepted my offer."

Jumping up, Nikki rounded the desk and drew Andrea and Ella into a hug. "Yay you." Nikki stepped back. "When can I see it?"

"Closing in thirty days. I can't wait to meet the Eckie House spirits."

****

Her feet propped on an ottoman, Andrea flipped through a decorating magazine. Ella watched the world and played with her hands in the stroller beside her, undisturbed by Andrea's mumbled questions. "Pink for your room, Ella. Ruffles. Or are you more clean lines and bright colors?"

Ella fussed, and Andrea looked up into familiar hazel eyes. "Couldn't stay away," Spencer admitted, a question in his eyes. "It's okay to visit, right?"

Ella's fussing turned to little cries. "Of course. Come on back, so I can put Ella down." They strolled the hallway to her room. New experience, a surprise visit from Dad, inviting him to her room. Her father settled in the desk chair while Andrea changed Ella and gently placed her in the bassinet.

He whispered, "Thanks for the pictures of your new house. It's one reason I came."

"Really? To see my house?"

"There's some of your grandmother's things in storage. Could you use them? I know you have plenty of money in your trust for furniture, but I wanted to offer."

Her mother redecorated the family home every few years and her taste tended toward modern, glass, and chrome. But her father had a storage unit full of grandmother's things? Did she know the man who raised her at all? "What sort of things?"

"Furniture, family heirlooms like quilts, and dishes. Here." He pulled out his phone. "I took these the other day." Picture after picture of furniture, decorative glass, paintings. "I can have it all moved here for you or you can pick out a few things or nothing."

"Everything. Move it all, okay? What I don't use I'll store for Drew." Noticing her father's wistful expression, she asked, "How did this happen? What made you put grandmother's things in storage?"

"Dorothy wanted all new. From our first house to our last, everything had to be new. When your grandmother died and the house sold, I put her things in storage. What else could I do? Someday you or Drew might want something from your grandmother, so I saved everything."

"I remember grandmother. When everything gets to Creekside, you come too. While we arrange furniture, you can tell me family stories I can pass on to

Ella. There has to be so much history wrapped in grandmother's things."

After dinner with her dad, and Ella's night ritual and late feeding, James called. "So, today you inherited a house full of furnishings. Busy day for you," James commented. "What trust?"

"Our grandparents set up trusts for Drew and me when we were born. At twenty-five, I gained control of mine."

"You're a trust fund baby?"

"Yep. It's how I bought the house. Ella's a trust fund baby too. Dad set up her trust the day she was born."

"Until moving to Creekside you lived in a small townhouse in a normal neighborhood. Not a typical trust fund baby."

"From the moment Nikki brought me home with her, I wanted to be like your family. You all worked, studied, played. So I did exactly the same thing." *I wanted to be just like you, part of a happy family where the children mattered.*

"It wasn't that way at your house?"

"No. The housekeeper worked, the nanny worked, the cleaning crew worked, the landscapers worked, my dad went to work, but I never understood what he did there. Mom played. Tennis, golf, cards. She exercised at the gym, attended yoga and spin classes, dragged my father to social events for charity. She worked at keeping herself beautiful and busy."

"You must have felt like you'd been dropped into another universe."

"Another universe where every person mattered. Know what seemed the weirdest to me?" *Beside the fact your mother talked to you every day, asked about your friends and school, listened to your thoughts and feelings. Is my sudden attraction to you a wish to tie you to me? A way to create a permanent place for myself in your family?*

"No idea."

"Ms. Effie. Nikki could hardly wait to help Ms. Effie make dinner. When your mom got home, everyone ate together in the kitchen, even Ms. Effie."

"Did you expect her to take hers home? After she cooked dinner, shouldn't she eat it?"

"Not only did she eat with you, she never did the dishes. Not once. Or cleaned off the table."

James remembered Ms. Effie and her cooking. "Mom said she who cooks is excused from cleanup. Plus I was never sure how old Ms. Effie was, but she was old."

"And patient, kind, good at homework, and an excellent cook."

"Yep. And she admired Patrick's and my skill with a lawn mower and hedge trimmers. Between our lawn and hers, we became experts. All the lawn mowing helped pay for college."

"I didn't know Ms. Effie paid you two for lawn work, though I knew you mowed many of the neighbor lawns."

"No. She did not pay us. Our sweat paid part of the after school and summer care bill so mom could work. Ms. Effie bragged about the great job we did, though. She was our entire marketing program."

Andrea climbed between the sheets. She pictured a gleaming, wooden table nestled under the kitchen window in Eckie House and Ella at age five, Andrea's age when Nikki brought her home from kindergarten like a lost puppy. Ella placed the silverware at three places around the table, knives and spoons on the right, forks on the left. Unlike Andrea on the first day, Ella knew just where everything belonged. Before her first dinner with the Bentons, Andrea never set the table or carried her own dishes to the sink. The nanny hustled her into the kitchen where she ate alone until Drew was old enough to join her. Andrea's eyes drifted closed; her breathing softened. Her last thought before sleep was she'd pass on to Ella everything Nikki's mom and Ms. Effie taught her about family.

She woke to the sound of Ella's cry. Victoria glided through the closed door heading for Ella's bassinet. She whispered to Ella whose cry slowed to a whimper. Victoria gazed directly into Andrea's eyes. Andrea threw the sheet back. Victoria disappeared, leaving a lingering scent of lavender. Another mother who couldn't leave a baby to cry.

Chapter Ten

Dear Momma,

I could see the tracks of your tears on your last letter and you can probably see mine on this one. After I sent Violet's letter off, she finally told me why she didn't want to go home. I wanted to run right down to Phoenix and attack that boy. How could anyone want to hurt our beautiful girl? George found us wrapped together on the settee in the parlor exhausted from tears. When he heard her story, he decided we both needed to know how to protect ourselves. So, you'll be proud to know Violet and I are learning how to fight back even though neither one of us is very big.

~from Beloved Wife, Mother, Sister, and Friend, A Biography of Faith Taylor Eckie by Emaline Eckie Benson

****

Coffee's comforting smell greeted Andrea when she opened the door. Eric must have arrived early. She paused at the sound of familiar laughter. James? James, leaning against the kitchen counter, a mug of coffee in his hand, laughed with Eric.

"Hey, you're here early," Andrea commented, drawing their attention.

"Good morning to you too," James answered. "Figured I'd get an early start. Eric just handed me the schedule."

"Nikki said every room is reserved. Where are you sleeping?" She blushed. Asking James about sleeping arrangements probably was not a good idea. Their late night conversations evolved from the casual checking in of longtime friends to discussions of values, dreams, and flirting.

James filled a mug with coffee, added a spoon of sugar, and handed it to Andrea. "Guy cave. The boys are already at Windsong. Patrick and I are sharing the guy cave because Nik rented our rooms out."

Andrea sipped, the hot liquid fixed exactly as she liked it. "Bellhop, right? Nikki assigned you bellhop?"

"Front desk, bartender sometimes." James grinned. "Only you would tell guests I'm the bellhop."

****

At nine o'clock, a million stars in a black velvet night greeted James when he stepped onto the upstairs veranda. He considered calling Andrea from here. Almost every night he called her, just checking in. The warmth in her voice helped him sleep except on the nights the flirting heated his blood. Then memories of the passion in their one kiss made him restless. It was time to find out what she wanted. Tonight, he could hear her live just by knocking on the door of Room 11, or he could call. Turning away from the view, he walked inside and locked the door behind him. One flight of stairs later he made a decision. He hiked the hallway, and then standing at her door, he raised his hand to knock. He sensed a presence beside him; Victoria looked his way, winked, and glided through the door. He knocked quietly; the door opened. Andrea stepped back. James pushed the door closed, flipped the lock, opened his arms, and pulled her against him. Ahh, her heart beat against his chest; her scent surrounded him.

"I wondered if you'd call," she whispered, "but this is better."

Their lips met, and through half-closed eyes, he watched her eyes close. Her sigh brushed his lips. He kissed the corners of her mouth, licked the seam, and she opened to him. Her hands glided against his cotton T-shirt, caressing his back. Heat fired his blood at the sound of her soft moan. Gathering his self-control, he gentled the kiss, finally looked into her passion-filled eyes, his voice slightly rough, he asked, "Do we move to the bed or the chairs?" He nuzzled her neck. "Take this farther, or cool it down?"

Taking his hand, she pulled him toward the bed and he mumbled, "Thank God." Facing each other, standing beside the bed, they watched each other undress. Andrea slipped between the sheets. James sat and yanked off his socks, stood and dropped his jeans. Pulled a condom from the pocket and tossed it on the nightstand. He caught her watching and mumbled, "My turn." He yanked the sheet away from her, his eyes focused on her smooth skin. "You're beautiful."

"So are you."

He lay beside her. "Let's see. Where were we? Here?" His tongue darted around the edge of her ear. "No? Then here?" He nuzzled her neck, placing soft kisses in a trail leading to her collarbone. Her breast cradled in his hand, his thumb rubbed softly against the nipple. "Or here?" Their lips met. Locked together, he rolled her under him, balancing his weight on his forearms.

Andrea caressed his back, gentle touches then

massaging the tense muscles holding him up. Her hands slid downward, over his butt. James moaned. His kisses traveled the length of her body, her collarbone, her breasts, hipbones, soft tummy. He stopped. Andrea opened her eyes slightly. James lifted an eyebrow. "May I?" Taking her sigh as a yes, he kissed her intimately. When she reached the knife-edge, he moved up her body, placed his lips against hers, thrust inside slowly, and over they went.

****

Dressed only in jeans, James whispered to Ella as he changed her diaper. Grabbing a T-shirt from the pile of garments on the floor, Andrea pulled it over her head and commented, "She's probably hungry."

Giving Ella a last tickle, he lifted her into Andrea's arms. While Ella nursed, James searched for his scattered clothes, picking up and folding Andrea's as he searched. "My shirt looks good on you."

"Sorry, your shirt was on top."

"No problem. It's three o'clock, and chances are no one will see me cross the hall bare chested." He buzzed her cheek. "See you in the morning." Across the hall and down the steps to the guy cave he strolled, his body so relaxed he could hardly wait to flop on the bed and sleep. A dim light crept under the boys' cave door. Patrick left the light on, one advantage to an older brother who always looked out for you. Finally, he climbed between cool sheets.

Waking to the shower's sound, hands behind his head, James wished he'd wakened in Andrea's arms. Would she welcome him tonight? Too soon to move into her room.

The shower stopped; Patrick, towel wrapped

around his waist, stared down at him. "You know if you hurt her, the rest of us will make you pay?"

"And if she hurts me?"

Patrick shrugged. "Your problem. Figure you can take of yourself."

****

Glasses of wine in hand, Patrick and James lounged on the upstairs veranda. The moon peeked between the clouds and the stars winked on in the black sky.

"So did we complete Nikki's list?" Patrick asked, his head resting against the chair's high back, his eyes closed.

"Everything except chasing the guests off the upstairs veranda and locking the doors," James answered.

"Well, we're not really guests. We're staying in the guy cave."

James glanced at his brother, surprised how relaxed he looked. "Anyway, we own the place, sort of."

"Yeah, or at least part of it. Right now we own this part."

"Yep. Tonight our little sister appreciated our help for a change. She didn't hesitate to leave us in charge."

"Sam was desperate to join the other guys at the ranch, and Nik was anxious to spend the night with her husband," Patrick added and sipped his wine. "She and Alex missed the honeymoon phase, went from engaged to married with children."

"Yeah, well I offered to take over the hotel and the boys for a month after the wedding and she turned me down," James admitted. "The first weeks of January are usually pretty slow at work anyway."

"I offered too. Thought the newlyweds deserved a little time without kids and jobs. Guess they were ready to start building their life together."

Creekside night sounds of traffic and music seemed very far away. Tomorrow night it would be a full house, not one room open to rent for rest of the holiday. Thinking about rooms, James asked, "How's the house sale going? Any nibbles?"

Patrick lifted his glass in a mock toast. "Sold it."

"Hey, good for you. So, when are you moving to the beach shack?"

"Not moving to a beach shack. Moving to Creekside. One more room in the Palace occupied by a Benton."

Surprised, James asked, "What about your law practice?"

"Sold the practice too. Partners bought me out."

"Why?"

"Why not? Amy picked the house. Stayed there because of Scott. He's not coming back, why stay any longer?"

"Oh, I get selling the house. But you love the beach, surfing, sailing, all the California life. You loved the beach even when we were kids and lived in the desert."

"Yep. Love the beach, but I'm ready for a different life."

"And the law practice? Are you ready for something other than law?"

"For a while, I'm going with innkeeper. Eventually, I'll probably open a law office. I still have an Arizona license."

What do you say when your older brother says he's

totally changing his life? Congratulations? Best wishes? Are you crazy? "So, does Nikki know?"

"Not yet. But she will soon."

"Thirty day closing?"

"Yep. When the baby comes, I'll already be here making sure our sister gets all the help she needs."

"I'm sure she'll appreciate it. Not. And you'll be closer to Scott."

"That too."

"Speaking of Scott, look over there." A familiar small SUV pulled in front of the hotel. Lights doused, engine turned off. Silence. Eventually, the passenger door opened. Scott climbed out. Engine revved, lights on, car eased out of the parking space and disappeared around a corner. Scott jogged around the building.

Patrick handed his glass to James. "Take care of this." He disappeared out the door; his steps echoed on the stairs. Must be tough when your only child is suddenly a man. Especially a man with his own ideas about where he should live, who he should love. Patrick's concern was understandable. Scott and Casey were both starting college at NAU in September, both dependent on their families. Biggest concern, each other's first love. Just like Nikki and Aaron. He used to like Aaron until he walked out on Nikki. How could Aaron sleep at night knowing he deserted Nik when she needed him most? What Aaron did wasn't as terrible as some of what he'd seen working pro bono for the women referred by the crisis shelter. But Aaron's betrayal was personal.

Andrea opened the door to his knock, a finger to her lips. Door pushed shut and locked, James opened his arms, pulling her tight against his chest. "Better."

"Better than what?"

"Better than a starry night viewed from the veranda, better than conversation with my older brother, better than a final glass of red wine."

"I'm flattered. You love Patrick, starry nights, and red wine," she teased.

"But holding you is better." How did this happen? When? Tonight, holding Andrea, hearing her voice, seeing her smile was the best part of his day.

"Where are your thoughts? Is everything okay with Patrick?"

"Just making tough decisions."

"What decisions?"

"Do we keep our clothes on and talk sitting in the chairs, or do we take our clothes off and talk lying in bed?" He sighed. "Very tough decision."

"Oh. And do I get a vote?"

"Your vote carries the most weight." His arms still encircling her, he kicked off his shoes. She placed her hands on his chest and started unbuttoning his shirt. "Perfect. It's unanimous. No clothes, bed."

****

Tuesday. Clear sky, a gentle breeze pushed a few stray leaves along the grass. Tourists strolling the sidewalks, conversation occasionally punctuated by sudden laughter. Ainsley wove her way along the sidewalk heading to The Palace for a tea party. She glanced up at Room 15. Victoria waited partly hidden behind a lace curtain. Ainsley started to raise her hand in a wave. Time stopped. Scattered across the veranda, ladies wearing colorful 1920's dresses gathered in small groups, teacups in their hands. Ainsley blinked; the vision disappeared. Catherine, Nikki, and Andrea lounged on the Palace's front porch, baby Ella asleep on her mother's lap. "Afternoon tea?"

"Exactly," Nikki responded. "Ahh. Here comes the food." Mary Beth from Cuppa Joes carried a tray up the veranda steps. "Thank you."

Mary Beth set the tray on a table. "Way I understood it, if I didn't deliver the food, there was trouble on my horizon from the law."

"Little overprotective, my Alex," Nikki admitted.

Mary Beth arranged the service on the table. "Well, why should you pick up a tray when I was invited to the party?"

"True. Shelby's on her way. Maybe she'll write our tea party up as a major social event with catering provided by Cuppa Joe's."

"My ears are burning. Were you talking about me?" Shelby asked as she plopped in a chair and reached for the pitcher of iced tea.

"Guilty. I thought you might give Mary Beth a plug by writing up our tea party as a social event," Nikki answered.

"Wouldn't be the first time tea at The Palace made *The Reporter*," Shelby answered. "Lately, I've spent lots of time reading old copies of *The Reporter*. In the 1900s, tea parties, weddings, engagements, new residents, new businesses all warranted thorough descriptions."

"Hi, ladies." Scott walked onto the veranda. Spotting the tray of cakes and tiny sandwiches, he added, "There's food and you didn't invite me?"

"Help yourself, but hand me the phone first," Nikki commented. "You finished the pictures?"

"Yeah." Nikki took the phone while Scott loaded a

plate. "Piles of furniture in the basement, Aunt Nikki. You only have to choose."

"Pictures?" Catherine asked.

"We're furnishing the third room in the attic for Patrick," Nikki answered. "He's moving into The Palace at the end of June."

Shelby asked, "Temporary or permanent?"

"Permanent," Scott answered. "He sold the house and his share of the practice."

Nikki handed the phone back to Scott. "Mark what you think he'd like. Then I'll make a decision."

He flipped through the pictures, moving his favorites to an album. Handing the phone back to Nikki, he asked, "Anything else?"

"Nope," Nikki answered. "You can go to Casey's now."

Scott blushed. "Thanks, Aunt Nikki."

"So, Patrick's moving in before the baby comes?" Shelby asked.

"That's the plan. He'll move in just about the time Andrea moves out. He thinks he's taking over running the hotel."

"Well he does own part of it," Andrea commented. "Why shouldn't he help out?"

"Oh, I'm happy for the help." Nikki poured a glass of tea. "Patrick takes over, though. Oldest child syndrome."

"Hey, won't it be great to have some time just being a mom?" Shelby asked. "Even *The Reporter* pays six weeks maternity leave."

Nikki sipped her peppermint tea. "But getting control back from Patrick won't be easy."

"Maybe Henderson will finally retire and Patrick

could take over the law office," Mary Beth suggested. "In fact, I think he was looking for a partner so he could cut back. The man's seventy if he's a day."

"That would be perfect. Patrick in Creekside not running the hotel would be perfect. Maybe Alex will mention Creekside's need for an attorney to Patrick."

"He's not even here yet, and you're looking for ways to keep him away from The Palace."

"Exactly," Nikki admitted. "Outwitting either of my brothers takes cunning and thorough planning."

"Speaking of planning, no more delays. Let's plan a baby shower and housewarming for Andrea," interjected Mary Beth. "When do you move in?"

"June 15. We also need a baby shower for Nikki," Andrea answered. "Let's combine everything into one celebration."

****

Shadows drenched Room 11, broken only by the desk lamp shining on Andrea's list. First, a page with furniture for Ella's room, and another with supplies for the kitchen and pantry. June 15, moving day, a big change from a hotel room to a house, a home. Would James drift away when she moved from the hotel? She flipped off the lamp and climbed into bed. Would their relationship survive her move? With Laurence, she accepted the relationship was temporary. How long could anything last when the future stretched out more of the same? Evenings spent with people she found interesting but never developed a close connection with. Nights spent in bed with someone whose primary topic of conversation was himself. Two years together and she doubted he knew her favorite color or even her favorite restaurant. He proved he had no idea of her values when he demanded she get an abortion. She would not let it happen again. She'd rather be alone than with someone who never bothered to know her. She closed her eyes and drifted into sleep.

Ella's whimpers woke her from a dreamless sleep. In the shadowy room, Victoria glided through the door. The spirit leaned over Ella's bassinet and adjusted the blanket. Andrea tossed back the sheet and rolled out of bed. Victoria disappeared.

Andrea stripped off Ella's diaper, cleaned her with a wipe, and anchored the fresh diaper with its sticky tabs. "Will you miss Victoria?" she whispered to her daughter. "Will other spirits visit you in Eckie House?" She lifted Ella in her arms and swayed slightly left to right. "When you grow up will you remember the time we shared a room in a haunted hotel and Victoria appeared to comfort you?" Ella's breathing evened and Andrea nestled her in the bassinet. Would her daughter have any memory of living in The Palace?

Chapter Eleven

Merry Christmas Family!

Hope your Christmas is filled with joy. Violet, Emaline, George, and I had so much fun finding gifts for everyone. We wish we could be there to see you open the box. Be very careful. In the bottom is a special gift for Momma and Daddy. Creekside celebrated the holiday in style with a community Holiday Party hosted by the local churches. There was food, music, games, and small gifts for every child. Oh, Momma, sometimes it's hard to see the children who don't have as much as we do. At least the community united to make sure every child had one gift and every family received a basket of holiday goodies.

~from Beloved Wife, Mother, Sister, and Friend, A Biography of Faith Taylor Eckie by Emaline Eckie Benson

****

Sun glinted through the lobby windows making the old wood floors shine. The Beatles claimed "I Get By With a Little Help From My Friends" and Andrea, buckling the stroller strap around Ella, grinned at the sound of Nikki's off key humming. As Andrea straightened, Nikki asked, "Ready?"

Squaring her shoulders, Andrea nodded. "Ready."

"Let's do it. Scott, you're in charge of the hotel." Nikki handed James a basket and a broom. "Here, make yourself useful. You can carry this."

"What is it?" James asked. "Besides the broom."

"Everything needed to make moving positive and prosperous for Andrea," Nikki answered.

James mumbled about superstitious nonsense and took the basket and broom from Nikki's hands.

Walking toward Eckie House, Andrea pushed Ella in the stroller and whispered to Nikki, "So what's in the basket?"

"Well, you have a new broom to sweep away the old troubles. Burn the candles the first night you stay in the house. The candles bring light and push away darkness. A house blessing."

"Nikki, did you burn candles your first night in The Palace?"

"Yeah. And replaced my old broom with a new one, leaving my problems behind."

Eckie House rose before them, her lawn mowed, bushes trimmed, glass sparkling in the sun. Jackson waited beside the front door.

"Go." James took the stroller handles.

Andrea climbed the steps to the porch and joined Jackson at the front door. He handed her the key. "It's all yours."

Andrea, key in hand, looked back at James and Nikki. Her face lit with a smile. "Welcome to my new home."

Inside, Andrea and James strolled through the downstairs rooms. Nikki pleaded swollen ankles, lifted Ella from her stroller, and cuddled her, sitting on the stairs. Andrea's and James' voices drifted away, replaced by the comforting sounds of an old house settling. Humming a lullaby, her mind wandering,

Nikki suddenly heard childish giggles and the living room filled with children playing board games on the hardwood floor. Dolls perched on shelves, books piled in a corner. Andrea's laugh carried from the other end of the house and the children disappeared, leaving an empty room, dust motes dancing in the sunlight filtered through the windows. A happy home, Andrea owned a happy home. Nikki rose, Ella in her arms, and met Andrea and James in the foyer.

****

Moving day. Andrea pushed open the Eckie House front door just as the sun peeked over the horizon. Wood floors shone from a recent cleaning, polished and waiting. Built-in bookcases glinted in the early sunlight. Kitchen counters gleamed, the refrigerator hummed, every cabinet shelf boasted new paper. The ramp Donaldson installed created a gentle slope from the back porch to the ground. The only thing missing was a plan.

When she moved into her townhouse, she'd had a plan and a contingency plan in case something didn't look the way she expected. She assigned a place for every piece of furniture. She'd looked at the pictures of her grandmother's furniture, but everything was out of context, nothing to compare for size, no measurements. Today's move reminded her of her life since finding out she was pregnant.

Plan A before Ella included college, success in her profession, her own home, and someday a loving husband and children. After six months with Laurence, she knew he wasn't loving husband material, but he was good company, enjoyed trendy restaurants, charity galas, and movies. She was busy establishing herself in her profession and learning to administer her trust. Being with Laurence was easy; they had no expectations of each other, no deep conversations. When the doctor confirmed her pregnancy Andrea suddenly figured out why her relationship with Laurence was easy but not satisfying. They were living her mother's life.

She climbed the stairs to the master bedroom and Ella's room. Boxes sat on the floor. Ella's crib, ordered online, and a changing table and dresser waited for assembly. Every bedroom door bore a label; at least, she could direct the movers to a specific room. Probably wouldn't do much good since there was no plan. A small elevator, hidden behind panel doors in the kitchen, could carry one piece of furniture at a time. The dumbwaiter ran from the laundry to a closet on each floor. Startled by the doorbell's chiming, Andrea dashed down the stairs.

****

Exhausted, Andrea dropped into a wing chair. Ella, finally settled comfortably at the breast, nursed. Sam, Hope, and Lily played a board game on the floor. She should help James assemble and arrange Ella's room, or help her dad put sheets on the beds. While Ella nursed, Andrea's eyes drifted shut. Automatically, she transferred Ella to her shoulder, patting her little back. A callused finger touched her cheek. Andrea's eyelids lifted and she gazed into James' familiar hazel eyes.

He lifted Ella from her arms. "Dinner's here." She took his offered hand and rose.

Standing on the back porch, admiring a black velvet sky filled with stars and a sliver of moon riding high, quiet surrounded Andrea. Claiming a mixture of exhaustion and emails waiting for a response, Spencer retired an hour ago. Her tummy full, exhausted after a bath, Ella slept in her new crib. Taking a final sip of the red wine she'd nursed since dinner, Andrea opened the French door and returned to the kitchen. From the top shelf of the pantry, Andrea retrieved the small box Ainsley gave her the day she closed on Eckie House. Curled up on the sofa in the main parlor, she carefully removed the wrapping. Inside, she found a framed watercolor miniature of a young woman wearing old-fashioned clothing, a baby wrapped in a pale blue blanket in her arms. A little girl, perched on the woman's knee, leaned toward the baby. Chance Pagent's signature rested in the bottom right corner. On the back a small plaque: Perfect Love, Faith, Emaline, and George Jr. Andrea stood the miniature on the picture rail beside the mantel in the main parlor and whispered, "Welcome home." She checked the locks on every door, turned out the lights, then climbed the stairs to Ella's room. Ella slept, her tiny fist pressed against her pink lips. In the master bedroom Andrea flipped the monitor volume to high and listened to Ella breathe. Dressed in a summer nightgown, Andrea slid between soft, white sheets and drifted to sleep.

Hours later, she startled awake to the sound of a wooden chair scraping against a wood floor. Blinking her eyes to adjust to the low light, Andrea focused on a young woman slipping into a wooden chair pushed up to a small desk. In the stillness, Andrea heard the desk drawer open, then close. Now the woman held a fountain pen in one hand and a small book lay open on the desk. The woman's face lit with a smile. Beside her, a small girl dressed in a white nightgown appeared.

"Momma," she whispered, "come tuck me in." The wooden chair scraped again, the woman rose, taking the child's hand. They disappeared. Perhaps she wouldn't miss Victoria after all.

****

Celebration. Conversation, music from a borrowed speaker, the tinkling of glasses touched in a toast. High heels beating a tattoo on wood floors, the whir of a blender, the pop of a cork, the clink of ice in a pitcher of iced tea. Appetizers arranged on sparkling platters, baby gifts in neat piles on a long table in the library, housewarming gifts on her grandmother's desk in the parlor. Celebration of new home, celebration of new life. Six-thirty, an exodus, hugs, best wishes, congratulations, compliments on the house, on Ella's beauty, on the party. Ainsley, Catherine, Nikki, and Andrea paced through the rooms gathering glasses, plates, napkins, and silver, delivering them to Patrick and James loading the dishwashers in the kitchen. Andrea stopped on the living room threshold. Her father, wearing a white dress shirt with sleeves rolled to the elbow, sat cross-legged on the rug. Ella, on a blanket, laughed her baby laugh showing off her latest accomplishment, a roll. Flashes from her own childhood flipped through her mind—moments when her father held Drew, spoke to her in his gentle voice.

In the kitchen, Ella, ensconced in her swing, concentrated on watching the colorful plastic rings suspended from the swing's top move back and forth. Left over appetizers spread between them on the kitchen table, Andrea and Spencer created dinner. "Great party. I've never been to a baby shower," Spencer commented. "I like your friends."

"They do love a reason to celebrate."

"What are your plans for Eckie House? I heard lots of theories from your neighbors."

Andrea lifted her water glass and sipped. "No one believes I might just live in Eckie House with Ella. It's zoned for a bed and breakfast."

"Is that what you're planning?"

Andrea shrugged. "Right now I plan to get everything put away, all the moving boxes emptied."

"Well, whatever you do, please save me a room." Spencer tapped Ella's colorful rings and made them dance. "I'll need lots of time to spoil my grandchild."

"I don't need to run a bed and breakfast to fill the rooms," Andrea admitted. "One for me, one for Ella, one for you, one for Drew and Jodi, only three left. Plus the apartment over the garage and the housekeeper apartment."

Ten o'clock, Andrea climbed the stairs, checked on sleeping Ella and, dressed in cut-off sweats and a tank top, tumbled into bed. Of course, her neighbors speculated about plans for Eckie House. What did a single woman with a baby need with so much space? They didn't understand she needed a permanent home, a home that surrounded her with warmth and comfort. Home where family was always welcome, family by blood and family by choice. Her cell phone rang James' ringtone "Save a Horse."

"Didn't I just talk to you a few hours ago?" she asked.

"Yeah. But other people surrounded us. Great party by the way."

"Yep, excellent party. Are you going home tomorrow?"

"Have to. Work beckons. I'll stop by in the morning to say goodbye."

"You could have stayed here tonight," she offered. "I've plenty of room."

"Couldn't. Not with Spencer there."

"Why not?"

"Embarrassing if I slept in your room with your dad down the hall."

"You could have your own room."

"That would be worse. Too much temptation to find my way down the hall to your bed in the middle of the night. Awkward if I ran into your dad."

"Does it bother you people assume we're sleeping together?"

"No. Not at all. We're single, consenting adults. Anyway, I'm proud you want to sleep with me."

"But not in front of my dad?"

"It's different. One thing to know your daughter sleeps with a guy, something else to have it thrown in your face. Anyway, I plan sleeping with you for a long time. Don't want to start pissing off your dad."

Finally, she drifted into sleep, her last thought he planned to sleep with her for a long time. Good sign.

Blue sky, white clouds, bright sun, and Ella in her arms, Andrea stood on the front porch and watched her father drive away. Before she could open the front door, James pulled up. His car door slammed. He bounded up beside her on the porch, leaned over, and buzzed her cheek. "Spencer just left?"

"Yep. Good morning to you too." She lifted on her toes and kissed his lips. His arms circled her, trapping Ella between them. He deepened the kiss, sending warmth from her lips to her toes. "Mmm." Andrea pulled back. "Better. Much better good morning kiss."

"Definitely, though you bruise my manly ego with your complaint." He handed her a small wrapped package. "I've brought you a housewarming gift."

"What is it?"

Ella in his arms, James opened the door using a hand on the small of her back to encourage her inside. "Can you spare a cup of coffee while you open your gift?" he asked.

"Of course." She led the way to the kitchen. They sat at the kitchen table, Ella belted in her swing. Andrea pulled the bow, and it dropped to the table. Carefully she used a fingernail to lift the tape.

James sighed. "You always did take forever to open a gift."

"The anticipation is usually the best part."

"But tough on the other people waiting to know if you like it, waiting for their turn."

Andrea peeled back the paper. A book, a very old book bound in blue with gold lettering on the front. *Beloved Wife, Mother, Sister and Friend. A Biography of Faith Taylor Eckie by Emaline Eckie Benson.* "Where did you find this?"

"I can't take the credit. One of my clients deals in old and rare books. He found it," James admitted. "The Historical Society wasn't interested in selling me their copy."

"Thank you. It's perfect."

James rose, set his empty mug on the counter, and drew Andrea into his arms. "I'm glad you like it." He tightened the embrace. "You feel so good. I missed you the last few nights."

"I offered you a room."

"Sorry, can't share your bed with Spencer in the house. Next time maybe he won't stay so long or I'll come when he's not here." Ella started whimpering, preparing for a full-on cry. James released Andrea. "I'd better go." He lifted Ella from the swing. "Eww, stinky." He handed her to Andrea and disappeared out the kitchen door.

Ella nestled in her crib for a morning snooze; Andrea grabbed the monitor and climbed the stairs to the third floor. The rush to get furniture out of the moving van and then prepare for the housewarming meant she couldn't remember what the three bedrooms contained. She ambled into the largest of the rooms. A double bed held pride of place, its mahogany four posters elegant sentinels; a star quilt covered the mattress. Beside the bed, a wooden rocker dressed with a needlepoint cushion waited. Andrea dropped into the rocker and fingered the quilt. Tiny hand stitches anchored each piece of the star. She lifted the bottom hem and read, "For Anna Lea to keep you safe and warm. Love Mother." Her great-grandmother's quilt. Family history. Odd she did not know much of her family's history, not on either side. She remembered her grandmother's funeral more because she held Drew's hand or trapped his four-year-old body on her lap through the service. Next time her father visited they needed to talk about family history.

Chapter Twelve

Dear Momma,

Happy New Year 1908. I'm so glad you liked the family portrait. You know I stole the idea from Jacob and Lila since they sent us one of their wedding pictures in a frame. We decided to make the portrait an annual event. A second annual event is the New Year's Eve Party on the Square. After seeing the number of families just getting by a group of us decided to place a donation box at the Square during the New Year's Eve Party. Everything collected we put in the Community Exchange. We wanted to be careful of people's pride so no prices on the goods just bring something to add and you can take something you need. You'd be proud of Violet. She convinced some of her friends to donate time to the Community Exchange after school.

~from Beloved Wife, Mother, Sister, and Friend. A Biography of Faith Taylor Eckie by Emaline Eckie Benson

****

Startled by "One Less Bell to Answer," Andrea glanced at Ella sleeping in the portable crib undisturbed by the doorbell's song and dashed to the front door. An unfamiliar young, blonde woman waited on the step.

"Hi. Are you Andrea Hamilton?" she asked.

Surprised, Andrea answered, "Yes. And you are?"

"Carly Edwards. Laurence Edwards is my father."

"Come in, Carly Edwards." Andrea motioned her inside. "Have a seat in the living room. I'll be right back." Leaving Carly to find a seat, Andrea sprinted to the bookroom. Ella slept in the portable crib. "Lucky you, Ella," Andrea whispered, touched Ella's cheek, and grabbed the monitor. Returned to the living room, she sat across from Carly. "What can I do for you?"

"I want to meet my sister."

Andrea tried to remember Laurence's comments about his oldest child. Money pit, scatterbrained, silly. Nothing scary, no stories about real trouble. Dressed in jeans, T-shirt, low boots, and carrying a small backpack, Carly looked the college student she was. "Why?"

A surprised look crossed her face. "Because she's my sister?"

"Only through biology," Andrea answered. *He'll never really be Ella's father.*

"I know. Dad forfeited his parental rights."

"He told you?"

Blushing, Carly admitted, "Not likely. Eavesdropping. I overhead him talking to his lawyer." Carly raised her hands in an attitude of surrender. "I know it doesn't sound good, but we were at dinner and Dad answered his cell. Hard not to hear."

Familiar with Laurence's penchant for letting his cell interrupt meals, Andrea accepted the answer. "Still doesn't explain your interest in Ella."

"You know Scott Benton?" Andrea nodded. "I met him and Casey at freshman orientation at NAU. They talked a lot about his Aunt Nikki and her haunted hotel."

"And they mentioned me?"

"Yeah. Only in a good way and because you lived for months in the hotel. Please, I just want to see her. She's almost family."

Andrea gazed into Carly's pleading eyes. What could it hurt? Ella wouldn't know the difference. "Okay. Come with me." Andrea hesitated at the bookroom door. "She's napping." She led Carly to the portable crib. Ella rolled over and opened her eyes, grinning her toothless grin. Andrea lifted Ella from the crib. "Let me change her." Now dry, Ella cooed as Carly held her. Sisters sort of. Laurence's daughters. Though Carly spent time with Laurence, benefited from his financial support, Andrea believed Ella was better off without him. Better no father than one who didn't want you. Ella fussed; Andrea took her from Carly with, "Time for food for this one."

Carly rose. "Andrea, can I visit again?"

Andrea, Ella in her arms, nodded. "Next time call, though; we're not always home." They exchanged numbers and Carly was gone.

Random thoughts of Carly intruded all afternoon as Andrea focused on Ella and work. Would Carly visit again? If the tables were turned, if Andrea discovered a half sibling what would she do? Some of her friends came from blended families. Sometimes a close bond grew among the children, but most seemed decidedly cool toward each other, especially when the children lived at least part of the time with a different parent. Jealousy, resentment, possessiveness? Why did some blended families work and others not? Nikki's family represented more blending than most with Alex's sons, Sheri's son, and soon their baby girl. Yet her friend was happier than she'd ever seen her. The older boys pulled

Sam into their tribe, and both Colin and Mitch were gentle with Nikki, tender and watchful the closer she got to term.

The cell phone ringing interrupted her thoughts. It was Patrick. "Andi, baby's coming. Can you take over as innkeeper?"

"On my way." In ten minutes, she sat behind the front desk, Ella beside her in the stroller. Moments later, Chance dashed through the door.

"As ordered," he saluted. "I'm removing your daughter to a better place."

"Exactly what makes Sanders House better than The Palace?"

"Hope, Lily, and Catherine are waiting patiently for their favorite baby." He grabbed the diaper bag, picked up the stroller, Ella included, and sauntered out the hotel's front door.

****

Midnight, she woke to the sound of James' ringtone. "She's here. Michele Elizabeth Stark. Momma and baby both doing well."

"James? You're at the hospital?"

His baritone chuckle rumbled through the phone. "I woke you up. Again."

She gave herself a moment to clear her head. "They're both well?"

"Yep. Can I stay with you tonight?"

Suddenly, Andrea was wide awake. "Yep."

****

Warm summer air, black velvet sky, faint new moon greeted James outside the hospital. He flashed to his last sight of Nikki and baby Michelle. Baby nestled in her arms, Nikki rested propped up in the hospital

143

bed. Beside the bed, Alex slept in a chair, his head next to Nikki on the bed, his hand on her hip. James planted a gentle kiss on his sister's forehead and the fuzzy head of his niece and left the family to sleep.

The porch light cast a soft glow when he reached Eckie House. Inside, he quietly climbed the back stairs and checked on Ella in her nursery. In Andrea's room, he stripped to boxers and climbed into bed beside her. She opened one eye then opened her arms. Accepting her invitation, he pulled her against his chest, heart to heart.

She whispered, "Welcome home."

He stilled. Her breathing evened and he knew she slept. Home. Was Eckie House his home? Sleep took him before he found an answer.

Andrea's quiet voice through the monitor woke him. Yesterday's clothes he found folded on a chair and his small duffle bag sat beside the bathroom door. Showered and shaved, he followed the scent of coffee to the kitchen. "Good morning. Coffee ready?" he asked.

"Yep. Mugs are above the coffee maker."

He filled a mug, and then grabbed the silver, napkins, and plates, setting the table exactly as they'd been taught. "You make a pretty picture fixing breakfast in the sun." In concert, they dished up breakfast, buttered the toast, and sat down. Ella, strapped in her high chair, pounded her spoon on the tray. "Is she hungry?"

"No. She's eaten." Andrea made a face and Ella responded with a laugh. "We sit at the table for breakfast most days. She's not much of a conversationalist, but she's a great listener."

"She watches every move you make."

"Yep. Heady feeling knowing she finds me fascinating," she answered, watching Ella watch her lips.

James touched her hand, bringing her attention to him. "I find you infinitely fascinating."

Time flew and then he was gone, again. What was their relationship? Of course, they were friends and now occasional lovers. Laurence spelled out exactly what he wanted on their third date. A beautiful escort, an intelligent companion, and frequent sex. In return, he took her to glittering social events, business dinners in five-star restaurants, and golf vacations at four- and five-star resorts. All things she could afford on her own with the trust fund, but having an escort was nice. Andrea plopped in her favorite chair, Ella in her arms. Yuck, her life with Laurence was exactly like her parents' marriage except she held down a full-time job. No wonder she'd felt vaguely uneasy most of the time. She was living someone else's life, not the life she wanted. Not anymore. Parenting Ella, owning Eckie House, building a new relationship with her dad, sleeping with James, all her choices. Yeah, no matter what came next, this was her life lived her way.

Blue sky, midsummer heat, Andrea propelled the stroller down the ramp, onto the walkway, and around Eckie House to the sidewalk heading toward The Palace. Thinking of baby Michelle, soon to be her goddaughter, she quickened her pace. A block from the center of town, tourists meandered and stopped, peered in shop windows, checked out restaurant menus displayed in windows, and crowded the sidewalk. Maneuvering the stroller around a line in front of

Willie's Pizza, she glanced up. There was Patrick, waiting in line. "Getting lunch?" she asked.

"My assignment for this afternoon. Lunch. On your way to visit Michelle?"

"And Nikki." He waved her on.

In front of The Palace, she peered up at Room 15 No Victoria today. What would Mother think of her searching out the company of a ghost? She pushed the stroller through the hotel's parking lot After tapping in the code for the back door, she entered the quiet hallway. Victoria stood in front of the door to Room 10, Nikki's sitting room door. Their eyes met. Victoria turned and glided through the closed door. Andrea raised her hand to knock and the door opened. "Hey Mitch, perfect timing. How'd you know I was about to knock?"

"Hi Aunt Andi. Scott heard you open the back door and texted me." Scott peeked his head into the hallway and waved at her from the lobby.

Andrea pushed the stroller into the sitting room, spotting Nikki ensconced in a rocking chair. Michelle, wrapped in a pale green blanket decorated with dancing tigers, nestled in her arms.

Ella in her arms, Andrea switched to a chair beside her best friend. For a moment, superimposed over Nikki, Andrea saw another woman, another rocking chair, a baby wrapped in a yellow blanket in her arms. Andrea blinked. Victoria disappeared.

"Need anything, Nik?" Mitch asked, his hand on the door.

"Not a thing. You going out front with Scott?" Mitch nodded and disappeared out the door.

Holding Michelle, Ella in Nikki's arms, Andrea

commented, "Quiet in here. Where is everybody?"

"Patrick's getting lunch, Sam and Colin are at the ranch, Alex is keeping Creekside safe, and now Scott and Mitch are out front. Finally, not one hovering male in the place."

"So, why is Mitch here if the others are at Windsong?"

Nikki leaned toward Andrea. "He has a date, in town, at the movies."

"Oh. A date. Just him and a girl?"

Nikki sat back and shook her head. "Not exactly. More like a triple date, Mitch, two friends, and three girls."

"So what's Alex think about Mitch going on a date?"

"He's not very happy. He worries. Remember Quinten?"

"Tall, blond, charming Quinten? Quinten, my prom date of the octopus arms?"

"Yeah." Nikki grinned evilly. "Wonder if he was able to father children after you stopped his wandering hands?"

"Hey, your brother taught me that move." They laughed.

Patrick walked in balancing pizza boxes, Mitch one step behind. "Hey, share the joke."

Nikki and Andrea laughed on. "Can't. Private joke. Girl joke," they answered.

****

Weaving expertly between clumps of tourists, Andrea pushed the stroller toward Eckie House after lunch. Shared childhood, shared secrets, and shared laughter, the foundation of her friendship with Nikki.

Was that part of her attraction to James? He figured prominently in her memories of elementary school. Memories of James, Patrick, and Craig tangled with memories of Nikki, Ms. Effie, and Nikki's mom. Pushing Ella's stroller up the ramp, her thoughts veered to Carly. Someday would Ella's childhood memories include a half-sister? And James, had he ever invested time in finding his half-sisters, his father's other family? Questions for another day.

Chapter Thirteen

1909

Dear Momma and Daddy,

Happy Easter. So many things to be grateful for at our house. Violet may have told you she won an award for her drawing of Eckie House. I had George take a picture of her picture with his new camera and it's enclosed. Also, Emaline is going to be a big sister in October. We're so excited. We both love the sounds of happy children and we can hardly wait.

~from Beloved Wife, Mother, Sister, and Friend, A Biography of Faith Taylor Eckie by Emaline Eckie Benson

****

Flinging the front door open, the world tilted and Andrea found herself engulfed in a hug and twirled in a circle. Drew set her on her feet. "It's huge, sis. What did you say you planned for Eckie House?"

"To always have room for family." She hugged her brother and turned to Jodi. "I'm so glad you're here." She led them toward the kitchen. "Lunch is ready, perfect timing."

Drew lifted the double chocolate brownie toward his mouth. "I don't need this, but I want it."

"It's yours. Now tell me what brought you to Creekside." She refilled their glasses of iced tea.

"A wedding," Drew answered.

"Really? Whose?"

"Our wedding. We want to get married here," Jodi answered.

"And it needs to be soon," added Drew.

"Not to be indelicate, but how soon?" Andrea asked, afraid to ask why.

"November, or sooner," Drew answered. "I'm being reassigned."

While they cleaned up from lunch, talk centered around the wedding, how big, when, pastor or justice of the peace, so many decisions. While Drew and Jodi took Ella on a stroll around the back yard, Andrea called Nikki.

"Getting married here, your little brother," Nikki commented. "What's your mother going to say?"

"No idea," Andrea admitted. "Not sure Drew will even invite her. Plus she found a new man, so if she's invited don't we have to invite him?"

"Really, it's up to Drew and Jodi. They decide who is and isn't invited," Nikki pointed out. "Can't picture your mom being very happy at a wedding in Creekside."

"Me either. Not her style, plus she won't have any say. But, Nikki, I'm going to need your help. Can you come tomorrow?"

"Hey, of course. I'll bring Ainsley and Catherine too," Nikki offered.

****

"Boy, I feel like the odd man out," commented Drew as he followed Jodi, Andrea, Nikki, Catherine, and Ainsley through the house. They stopped at each room, debating the best place for the ceremony, the reception.

"Not odd, Drew," Nikki answered and patted his arm, "just the groom."

"Yep, not odd," added Andrea, "but not particularly important. Don't you know the wedding is all about the bride?" She strolled into the large parlor. Beside the light switch, she pushed a button and panels in the wall slid into pockets, connecting the large and small parlors.

"Tricky," Drew commented. "Is the connection part of the original plans?"

"The connection, yeah. Using electricity to move the panels was added much later." Andrea continued, "Combined, the rooms should be big enough for the ceremony and reception."

"Or the reception outside, ceremony inside if the weather cooperates," added Jodi.

"Is inside and outside what you want, Jodi?" Drew asked. "Then inside and outside is what we'll have."

"See, little brother, that's what I mean. At this stage, you're superfluous. It's all about the bride." She pecked his cheek. "You gave exactly the right answer. Whatever the bride wants."

****

Sunday morning, Andrea, Ella in her arms, stood on the front porch. Bright summer sunlight reflected off the rental car's white paint. A single honk disturbed the quiet. Drew and Jodi drove away.

Surrounded by quiet, Andrea walked through Eckie House. In the main parlor, sunlight glinted through the windows. Already, dust motes danced in the air. Either she needed to close off a few of the rooms or hire help to keep the house clean. The housekeeper apartment and the garage apartment were both ready. Might find a housekeeper who needed living space, but the landscape service already arrived weekly, conquered the acres surrounding the house, and disappeared. Certainly didn't need the garage apartment for guests with seven bedrooms and a best friend who owned a haunted hotel a few blocks away.

In the kitchen, she secured Ella into her highchair. Immediately, the quiet ended as Ella pounded on the tray. Andrea kissed her cheek. "Chill, oh demanding princess. Lunch is on the way." She pulled food from the fridge and served lunch. Ella babbled and ate, creating both a mess and a cheerful noise. By the time Andrea cleaned up the mess and lay Ella in the crib, late afternoon sun peeked through the nursery curtains. Andrea grabbed the baby monitor and trooped down the stairs. The door chime played "One Less Bell to Answer." Andrea looked down at her blue T-shirt spotted with baby food, shrugged her shoulders. Whoever waited on the other side would have to accept her mess and all. She yanked open the front door and grinned at a familiar smiling face. "Ainsley. Hi. Come in."

"I didn't wake Ella, did I?"

Shaking her head, Andrea led the way toward the kitchen. "No worry. She's sleeping upstairs. I was just about to make tea. Would you like some?"

Settled at the small table, tea cups full, she asked, "What can I do for you, Ainsley?"

"What are your plans for Eckie House, other than hosting a family wedding in October?"

Andrea sipped her tea. She needed a plan for Eckie House for two reasons, to end the questions from interested friends and neighbors, and so she didn't commit to something she'd later regret. "So far, my only plan is to hire help keeping the house clean. I'll probably rent out the garage apartment eventually. With housing close to the square in short supply, seems a shame to let the apartment go empty." And having someone else living on the property was safer when she needed to be in Scottsdale for work occasionally.

"Perfect. I have a potential tenant for you," Ainsley admitted. "Fitting for Eckie House, she's a single mother."

****

Stretched out on the lounger, bare feet propped on the veranda rail, Andrea settled back to watch the moonrise. Soft jazz on the radio and the rustling sounds of leaves dancing in the summer breeze provided a calming counterpoint to Andrea's chaotic thoughts. Tomorrow she'd welcome the artist and single mother, Ronni Stephens, to Eckie House. Should she keep their relationship all business like the one she had with the tenants in her Scottsdale townhouse? Or, because the apartment shared Eckie House property, should she try for acquaintance open to friendship? Earlier, Patrick printed off a lease agreement and handed it to her with a warning to trust her gut. At the moment, her gut had nothing to say, no sense of impending doom or the beginning of a great adventure. The opening chords of "Save a Horse" played on her cell phone. "Evening, James. How was your company dinner?

"Excellent. Always fun celebrating with partners and staff. Russell's engagement is now officially celebrated. Another one bites the dust." His deep chuckle traveled over the phone.

"Are you the last of the Associates single?"

"Nope. We still outnumber the marrieds. Enough about my crew. What's new with you and Ella?"

"May have a tenant for the garage apartment," Andrea admitted. "Meeting her tomorrow and we'll see."

"That was quick. Thought you weren't sure you wanted to rent it."

"Still not sure, but it seems wasteful leaving the apartment empty," Andrea commented. "Anyway, I've started reading the biography you gave me. Faith Eckie provided a home for women and children. I'm just continuing the tradition."

Good nights exchanged, Andrea dropped the phone in her pocket, locked the back door, and wandered through the hallway, turning off lights as she passed. Andrea flipped the lights on in the main parlor and crossed the room to check the window locks. She returned to the main light switch and placed her fingers on the switch. Her grandmother's furniture disappeared, replaced by old-fashioned chairs and settees arranged in groups on one side of the main parlor. On the other side, small tables and chairs, toys, games, and dolls filled bookshelves and everywhere children played. Andrea blinked. Grandmother's furniture again filled the parlor, but in the quiet room the sound of children's laughter floated on the air. Andrea climbed the stairs, her gut finally giving her a message. Renting the garage apartment to Ronni Stephens and her daughter was exactly what she needed to do.

"One Less Bell to Answer" echoed through the house. Ella woke with a startled cry. Perfect timing. Andrea had just glanced in her room checking on her.

She grabbed Ella in her arms, cuddled her against her chest, felt the squishy diaper against her forearm. "Oh baby, soon as I answer the door I'll get you out of that yucky thing." Ella's cries turned to whimpers as they hustled down the stairs. Yanking open the door Andrea blinked, tried to focus against the onslaught of sunlight.

"Oh no, did we wake Ella?" Ainsley grimaced when Ella renewed her cry.

Shaking her head, Andrea stepped back, letting them inside. "She needs changing. Come back to my office, and I'll get her changed so we can talk." She led the way. Ella's cry turned back to a whimper as they walked. "Welcome to Eckie House. Not exactly how I planned to meet you. Please sit down while I solve Ella's problem."

Ainsley offered, "Andrea, I'd like you to meet Ronni and Tina Stephens and Ronnie's brother, Nathan."

"Nice to meet you." Andrea greeted a brown-haired couple about her age and very young girl with blonde pigtails. "You're looking for an apartment, Ronni?"

Tina climbed off her mother's lap and wandered to the changing table.

Nathan rose from the sofa and followed Tina.

"Yes. Something big enough for Tina and me," Ronnie answered.

Andrea placed Ella in the playpen, setting a couple of toys just out of reach. Ella pushed herself up on her arms and grinned. "What brings you to Creekside?" Ronni looked at Nathan. He nodded slightly.

"Ainsley agreed to sell our art in Serendipity."

Andrea looked at Ainsley, who lifted an eyebrow

155

and shrugged. Ainsley had a gift for reading people. If she thought Ronni and Nathan were okay, Andrea would accept it. "Okay, let's go see the apartment." Ella held in Andrea's arms, Tina holding Ronni's hand, they trooped to the kitchen and through the back door. "There's a covered spot for a car next to the garage. At some point, half the garage was turned into a studio."

They crossed the lawn and walked the short path through a group of trees. Two stories tall, the garage sat perched on a small rise. On the second floor, a balcony stretched the length of the building.

"The stairs are inside." Andrea punched the code into the lock, swung open the door, and they climbed the stairs. On a small landing at the top, she entered the code again and held the door open for the others. Light from Creekside's mid-day summer sun filtered through the partly open shutters and glinted off the polished wood floors. "Two bedrooms with a bath between and a half bath next to the kitchen." Tina raced through the apartment, looking under the furniture, climbing on the beds, opening the kitchen cabinets she could reach. Nathan reached Tina just as she climbed inside the cupboard under the sink. He pulled her out, distracting her with tickles.

As they climbed down the stairs, Ronni asked, "Would you be interested in renting out the studio?"

Andrea shrugged. "Hadn't thought about it." She led the way around the building to a side door. As the others stepped inside, Andrea flipped a switch and the garage door opened, revealing blue sky, meadow, trees, and Granite Mountain towering in the distance. Tina slipped out of her mother's grasp and raced through the open door, Uncle Nathan on her heels. Laughter sang in the air as Nathan lifted Tina over his head, twirling her in a circle.

Black clouds floated across the blue sky. A cool breeze lifted Andrea's curls from her forehead as she and Ainsley stood on the front porch and watched Nathan, Tina, and Ronni walk through the front gate. When the Stephens disappeared around a corner, Andrea turned to Ainsley and asked, "What is Ronni afraid of?"

"I don't know," Ainsley admitted. "You felt her fear too?"

"Yeah. Do you think she's safe here?"

"Hopefully. Unfortunately, I read emotions, not the future."

****

From the window of his second story accounting office, James watched cars cruise slowly on Scottsdale Road. The unrelenting heat fueled driving tempers, and honking horns punctuated the hum of engines struggling to run air conditioners in stop and start traffic. In ten minutes, his one o'clock appointment should arrive. He wondered if Jacob Stanley intended giving himself an edge using the element of surprise. Amazing what you could learn about a person with a simple internet search. He always looked up new clients prior to their first appointment. Gave him an edge in helping them, retaining them as clients. Jackie's voice over the intercom startled him. "Your one o'clock appointment is here."

James pulled open the door and strolled to the reception area. "Mr. Stanley?" He stuck out his hand. Calluses roughened Jacob Stanley's large hand, his handshake firm. "Come back to my office." He offered coffee, iced tea, or water and settled Jacob Stanley in the client chair. He plastered a professional smile on his face and looked into a pair of hazel eyes surrounded by tiny lines. "What can Benton and Associates do for you today?"

"I believe we're related," Jacob blurted. "By marriage."

"You were married to my half-sister. Sorry for your loss. I understand she passed away several years ago?"

"Six years ago."

"And why are you here now, Mr. Stanley? What do you think I can do for you?"

Jacob relaxed back in the chair. "Nothing for me. But my daughter, Whitney, wants to meet you. All of you."

"How old is Whitney?"

Jacob sighed. "Seventeen. She's curious about aunts and uncles she's never met. I've put her off since her mom died but she claims she's old enough to decide."

James remembered the road trip to Tucson when he was seventeen. "I can't speak for Nikki and Patrick, but I'll be happy to meet your daughter."

"Lunch? Tomorrow at the Sugar Bowl?"

"I'll see you tomorrow at one," James answered as he led Mr. Stanley back to the reception area. "I'm looking forward to meeting Whitney."

****

Eight o'clock at night, wine glass in hand, James pressed a single number and dialed his brother.

"What's up, bro?" Patrick answered. "You coming up this weekend?"

158

"Maybe. You need me up there?"

"Well if you're coming anyway you can check over Mr. Henderson's books, see if it's worth my time to practice law in the booming metropolis of Creekside."

"Bored already with inn keeping?" James asked. "Or just tired of fighting our baby sister for control of The Palace?"

Patrick chuckled. "A little of both. I'm sure that's not why you called."

"True. Hey, remember our road trip when I was seventeen?"

"Oh yeah. Hard to forget," Patrick admitted. "We thought we were men, tough guys. Confronting Dad, getting answers. That was the plan."

"Didn't exactly turn out that way, though. We found him. Saw his other family."

"Lost our nerve, turned around, drove home." Patrick chuckled. "Didn't even have nerve enough to tell Mom we left town for a day. Not our finest hour."

"Were we afraid of the answers? Is that why we didn't ask?"

"Maybe. Bad enough to believe we weren't important enough or loveable enough to be his family. Painful to have our fears confirmed. What brought on this trip down memory lane?"

"Had a visitor today. Mr. Jacob Stanley. A contractor from Tucson."

"And?"

"He has a seventeen-year-old daughter, Whitney. She's our niece," James admitted.

"Ahh. Krystal's daughter. Her mother died awhile back."

"What? You've been keeping track of them?"

"Not exactly. Just checking occasionally. Especially after Krystal's mom died."

"Why?"

"Felt sorry for them," Patrick admitted. "The three girls weren't quite grown when their mom died. Can you imagine life if we'd been raised by Dad?"

"Nope. I see your point," James commented. Life couldn't be easy with a single parent as lacking in honesty and loyalty as their father. "Tell me what you know."

"Kyla moved to New York right after college. Kristen teaches high school in Hawaii. Both still single. Krystal married Jacob her last year of college. She worked for an executive search firm until she died six years ago. So what did Jacob Stanley want?"

"Lunch tomorrow at the Sugar Bowl. Whitney, his daughter, wants to meet me. All of us if she can."

"Why now?"

"Don't know. Because she's seventeen and curious? Because her aunts left Tucson long ago and she's looking for family connections? I guess I'll find out tomorrow."

The air conditioner's constant hum provided a backdrop for James' circling thoughts. Stretched across his king-size bed, staring at the surrounding dark, he remembered the road trip. Their big talk on the drive down in Patrick's old car. They drove by their father's house. He stood on the porch, his arm around a woman. In the driveway three teenage girls played basketball, laughing when they made a shot, groaning when they missed. Patrick turned the corner and drove through the neighborhood to a strip mall. Seated in a booth in a coffee shop, Patrick finally broke the silence. "I couldn't stop. Not the kids' fault Dad's a jerk. Maybe they don't even know about us."

"But we know about them," James pointed out.

"Yeah. Because their existence caused the divorce. They probably think their parents are married."

"Oh. Well, I don't want to be the one to tell them different." They finished lunch and walked out.

Exhausted, James drifted toward sleep. Their father's betrayal affected all three of them. Since his father worked one week in Tucson and the next in Phoenix, James didn't miss him much after the divorce. Most of his memories were of a distant man who showed up for dinner during the week, crashed in front of the television, and complained about what his mom spent. He couldn't remember a time he took a problem or question to his dad. If he couldn't confide in Mom, he asked Patrick. Typical of Patrick thinking Dad's other children might need him. Patrick, the family fixer.

****

Sunlight glittered on the windows stretched the length of the familiar pink building when James strolled the two blocks to The Sugar Bowl. Protected by a bright pink and white striped awning, Jacob waited beside a tall, willowy girl, her black hair confined in a ponytail. James nodded his head. "Mr. Stanley." He looked into brown eyes so dark they appeared black. "Miss Stanley."

She took his offered hand. "Uncle James?"

"Uncle James it is, Whitney. It's nice to meet you."

Seated on pink chairs at a table beside the window they consumed sandwiches, shakes, and sundaes surrounded by framed Bill Keane Family Circus cartoons. James drew Whitney out, learning about her school, friends, the dance team, college plans. Just as he scooped the last spoonful from his Tin Roof Sundae, Whitney said, "Now it's your turn."

James raised an eyebrow. "My turn?"

"Yep. Your turn to tell me about you, about your brother and sister. It's why I'm here. I already know about me."

He finished the last bite, enjoying the mixture of cold chocolate, frozen vanilla, and salty peanuts. "Hmm. I'm single, no children, and an accountant in Scottsdale. Undergrad and graduate ASU. Own my own firm. Play basketball a couple of times a week at the gym with friends, golf at Orange Tree Country Club some weekends, swim in the pool at my condo at night. My bookcases are full of an eclectic mix, and there's a stack on the coffee table waiting. My favorite people are either related to me or almost related to me and I spend as much time as possible with them." He shrugged. "Boring."

"What about Patrick?"

"Divorced, one son a little older than you. An attorney. Lives in the attic of a haunted hotel."

"No way."

"Yep. He's a lot more interesting than I am."

Whitney shook her head. "What about your sister, Nichole?"

He slipped the bill from the table into his shirt pocket. "Nikki's even more interesting. Owns and operates a haunted hotel in a town famous for its ghosts. Married to a police chief, has three sons and a baby girl." James pulled a business card from his pocket and dropped it in front of Whitney. "If you're curious, look up the hotel. Website's listed on the back." He pulled out a second card and handed it to Whitney. "My business number is on the front, my personal number on the back. If you have more questions or find yourself at loose ends in Scottsdale, call."

From under the bright pink striped awning, James watched Jacob and Whitney stroll away, their shoulders touching. Family...sort of. Ambling the opposite direction, he flashed back to the last time his father showed up for the scheduled weekend visit. They'd taken a basketball to the park. Shot a few baskets. Then, The Sugar Bowl for ice cream. It was the first time James really noticed the Family Circus cartoons. Framed on the restaurant's walls and sold at the gift counter, the perfect family laughed, cried, and ate ice cream. At seven years old, he'd wondered why their family wasn't like the cartoons. Momma, daddy, children, grandparents all smiling and laughing. As he climbed the stairs to his office, other memories intruded. Sharing the same table by the window with Patrick, Nikki, Mom, and Ms. Effie. Sometimes pushing two tables together to make room for Craig and Andrea. A booth in the back, he and Craig and their dates, ice cream after a high school dance. Meeting Craig and Catherine for lunch. Craig's terrified expression, "I'm gonna be a father." Shared laughter when Catherine popped him on the arm.

James pushed open the door to Benton and Associates. Jackie greeted him with a smile. "How was lunch?"

"Sweet." He grinned. "Had to be sweet. After all, it was The Sugar Bowl."

Chapter Fourteen

Dear Momma and Daddy,

Congratulations! You're now grandparents three times. George Wyatt Eckie Jr. entered Creekside at noon today. Junior and I are fine. As usual, George Sr. is exhausted. He claims it's the hardest part of parenting, watching me work so hard bringing our children into the world. He can't imagine going through it seven times like you and Daddy.

~from Beloved Wife, Mother, Sister, and Friend, A Biography of Faith Taylor Eckie by Emaline Eckie Benson

****

Sun glared off the windshield when James yanked the door open and burned his hand on the metal handle. Sunglasses perched on his nose, radio turned up, he pulled out of the condo parking lot into typical weekend summer traffic. The air conditioner's hum, the honking horns, squealing brakes, and sunlight glaring on the windshield didn't interrupt his circling thoughts. Since Nikki opened The Palace, his life had taken some odd turns. First Craig died leaving behind Catherine, two little girls, and a mystery. Catherine and the girls moved in with Nikki for safety. Then James was suddenly an uncle again, Sam's uncle because an accident turned Nikki from a godmother to a guardian mom. Creekside's coldest day of the year, Nikki married Alex, and James noticed Andrea in a new way. Was it just the wedding? Weren't weddings a cliché when it came to pairing up groomsmen and bridesmaids? Instead of meeting friends for happy hour or setting up a date with a beautiful woman for the weekend, James fought the weekend traffic to escape the heat.

Overnight bag in hand, he sauntered up the hotel's front steps and yanked opened the door. Wearing a bright blue Palace polo shirt and jeans, Patrick the innkeeper didn't look much like an attorney or a beach bum today. "Hey, bro. Which room did I draw this time?"

"Across the hall from me." He slapped a key card in James' hand. "Nikki's trying to keep us as far away from her suite as possible."

He ambled toward the stairs. "Have you been annoying our baby sister?" James asked.

"Yep. She's considering locking me in the attic and letting me out only to work the desk. She told me to let you know not to bother her when you check in. She'll text you when she and Michelle are available."

James pounded up the stairs two at a time. No surprise Nikki was already tired of Patrick's advice. Good thing he was considering going back to lawyering. James could be the better brother and stay away until she invited him. Maybe. James pushed open the door to Attic A. Standing in a shaft of sunlight from the skylight, a large gray dog wagged his tail, his tongue hanging out. From a distance a childish voice called, "Smokey, come here." Smokey leaped through the wall and disappeared. The attic must have been a favorite playroom for RJ and Smokey when RJ was young. Did RJ haunt the hotel, or was his spirit a manifestation of Victoria's haunting?

After pouring a glass of red wine from the bottle on the dresser, James perused the mini fridge in search of a snack. Wine glass in one hand and snack plate in the other, he lounged in the reading chair and propped sock feet on the ottoman. He flipped through a few channels on the remote and finally turned on music for company. Company? What was he doing alone at The Palace when he could be with Andrea at Eckie House? James glanced at the king-size bed covered with a crazy quilt and groaned. Yep, he could be with Andrea and Ella. But meeting Whitney reminded him of Dad. Andrea should marry and Ella deserved a father. Someone who got the whole long term, forever, build-a-family deal.

Not James, someone better. He needed to back off before someone got hurt. He dropped his head against the back of the chair and closed his eyes. He missed Andrea. The warmth of her body next to his, her arms held out, welcoming him into her bed. Damn. This wasn't good. Whatever made him think making love to Andrea was a good idea? Could they go back to being friends?

Grateful for the interruption, James jumped up at the sound of a knock on the door. The next few hours Patrick and James reviewed Henderson's financial records for the law practice. When Patrick gathered the papers and rose to leave James commented, "Well, you won't get rich in Creekside, but there is a need."

"Don't need to get rich. Just need something interesting to do away from the hotel," Patrick admitted.

"Hard to go from the rat race to a bunch of slow,

walking rats?"

"Something like that. What did you do to Andrea that you're staying here instead of Eckie House?"

"Nothing. Didn't ask to stay with her this weekend," James admitted.

Patrick grimaced. "Ouch. How's she feel about you staying here?"

James felt color infuse his face and rose from the chair. His phone rang. "Hey little sis, ready for a visit from your favorite brother?"

Nikki's laughter sang through the phone. "Yep, come on over if you're done with Patrick."

"All done. I'm on my way." He should have let Andrea know he'd be in Creekside for the weekend. He didn't mean to be thoughtless; he was confused and unsure. No excuse. He pounded down the steps and joined Nikki in her sitting room.

Settled in the rocking chair in Nikki's suite, James cuddled tiny Michelle. "She looks more like you every day."

"I think she looks like Alex, especially the shape of her eyes."

James shook his head. "God forbid she looks like Alex. Too pretty to look like your dad, right, Michelle?"

Nikki interrupted James' flow of nonsense. "So, besides checking out Henderson's books and talking nonsense to Michelle, what brought you to Creekside this weekend?"

Placing Michelle carefully against his shoulder, James slowly rocked. "Do you remember our dad?"

Shaking her head, Nikki settled back in the easy chair and plopped her feet on an ottoman. "Nope. Guess

I was too little when he stopped visiting you guys. Always thought of him as your dad not mine."

"A few days ago, I met his granddaughter, Whitney Stanley, age seventeen."

Nikki's eyes widened. "Really? How'd it happen?"

"She wanted to meet all of us. Guess she's looking for family since her mom died. Or she was just curious about the rest of her relations." He stopped the rocker and handed Michelle to Nikki. "I gave her your card from the hotel. She might call."

"I hope she does. There's always room for one more in the Benton tribe."

Chuckling at Nikki calling them a tribe, James walked out the hotel's back door, heading toward Catherine's. Definitely part of the tribe. He raised his hand to knock, but the door swung open. Two tiny girls and two tinier dogs rushed at him. "Uncle James, Uncle James." He bent down and gathered a girl in each arm, nuzzling their necks and making them squeal. In the entry, Catherine snapped her fingers and the dogs trotted inside.

"Good trick." Child in each arm he strolled into the entry. In the shadow behind Catherine stood Chance Pagent. James stopped, set the girls on their feet. "Am I interrupting something?"

"Only playtime in the backyard. We were just getting out the sprinkler for the girls." She gave him a hug. "If you're brave you can join us." He noticed Catherine wore a T-shirt over a swimsuit, Chance wore board shorts, and the girls sported little bikinis.

"I think I'm overdressed." He followed them through the house to the patio. The summer scent of fresh cut grass surrounded him. Colorful pool towels rested on a table along with a pitcher of iced tea, plastic glasses, and a bottle of suntan lotion. The girls followed Chance as he set up the sprinkler. Lily gave him directions in her piping voice; Hope pulled the hose away from the puppies. "So, does he spend a lot of time over here?" James poured himself a glass of tea and plopped on a chair.

Catherine blushed. "Some. We're training the puppies together."

Chance set the sprinkler down, kneeled, and Lily rushed into his arms.

"The girls like him."

"What's not to like? He adopted Ariel's littermate, Belle, and he writes children's books. He wrote a book and made Hope and Lily the heroines."

"And you like him," James stated and sipped his tea. Part of him rejoiced Catherine and the girls found Chance. He wanted happiness for Craig's widow; she deserved a partner, someone to love. Part of him ached another man would hold his best friend's wife, help raise his best friend's children.

As Chance shook the water out of his red hair and loped to the patio, Catherine whispered, "Yeah, I like him."

The combination of breeze and summer sun dried his shirt and chilled his skin. The little girls' goodbye included sopping wet hugs. He loved little girl hugs and he loved those two little girls. Muddy puppy prints decorated his jeans. James meandered along the quiet residential street. The familiar scents of fresh cut grass and late summer flowers drifted on the breeze. Chance's expression when he dropped onto the porch swing next to Catherine meant 'like' didn't come close to how he felt. James recognized the look. Alex wore a similar look. When Craig met Catherine, Craig wore the look. He stopped at the corner and realized he had turned away from the hotel. Down the block, towering blue spruces stood sentinel beside the sidewalk leading to Eckie House. As he ambled through the black iron gate and passed the spruce trees, two young women appeared in the rocking chairs on the front porch. Their hands flew as they knitted; their voices drifted on the breeze. James' foot landed on the first step. The women looked up and slowly dissolved. The empty chairs rocked in the breeze. The spirits welcomed him and he wondered if Andrea would. He plopped down on the porch swing, pulled out his cell and texted Andrea.

—*Standing on your front porch. May I come in?*—

The door swung open just as James reached for the doorbell. Her arm wrapped around a squirming Ella, Andrea invited him inside. "Yes, you may come in." She turned around and started for the back of the house. He closed and locked the door and used his longer strides to catch her at the study door. Her familiar scent surrounded him, a mixture of body lotion and Andrea.

"I'm sorry?" He followed her inside. Holding a wiggling Ella in her arms, Andrea pulled a baby gate across the doorway and sat behind her desk. She set Ella on the floor. Ella took off crawling toward James, grabbed his pant leg, and pulled herself up. "Look at you. Just about ready to walk." Ella laughed.

"What are you sorry for? Or what do you think you're sorry for since you don't sound very sure?"

Ella let go of his leg, plopped on the rug on her bottom, rolled over, and crawled toward Andrea's outstretched hand. She grabbed the hand and pulled herself up, wobbling for a moment. She let go and stood alone. Her arms flapped, she plopped on her bottom, and crawled across the room. "I missed you."

"Hmm." Andrea raised a single eyebrow. "You're sorry you missed me?"

"A few days ago I met my niece, Whitney Stanley," he admitted, "my half-sister's daughter."

"And?"

James looked up from the hands he'd clenched on his knees into familiar hazel eyes. "I still don't understand why he chose them over us. What was wrong with us? What made them better?"

Andrea switched from the chair to the small sofa and took his clenched fist in both her hands. "I never met your father, but I'd guess he took the easy way out. For your mom, finding out about the other woman, the other family, had to be devastating. A deal breaker." She shrugged. "For the other woman, either she didn't know or didn't care. Or maybe she saw the divorce as a win for her and her children. They would no longer share your father with another family."

His hands relaxed and he threaded his fingers through hers. "Yeah. Except my father was no prize." The warmth of her hand, her unique scent comforted him. "He only showed up to visit for about a year. Then he was gone."

She leaned against his shoulder. "When adults behave badly, their children usually think it's their fault. It never is." Ella let go of the sofa, toppled over, and let out a cry. Andrea jumped up and lifted the baby against her chest, rubbing her head. "You're okay, Ella. Were you just surprised?"

James wrapped them both in a hug, kissed the top

of Ella's head and Andrea's cheek. "Thanks, Andi. See ya tomorrow." He strolled out the door.

Tennis shoes slapping against concrete, James jogged toward the hotel. Is that all it was, laziness? It was easier to choose the other family. Easier to send the support check. Easier to remember the birthdays of the children he lived with. Easier not to face the woman and children he'd betrayed. What about him? Was he guilty of choosing the easier path like his father? He chose women based on their interest in him. If their interest became too intense, he ended the relationship. Unlike his father, he didn't promise anything he wouldn't give and never dated more than one woman at a time. Did he really believe each affair's ending didn't leave someone hurt and disappointed? How would Andrea feel if he ended their affair? James leaned against the hotel's back door. His breathing slowed. A few minutes later, he joined Nikki, Patrick, and Michelle for dinner in the sitting room.

"So, little sister, what do you know about Chance Pagent?" James pictured the look again. Would Catherine be safe with the artist?

"Catherine likes him. The girls really like him. The painting hanging in the library is his work as is the drawing in your room." She shrugged. "He's Ainsley's twin and they moved from Scottsdale about nine months ago."

"Yeah," Patrick added. "And thirty days after he met Catherine in The Palace lobby, he moved into Sanders House...right next door."

"Probably not a coincidence," Nikki said. "Just like adopting Belle wasn't a coincidence."

Above the mountain peak, the sun's descent

painted the sky orange and red. James meandered along the crowded sidewalks, skillfully dodging clumps of tourists. Sounds of laughter and music drifted in the air. A light rock band played in the square's gazebo, their giant speakers counterpoint to the antique building. Bars and restaurants, their doors open to the cool night air, pulsed with music. He ambled into the Irish pub, Duggan's, and plopped on a barstool. Downing a Smithwicks, he chatted with the bartender. Another drink later, he dropped cash on the bar and walked out with a wave. Back in The Palace, he climbed the stairs to his attic room. Just as he slipped the key card in the lock, the door behind him opened. Patrick offered, "Come over, I'll buy you a beer."

Patrick pulled the door open wide. James followed and stopped on the threshold. "I thought I was the favorite brother. How come you get a bigger room?"

Patrick handed him a bottle from the small fridge. "Because I'm the oldest and I live here full time. Welcome to my owner's suite." The room stretched nearly the length of the attic. In one corner, partially hidden by a three-quarter wall, a king-size bed dressed in a colorful quilt held pride of place. The main space boasted two comfortable chairs and a small sofa facing a big screen TV. A miniature kitchen tucked into a corner.

"What's Nik going to do with this when you move out?"

"Rent it as a suite?" Patrick shrugged. "Maybe I'll never move out."

"You planning on being the bachelor uncle tucked away in the attic? Someday you'll be a grandpa. Where you gonna put the visiting grandkids?"

Patrick shuddered. "Hope that's not for a long time." They settled in the two chairs.

James admired the suite. Compact but plenty of room. On the wall beside the door, a painting depicted a young boy and a large dog. The boy stretched out on the veranda railing, his back propped against a pillar. A smile wreathed his face, his hand rested on the dog's head. The dog sat on the porch, his head resting on the boy's knee, a blissful look on his face, his eyes closed. "Chance's work?"

"Yeah. Do you recognize the porch?"

James stood in front of the painting. In the shadows behind the dog and his boy, a familiar antique door guarded the entrance. James took a single step back. Outlined in the window, Victoria stood watching boy and dog. "The Palace?" He returned to the chair with a plop.

"Yep."

James stepped into his room and reached for the light switch. In the shadows, sounds of childish laughter drifted in the air. Two young boys raced across the room in sock feet and slid toward the wall. A large gray dog barked and raced with them, managing to trip both boys. They fell in a laughing heap. In the corner of the room, a woman appeared, her hands on her hips. "RJ, I can hear you two all the way out front."

The blond boy untangled himself. "Sorry, Mom." The gray dog bounded toward the woman, tail wagging. The dog barked again. The boys and woman dissolved like smoke. Laughter drifted in the air. James flipped the light switch on dispensing the shadows

James climbed into bed and extinguished the light. Victoria raised her son as a single mother. Patrick raised Scott alone. James' mother raised three children as a single parent. His mother claimed her children were her greatest achievement, her finest work. Would she feel the same way if she saw him now? Single, and before Andrea, his longest relationship only lasted a few months. His mom treated Andrea like a second daughter. Would she, like Patrick, be worried he'd hurt his sister's best friend? Or would his mom push him to examine his heart and decide what he wanted? Nikki filled her world with love, nurturing her children, sharing her life with Alex. Rather than stumbling around his empty house when Scott graduated from high school, Patrick moved forward searching for a new direction.

James remembered the day his mom visited his office the first time. She admired the discreet name on the door, the professional furnishings, and his office with a window facing Scottsdale Road. Started by three CPAs the firm grew to fifteen employees, including several like Catherine who worked remotely. At their last strategy meeting, they decided the firm was big enough. The other partners, the original associates in Benton and Associates, had wives and children now. Without the excuse he needed to focus on growing the business, what was his new goal? No answers, more questions. He drifted to sleep.

Chapter Fifteen

1910

Dear Momma,

Thank you for staying with me for so long. It did help. Momma, your advice to take each day with my children as a blessing reminds me I have to find happiness again for their sakes. For just a moment in the morning, I forget George is gone. I reach for him and find his side empty. Then I hop right out of bed like you suggested, get dressed, paste a smile on my face, and start the day. I lost my husband, my love, but Emaline and Junior lost their father. They deserve my best every day as their mother.

Like you suggested, I had a couple of sessions with the pastor. In my head, I keep wondering if I'd just distracted George for a minute more, held him a moment longer, given him one more kiss before he walked out the kitchen door, would he still be alive? Pastor Adam reminded me nothing I did caused George's death. The bank robber who pulled out a gun and started shooting killed George. He's the only one responsible. Not me, not God, not Mrs. Newell, who George pushed to floor and covered with his body.

~from Beloved Wife, Mother, Sister, and Friend, A Biography of Faith Taylor Eckie by Emaline Eckie Benson

****

Light diffused through lace curtains and glinted on the antique mirror over the dresser. Ella's cry, amplified by the monitor, pulled Andrea from sleep. Her bare feet hit the floor. "Coming, baby, momma's coming." She jogged across the hall. "Oh, my poor baby."

Ella stood white-knuckled hanging onto the crib railing with one hand. Tears coursed down her face. Between screams, she shoved her free fist into her mouth.

"Those teeth are really giving you a hard time." Andrea carried Ella to the changing table. As she wiped Ella down with a cool cloth and exchanged a wet diaper for dry, she glanced at the clock. Five o'clock. "Looks like we're starting our day early."

Andrea pulled a bottle from the mini fridge and plopped it in the warmer. At the light's flash to green, she pulled the bottle out, tested it, and handed it to Ella. "I need a shower, so you can finish your drink in the playpen in my room." By the time Andrea came out of the shower, the bottle was empty and Ella slept. The doorbell chimed the first notes of "Up, Up and Away." Andrea grabbed the monitor and trooped down the stairs.

"Morning, Andi."

She pulled the door all the way open. "Morning, James."

Taking her hand, he slowly pulled her into his arms and kissed her cheek. "You have any coffee?"

She led him toward the kitchen. "It should be about ready." They fell into a familiar dance. He poured coffee and dressed two mugs. She grabbed eggs, bacon, tomatoes, and cheese from the refrigerator. He washed the tomato and sliced it. She cracked the eggs and whipped them. The toast popped. James put filled plates on the table. Andrea added butter and jelly. They dropped into chairs, and Ella's cry rang through the monitor.

"Go ahead, eat while it's hot." Andrea jogged toward the servant stairs. She ran into her bedroom and screeched to a halt. Beside the playpen a young girl stood, her voice a low murmur. Ella's scream turned to sobs, then to hiccups. Ella reached one arm toward the young girl. She dissolved. Ella settled in her arms, Andrea headed down the servants' stairs. "So, Ella, you even disturbed the spirits with your scream."

While she belted Ella in the highchair, James pulled two full plates from the warming oven and pushed the microwave button, reheating the coffee. "You didn't have to wait for us."

"Came over to have breakfast with you." He placed their mugs on the table. "Defeats the purpose if I eat alone." Kitchen cleaned up, they took Ella and second cups of coffee onto the back veranda. "Hey, clever idea." James admired the childproof fencing surrounding a large portion of patio. "Who did this?" A colorful outdoor rug covered the floor.

Andrea pulled toys from a deck box and set Ella on the carpet. "Patrick and Scott." She joined James on the loveseat. "You do realize Patrick's already bored living in Creekside?"

James put his arm around her shoulder. "Yeah. Maybe working with Henderson will make him happier."

Andrea relaxed against his arm, rested her head on his shoulder. The unique scent of aftershave and James surrounded her. "Is that why you're here this weekend? To work with Patrick on partnering with Henderson?" How far should she push him? She had no claim, their relationship beyond friendship too new. But she hurt he couldn't come to her with family problems. He didn't need or want her comfort.

He shrugged. "And to tell Nikki about Whitney."

"And she said 'good. There's always room for one more in our tribe.' Right?"

"What? Did you talk to her?"

Andrea shook her head. "Nope. Didn't need to. Nikki's the most inclusive person I know." She watched Ronni jog toward them across the meadow. "Wonder what's wrong?"

Ronni stopped at the railing, tears ran down her face, her labored breathing loud in the afternoon quiet. "Have you seen Tina? Is she here?"

"No. What happened?" Andrea lifted Ella. "How long has she been gone?"

"Ten minutes? Maybe fifteen?" Ronni's tears slowed. "We were working in the studio. Tina was playing inside the play yard fence. We just took our eyes off her for a minute."

"How'd she get out of the yard?"

"She knocked the fence down. Nathan's out looking in the area around the studio but I thought she might come your way. She says there are children at your house to play with."

Andrea pulled Ronni into a hug. "We'll find her. The property's fenced." She looked at James. "Can you walk the fence line? Make sure all the gates are latched?"

"Sure. I'll call Patrick and have him help." Phone

pressed to his ear, James loped off toward the fence. He dropped the phone in his pocket and upped his pace. His shirt stuck to his chest, sweat dripped into his eyes. Jogging on uneven ground in hot sun very different from his usual ten miles on the treadmill. At the gate, he slowed, stopped, checked the latch, and ran on. At gate two his phone vibrated. Patrick and Scott were headed toward the orchard. Ronni and Andi were checking the front yard. James slowed at the next gate. From here, he could see the orchard's final row. Whisper Creek ran just on the other side. A tiny voice whimpered, "Mommy."

He followed the sound through the trees to the creek. Tina, her shirt ripped, hair a tangled mess, sat on the creek's edge dangling her fingers in the trickle of water. James sat down next to her. "Hi, Tina."

She turned her face away from him. "Go away or I'll scream. I can't talk to strangers."

"Okay if I sit here? I'm very tired."

Tina looked down at her fingers in the water. "Can you go get my mommy?"

"I could carry you to her."

"No! If you touch me, I have to scream." Big tears fell down her cheeks.

"Are you hurt?"

Tina pointed to her foot. James grimaced. A swollen ankle peeked over pink tennis shoes. James texted Patrick. —*Get Ronni or Nathan. We're at the creek about halfway along the fence line.*—

A warm breeze rustled in the trees, the canopy cooled the air, and into the silence James' low voice told Tina a story of running away from home and getting only as far as the end of the street.

A familiar voice came through the trees. "James?"

"Here." Patrick, Nathan, and Ronni appeared.

Nathan lifted Tina in his arms, pulled her tight against his chest. "You scared us."

"I hurt my foot."

Ronni grabbed James in a hug. "Thank you." She dropped her arms and joined Nathan and Tina as they walked toward their apartment.

"You couldn't carry her out?" Patrick asked as they walked through the meadow.

"Couldn't pick her up. If a stranger touches her, she has to scream." The Stephens disappeared through the garage door. "You coming in?"

"Nope." Patrick shook his head. "My work here is done. Scott, wait up." He loped off, catching up with Scott as they reached the driveway. Their identical blond heads glinted in the sun. They rounded the house and disappeared. James stopped, turned around, and faced the orchard. A breeze rustled the leaves, and shadows danced on the ground. He stilled. Children raced among the trees. Their silent laughter echoed in his mind. He blinked. They disappeared. James jogged across the meadow toward Eckie House and Andrea. He wondered if Tina escaped the play yard because she was chasing the spirit children.

In the library, he stepped over the baby gate, plopped on the sofa, and guzzled a bottle of water. Andrea sat in the wing chair. Ella crawled to him, climbed his leg. Holding on with one hand, she waved her other fist in the air. "Want to come up?" He reached for her. She dropped to her bottom and crawled away. "I guess not." He lounged against the sofa back.

"Tina wouldn't let you bring her home?"

He shook his head. "Nope. Stranger danger rules, I guess. If I touched her, she would scream."

"She's right. Scream and run."

"She couldn't run; her ankle was twisted."

"Oh. Poor Tina. Do you think it's broken?"

"Doubt it, but don't know for sure." He closed his eyes. "Andrea, will Ella be like Tina? Running head first into trouble the minute you turn your back?"

Ella pulled herself up, hanging on to the desk. She grabbed for the desk chair. It rolled away and Ella collapsed to her knees. Andrea pushed the desk chair against a wall. "Probably. The day Ella starts wearing shoes, I'm fencing the area near the back porch. No chasing this one through the orchard."

"Chasing through the orchard." He sighed. "I saw them today chasing each other through the orchard."

"Who?"

"The Eckie House children. I saw them after Ronni and Nathan picked up Tina and Patrick left." Ella crawled to the desk chair, pulled herself up, and pushed the chair against the wall with a bang. James rose and walked to Andrea. He took her in his arms and, to the sound of a desk chair banging against the wall melded with Ella's giggles, kissed her. Andrea's lips softened against his, parted slightly. Her arms circled his waist. An invitation. He slipped his tongue inside. Her sigh heated his blood. Her scent surrounded him. He moaned. Loosening his hold, he gentled the kiss. "Andrea, can I spend the night here?"

"Will you be sorry tomorrow?" She stepped back. "Or think you're sorry?"

He shook his head. "No. Never sorry for being with you." He leaned in and kissed her cheek. "Let me stay. I promise you won't be sorry either."

"Okay."

He drew her into a hug. "Great." He dashed to the door, vaulted over the baby gate, and jogged down the hall. James sauntered through the hotel's backdoor. Nikki's voice carried from the lobby. He rounded the front desk, waved to his sister, and climbed the stairs. Yanking open the attic door, he stilled. In the shadow at the end of the hallway Victoria's arms wrapped around a tall man, their lips locked. He dropped a small leather bag, pulled her into an embrace. A large dog bounded down the hallway and slid into Victoria. Her laughter filled the room. They disappeared. Was the kiss a homecoming kiss or goodbye? Was tonight a last time with Andrea or just the next time? Tonight, he needed to hold her, love her. Tomorrow on the drive back to Scottsdale, he would organize his thoughts and decide what next.

James zipped up his leather duffle, made a final check of the hotel room, and texted Nikki. —*Checking out now. Thanks for the room. If you need me to cover The Palace just call. Love u.*— He grabbed the bag and sauntered through the door.

At the bottom of the stairway, Nikki blocked his exit. "Oh. Checking out early? Got a better offer?"

James dropped his bag and wrapped her in a hug. He whispered in her ear, "None of your business." Grabbed his bag and jogged out the front door to the sound of Nikki's laughter competing with The Beach Boys "Good Vibrations."

He loped down the sidewalk, zigzagging around clumps of tourists until the landscape changed. Bungalows, duplexes, Craftsman-style houses marched side by side with three-story Victorians. The sounds of music faded, replaced by the whir of razor wheels against the sidewalk, children's laughter, and lawnmowers. He dodged a boy on a bicycle. Scents of fresh cut grass and summer flowers filled the air. The clang of Eckie House's front gate added one more note to the music of summer. Eckie House. His shoulders relaxed, he left the sidewalk and strolled around the side of the house. At the back porch, he climbed the steps, lifted the latch, and headed for the back door. His lips curved. She'd invited him. Relief loosened the tension in his chest. Or he'd invited himself and she agreed. Close enough. He found Andrea behind the desk in the library with Ella asleep in the portable crib. He opened the baby gate and leaned against the doorframe. Andrea looked up from her laptop and his lips turned up. In three long strides he reached her, swiveled the chair, and lifted her into his arms. Her laughter filled the room. "Can you get a babysitter for Ella? It's time we went on a date."

"Date?"

He gave her a smacking kiss and set her on the floor. "Date." He nodded his head. "You know, two adults, dinner someone else cooks, bottle of wine, dancing. No clean up."

She picked up her cell phone. "Give me a few minutes."

James grabbed his duffle and kissed her cheek. "Excellent. I'll hit the shower." He jogged through the doorway, his running shoes a rhythmic thwack on the hallway's hardwood floor.

****

"Do we have everything?" James asked as he

picked up the diaper bag and slung it on his shoulder. "Ugh. What's in here?"

Andrea belted Ella in the stroller. "The bare necessities."

The summer sun began its descent, tinting the blue sky with streaks of orange and red. Scent of fresh cut grass joined the appetizing smell of grilling meat. Children on bicycles zoomed down the street dodging parked cars. "Catherine volunteered babysitting duty?"

"Yep. They're having a movie night at home. Classic animated films. We exchange childcare sometimes. It helps since we both work from home."

By the time they left Catherine's, the sun had disappeared behind the mountain, and brilliant orange and red lit the sky in the last moments before dark. Andrea's small hand rested in his larger one, her smooth, soft skin and bright turquoise nails a counterpoint to his callused palm and short nails. "Were you surprised Chance joined them for movie night?"

"Nope. From what Catherine says, when he's not working in his studio, he's at her house."

"And she's okay with him around all the time?" James asked. He wondered if Chance plotted a strategy to win over Catherine or was it happenstance? Did he simply enjoy the company of young children or see the girls as a great path to their mother? He wrote children's books; children were definitely important to him, all children. Plus, he wore the look of a man fascinated by a particular woman.

"Must be or she'd send him home," Andrea pointed out. "I wouldn't be surprised if they end up married."

Streetlights blinked on as they strolled the few blocks to the square. The last of the sunset disappeared and the black velvet sky filled with stars. No, he wouldn't be surprised if Catherine and Chance married. Catherine enjoyed marriage and Chance spoke to Catherine and the girls with a quiet tenderness. They wove around clumps of people on the sidewalks. "First, the gallery."

"I wondered where we were headed." They walked beyond the busy square and turned on a side street.

Lights shone through the front windows and propped open door of Winter's Gallery. Classical music competed with the hum of conversation. Inside, Paul Winter greeted them and pointed toward a wine bar set up in the rear of the gallery. Glasses in hand, they meandered among the artwork. They turned a corner and Andrea stopped. "Good Grief." She took two steps back, pulling James with her. He hadn't been paying much attention to the paintings, his focus mostly on Andrea. Now he did. A sizeable painting surrounded by blank white wall hung in front of them. Eckie House rose three stories from her front porch. Sunlight glinted on the windows. Wispy white clouds peeked from behind her gabled roof. The spruce trees guarding her gate were small, hardly more than bushes. Beside one spruce, a young girl sat on a blanket sketching, her profile hidden by a huge hat. On the porch, a young woman perched in a rocking chair holding a tiny baby, her face in shadow. Andrea pulled James forward. "Can you read the artist's name?"

Before he could answer, Paul Winter stood behind them. "Violet T."

Andrea turned to Paul. "Where did you get it? Are there others?"

"Last question first, I have no idea if there are

more," Paul answered. "This is the only painting I've ever seen by Violet T."

"And where did you get it?"

"Bought the painting outright from a young man who claimed he inherited it from a great-great grandmother." Paul shrugged. "His story checked out. I bought it."

"Will you sell it?" James asked.

"Maybe. Talk to me next week." He nodded and walked away.

Andrea and James drifted through the gallery and stopped in front of various paintings. Wine finished, James, his hand on the small of her back, guided her outside. He took her hand when they reached the sidewalk, leading her back toward the Square. "You wanted to buy the painting."

"Oh yeah," she admitted. "The artist, Violet, was Faith Eckie's younger sister." They climbed the steps to Wellington's. A host seated them immediately at a secluded table by the window. James held her chair and slid it close to the table. The moment he was seated, the waiter returned with a bottle of Rosé and two glasses. The ritual approval completed, he poured the wine. Andrea sipped then asked, "So what's for dinner? Looks like you planned ahead."

"Whatever you want from the menu," he admitted. "Nikki gave me the name of your favorite wine. I know better than to order dinner for any woman. Not if I ever want another date."

Through dinner, they compared stories of dates turned into battles for control. By the time the Walnut Turtle Pie arrived with two forks, they moved on to dates who lost control. James groaned when Andrea took a tiny piece of the pie on her fork and slipped the sweet between her lips. A satisfied smile lit her face. His blood heated. What was it about this particular woman that made watching her eat an erotic experience? Her obvious enjoyment? The way she closed her eyes and touched her tongue to her lips? He shook his head. Cool off. The last crumb of chocolate crust disappeared at exactly the moment the waiter reappeared. Check handled, they made their way through the restaurant.

"Where to now?" Andrea asked as James took her hand. "We've had art, appetizers, dinner, and dessert."

"Dancing," James answered. "Or what passes for dancing at the Lone Star." After a whispered conversation with the bouncer, James grabbed Andrea's hand and led her inside. From a table in the corner, Nikki waved. For the next few hours, the sound of laughter and conversation mixed with country music from a cover band. James pulled Andrea onto the floor and wrapped his arms around her. The band played "Better as a Memory" and they swayed to the music. Andrea's scent surrounded him, flowery soap and woman. Through their summer shirts, James felt her heart beat; her breath tickled his chin. Nikki and Alex danced nearby, her head nestled against Alex's shoulder, and his arms encircled her.

After good-byes, James and Andrea strolled away from the Lone Star and walked through quiet residential streets toward Catherine's. James' arm rested across her shoulder, hers circled his waist. From Catherine's to Eckie House they strolled in companionable silence, Ella a sleeping presence in the stroller. James held the gate and Andrea pushed the stroller through. At the steps to the front porch, Andrea lifted Ella from the stroller and James folded it, tucking it under his arm. His hand on the base of her spine, they took the first step and stopped. At the front door a woman waited, her hand raised to knock. In her arms, a little girl wiggled, and a carpetbag sat at her feet. Her hand dropped, she picked up the carpetbag and glided through the closed door. Another woman and child found a welcome at Eckie House.

"Have you seen that particular woman and child before?" James asked as they climbed the stairs. "Do you know who they are?"

"I have seen them, and I think they are Autumn Rose Grantley and her daughter Rose," Andrea answered. When they reached Ella's room and nestled her in the crib, she continued, "Autumn Rose was the first woman Faith Eckie offered shelter to."

"And you know this, how?" he asked.

"She's described in the book you gave me. The biography," Andrea answered as she disappeared behind the bathroom's closed door.

"I hope she stays out of this room," James teased. "I have plans which do not include an audience."

Chapter Sixteen

1911

Dear Momma,

Thank you so much for the birthday gift. The quilt is exactly the right color for my bedroom. I've put the wedding quilt you made us away in a cedar chest. I'll probably give it to Emaline eventually, but that's a long time down the road.

Today, I hired more help for Mrs. Hunter. Doesn't it sound decadent; I hired help with the house? Mrs. Grantley, a widow, arrived on my front step, her little girl in her arms, a carpetbag stuffed with everything they owned at her feet. Seems her husband worked on the Stark ranch and they lived in a small house on the property. He died when he was thrown from his horse during a storm. Now she needs work to support her daughter, Rose. Mrs. Autumn Rose Grantley and Rose Grantley now live on the third floor of Eckie House. Today, my heart feels lighter. George and I meant to fill Eckie House with children's laughter, that's why he built it so big. After dinner, I heard Emaline and Rose laughing over a silly game. It's a start.

~from *Beloved Wife, Mother, Sister, and Friend, A Biography of Faith Taylor Eckie* by Emaline Eckie Benson

****

In the mirror, a man either needing a shave or sporting the scruffy look stared back at him. James rubbed his jaw with his palm. Too rough for Andrea's soft skin. He shaved. Wearing only navy boxers, he flipped the bathroom light off, opened the door, and searched the shadows. A definitely female silhouette stood before the bedroom's French door. He padded across the thick Aubusson rug, stopped behind her, and breathed in her unique scent. She reached behind and gently grabbed his hands, wrapping them around her waist, the cotton of her long T-shirt soft against his hand. "Look." She nodded toward the sky. A crescent moon rode high surrounded by a blanket of stars. She turned in the circle of his arms and placed a brief kiss on his lips. "Thank you for a lovely date."

He leaned in and retuned the kiss. "Were you impressed?"

Her chuckle rumbled against his cheek. "Were you trying to impress me?"

Nuzzling her neck he whispered, "Oh, yeah." His lips floated along her cheek, nuzzling, licking, placing tiny kisses. He lifted her in his arms. "And I'm not done yet." He lay her gently on the cool, cotton sheets and dropped down beside her. His hands roamed her body, sliding over soft cotton to her thighs and softer skin beyond. "So soft." She caressed the hair on his chest. "Does it bother you?" He stilled.

"What?"

He sighed. "My hairy chest."

"Nope. Not at all." She pulled at the hair in the center. He grimaced. "I've always wanted to do that. I remember when there was no hair."

"Yeah. The disadvantage to knowing me from age

eleven." He kissed her neck, ran his tongue along the T-shirt's neckline. "Let's lose this?" She nodded. He sat back on his heels, grabbed the hem, and slowly raised the shirt, tugging it along her skin in a caress. "Almost like you unwrap a gift. But better." He pulled the shirt over her head and tossed it to the floor. His forearms rested beside her shoulders holding himself up. He kissed her cheek, nose, ears, and jaw. He placed his lips on hers, deepened the kiss, and ran his tongue along her seamed lips. She breathed a sigh, and his tongue entered her mouth, gently mimicking intercourse. She answered his kiss; her tongue dueled with his. He pulled back, ended the kiss. Kissed her shoulder, licked her nipples, ran his tongue inside her belly button. She squirmed and reached for him. Caressed his shoulders, ruffled his hair. He kissed a wandering trail down her body, her hipbones, rounded tummy, the fragile seam between thigh and hip. His tongue darted out and softly licked her intimate folds. He looked up into her passion filled eyes. "Okay?"

She sighed. "Oh yes."

He kissed her intimately. She exploded on his tongue. He grabbed the condom, suited up, and slid inside. Her pulsing internal muscles sent him over the edge. Spent, he rolled to the side taking her with him, nestling her head on his shoulder. She opened her drooping eyes. "Great date." Her eyes closed. Her breathing evened. She slept.

The scents of spent passion lingered in the air mixed with Andrea's scent of soap and woman. She turned her back. He crawled out of bed, careful not to disturb her. In the bathroom, he tossed the condom and faced the stranger in the mirror. Already a hint of stubble darkened his jaw. He pictured another man touching her soft skin. His eyes narrowed, his dark brows drew together. No. Shutting the light off, he left the bathroom and crawled into bed. He pulled her into his arms, chest to back. He slept.

A screech woke James from a deep sleep. He forced his eyes open just in time to see Andrea, dressed in a giant ASU T-shirt, disappear through the door. He rolled out of bed, yanked on his boxers, and padded across the hall. The nightlight cast a rainbow of color and shadow in the nursery. At the changing table, Andrea spoke softly to her wiggling daughter. Beside the crib stood two young girls, their white nightgowns a beacon in the dark. They glided next to Andrea, their focus on Ella. Ella stilled. James stepped inside the room. The children disappeared.

Ella settled, sleeping in her crib; James tugged Andrea back to bed. "Does she often wake with a scream?"

Andrea shrugged and slipped between the sheets. "She sleeps about eight hours at night. Just doesn't happen to be the same eight I sleep."

"At least she goes right back to sleep." He spooned her, placing his big hand on her stomach.

Her eyes drifted closed. "Yeah. She just hates being wet. Sensitive skin."

James listened to her even breathing and closed his eyes. He snuggled closer. Would she find someone else when he was gone? He tried to imagine another man picking up Ella. Another man spooning with Andrea. Loss squeezed his heart. Foolish feeling. Even if she found someone else, she wouldn't disappear. They were part of the Benton tribe, Benton history. Her riotous curls tickled his cheek. He sighed. Maybe things would stay the same. The years go by and they'd still be together when they could. Look how long she'd stayed with Laurence. Ahh, but he knew better. If nothing else, he'd learned one truth in his thirty-nine years, things always changed. He drifted into sleep.

Bright summer sun glinted through the kitchen window. Aretha Franklin's demand for "Respect" competed with the bang of Ella's spoon on the highchair. The scent of bacon blended with the aroma of coffee. Toast popped and Andrea set two plates of pancakes on the table. James grabbed silverware and mugs of coffee.

Seated at the small breakfast table, James lifted his mug in a toast. "To breakfast." They clicked their filled mugs.

Andrea sighed. "I'm gonna miss this."

"There's no reason you can't make breakfast for yourself." James sliced into pancakes.

"Not worth the trouble just for me. Ella's diet's pretty bland."

James nodded toward Ella. "She likes the pancakes though." Smashed food decorated Ella's grinning face. She squeezed a small pancake in her fist.

Breakfast over and the kitchen cleaned, Andrea lifted Ella from the highchair. "Now to clean you up, young lady."

"Time for me to go." James wrapped them in his arms. "Sweet cheeks." He buzzed Ella's cheek and she giggled. "Andrea." His lips met hers, gently. His tongue darted out. She opened for him. "Mmm." He pulled back, placed a quick kiss on her cheek. "I'll call."

The air stilled. Standing beside the table, a toddler

in her arms, a young woman laughed. An older man lifted a little girl high in the air, her giggles lighting the room with music. Little girl now balanced on his hip, the man joined the woman at the table, leaned over, and kissed her lightly on the lips. He set the child down and walked out the back door. The woman and children disappeared; the familiar hum of the refrigerator filled the room. James grabbed his duffle from the kitchen floor, gave Andrea a grin, and sauntered out the back door. Did Andrea see the spirits at the table? Did their appearance just as he was leaving mean something? He wished he could go back and borrow the biography.

****

On Tuesday, blonde baby fuzz forming a halo around her face, Ella took two steps and toppled face first to the carpet in the bookroom. Her cry brought Andrea up from concentration on a client's whining email. She sat on the floor and lifted Ella in her arms. "Good thing you're built close to the ground, little one." Cuddling Ella in her arms, they rocked side to side until Ella quieted. "Ready to try again?" She set Ella on her feet, keeping hold of her hands. "Let go when ready." Ella let go, clapped her hands, and plopped on her bottom with a laugh. Andrea returned to her desk chair. "That was certainly more fun than listening to this guy's whiny rant." The opening stanzas of "One Less Bell To Answer" played through the house announcing a visitor. The grandmother clock chimed ten o'clock. Andrea grabbed Ella in her arms and dashed down the hallway. Her appointment had arrived. At the door, she stopped, adjusted Ella in her arms, and plastered a smile on her face. No point thinking about her hair. Ella's tiny fingers yanked on the curly strands. Andrea pulled open the heavy door.

"Hi. I'm Rose Peterson. You were expecting me?" A tall, blonde young woman offered her hand.

Andrea clasped Rose's soft hand and answered her firm shake. "Come in. Let's start in the bookroom." They strolled down the hallway. The heels on Rose's flats made a clicking noise on the wooden floor. "Jackson tells me you wanted a tour of Eckie House for a college project?"

"My master's thesis. I really appreciate you showing me the house." She admitted, "Jackson wasn't sure you would."

Andrea shrugged. "How long have you known Jackson?"

They entered the bookroom. "Three generations worth? He's handled my family's property in Creekside for three generations."

"But this is your first time in Eckie House?"

"Yeah." Her eyes widened. "Wow. No wonder it's known as the bookroom. Are the built-in shelves original?"

"I think so. They're approximately the same age as the house." Rose asked questions about the house as they visited the public rooms and climbed the main staircase. On the second floor, Andrea settled Ella in her crib for a nap and grabbed the monitor. They climbed the main stairs to the third floor and eventually returned to the first floor via the back stairs leading to the kitchen. Andrea pushed the door open, holding it for Rose.

Sun glinted through the kitchen windows and danced on the stainless steel countertops. Leafy herbs growing in small white pots decorated the kitchen windowsill. Rose turned in a circle, her eyebrows raised. "This is beautiful, but..."

Andrea chuckled. "But the commercial kitchen doesn't quite fit in a historic house?"

"You didn't do this?" Rose shook her head.

"Nope." Andrea gathered two glasses and a pitcher of iced tea. "The prior owner planned on turning Eckie House into a bed and breakfast, small five-star restaurant, and event venue. Have a seat at the breakfast table. Would you like tea, soda, or water?"

"Tea's great." Rose walked to the window. "Are the trees the end of the property?"

"Almost. There's a strip of land between them and the fence." Andrea poured the tea and dropped into a chair. Rose joined her at the table, adding sugar to her glass.

Rose sipped her tea. "What do you plan for Eckie House?" Andrea lifted her eyebrow, surprised by the question. Until now, Rose's questions concerned Eckie House's past. "My house is just the other side of your trees. What you decide affects me."

"Did your family buy the house from Faith?"

"My great, great grandmother moved into Eckie House in 1911 with my great grandmother in tow. They moved into one of Faith's houses in 1916. Much to the dismay of my brothers, uncles, and cousins, the house is always given to the oldest daughter when she turns twenty-five." She grinned. "This generation that's me."

"And what will you do with the house?" Andrea asked as she put the glasses in the dishwasher and they walked toward the front door.

"Right now, I've hired help fixing the house up. The last tenant didn't vandalize it or anything, but the house looks tired." She shrugged. "Then I'll probably rent the house out again."

"Shouldn't be a problem. Rentals close to the Square are hard to find."

At the door, Rose reached out her hand. "Thank you for the tour, Andrea. I probably won't use Eckie House in my thesis. If I do, I'll send you a copy." Andrea pulled open the door and faced Nathan, his hand hovering over the doorbell.

"Hey Nathan, what brings you here?" Andrea pulled the door wide. "Come in." She watched his eyes light as he stared at Rose. "This is Rose Peterson. Rose, Nathan Stephens."

"Hi, Rose." He blushed. "Actually, you're the one I want to see. Jackson sent me."

"Told you property near the Square was scarce," Andrea commented. The monitor in her pocket squealed and a tearful voice cried, "Momma."

"You can talk in the parlor or outside, but I need to answer Ella's call." Andrea pointed to a small room near the front door. Nathan and Rose walked outside. Andrea closed the door and sprinted up the stairs. A cleaned-up Ella in her arms, she headed down the stairs. How did an instant attraction so strong the mind stopped happen? Nathan stared at Rose for the length of several heartbeats before he gathered his wits to speak. When Chance first saw Catherine, he stopped halfway down the stairs, his face flushed. Love? Passion? Or a recognition of potential for both?

The porch was empty, her visitors gone. Fixing lunch, she realized she'd loved James forever or at least since the first time he balanced Nikki's bike and taught Andrea to ride. That love would always be there.

Would the passion remain? Was passion strong enough to build a future?

Just before dawn, Andrea woke to the sound of a deep voice humming a waltz. In a shadowy corner, a dark-haired man with a handlebar mustache held a woman dressed in a flowing white gown in his arms. They danced around the room to the rhythm of the waltz; her gown floated, revealing her bare feet. Her laughter filled the room. The couple stopped. He pulled her tight against his chest, leaned down, and planted a kiss on her lips. They disappeared, though her laughter still floated in the air. Andrea closed her eyes and slept.

Chapter Seventeen

1912

Dear Momma,

Today, I met the new attorney in town. Mr. Henderson seems very young; does that mean I'm getting old? He offered to visit me at Eckie House when I made the appointment, but the only downside to a house full of women and children is a lack of quiet. I'm finally ready to sell a small piece of the property complete with house. Mrs. Gantley is ready to move into her own home. I needed to be sure if something happened to me no one could take the house away from her. I decided to build the houses beyond the creek and orchard. Violet made all the drawings. When she starts at Arizona Normal School in the fall, she'll be sorely missed.

~from *Beloved Wife, Mother, Sister, and Friend. A Biography of Faith Taylor Eckie* by Emaline Eckie Benson.

****

Sun through the stained glass windows decorated Pastor Tim's white vestments in rainbow colors of red, green, and yellow. Michelle's whimpers competed with Tim's deep voice as he intoned the liturgy of baptism. Standing beside Nikki, Andrea repeated the familiar words, a promise of faithfulness and support for the daughter of her best friend, sister of her heart. At Tim's signal, they turned toward the congregation. "It is my pleasure to introduce you to Michelle Elizabeth Stark." The congregation stood and clapped. Michelle, held in her mother's arms, looked around, closed her eyes, and lay her fuzzy head on Nikki's shoulder.

Eckie House rang with the sound of conversation. Grandmother's dining table groaned under the weight of food. One corner of the large parlor boasted board games, toys, and art supplies suitable for a variety of ages. Andrea watched her father fold his long legs and sit on the floor in the play area. Immediately, the younger children surrounded him. Ella crawled over and climbed on his lap. Andrea pulled her cell from her pocket and snapped a picture.

James' arm slid across her shoulder. She looked up, and he nodded toward Spencer. "Different view of your father. He's working hard at the grandpa gig."

"Yeah. Whatever I thought of him as a father, he's become an excellent grandpa."

"Did you meet Jacob and Whitney?" He nodded toward the buffet table where Whitney laughed with an unfamiliar young woman.

"Yep." She chuckled. "Nikki introduced us. Nik's thrilled about adding more family."

"Who's with Whitney?"

Andrea took his hand and towed him toward Whitney. "Carly Edwards."

"My half-niece and Ella's half-sister." He shook his head. "This family gets more complicated by the minute."

On the way, Andrea stopped in front of Spencer. Ella sat on his knee and looked ready to scream. Andrea grabbed her. "Oh dear. Looks like someone needs a change." She glanced at her dad and grinned. "Two someones."

Spencer looked down at the spreading wet spot on his khaki pants. He unfolded himself from the floor and said, "Hazardous duty. I'll go change."

Ella in one arm, she towed James to Whitney and Carly. "Hi, Carly, this is James." She let go of his hand. "Excuse me, but we have a costume malfunction." She strolled to the bookroom. After cleaning Ella up, Andrea detoured to the kitchen. "Let's see if you're ready to eat, Miss Ella." Ella balanced on her hip, she glanced out the kitchen window. Led by Mitch and Colin, children ages four to fifteen played croquet, their laughter ringing through the window. Three-year-old Hope swung her mallet and missed. Mitch moved behind her, held her little hands in his and together they made the shot. The angry Mitch was gone, replaced by a kind, patient teenager. Blended family, that's what Ella had, family connected by love, biology, and choice.

The kitchen door swung open and a red head peered around the corner. "Okay if I come in?"

"Of course, Chance. What's up?" She secured Ella in the highchair with the belt. "Checking up on the girls?"

"Yeah and I wanted to ask you something?" He blushed. "Could you watch the girls one night next week?"

She raised her eyebrows, surprised Catherine didn't do the asking. "Sure. Just pick a night. Got a date?"

The red on his cheeks deepened and he nodded. "Dinner with Catherine, at Sanders House."

"So, do you want us to stay the night?"

"No. Catherine's not willing to stay all night." He sighed. "Someday. But not yet." He glanced out the window. "The girls are enjoying themselves. I'll text you tomorrow." He disappeared through the door.

Andrea cleaned up Ella and the kitchen, smiling at Chance's embarrassment. Hard to ask a friend to babysit when your plans included passion and the babysitter could tell. Of course, she hadn't been embarrassed asking Catherine to watch Ella for her date with James. Why? Maybe because they'd planned a date first? Maybe because they'd never hesitated to make love with Ella in the house? Maybe because unlike Chance, Andrea didn't ooze sexual tension every time she mentioned James' name. As though thinking about him conjured his presence, James appeared in the kitchen doorway. "Hey. Ready to rejoin the party?" He lifted Ella in his arms. "Aren't you the hostess?"

"But not the guest of honor. Anyway, Ella doesn't care about the party much when she's hungry or wet." They strolled down the hallway toward the sounds of music and animated conversation. At the base of the staircase, the air stilled. On the bottom step, a boy of about ten stood, one hand on his hip, the other in the air. He brought his arm down, and a little girl zoomed down the bannister, her dark braids flying. The boy grabbed her at the bannister's end and set her beside him on the stair. Giggles whispered in the air. The children disappeared. The sounds of the party returned.

"Do they appear often?" James nodded toward the stairs.

Andrea shrugged. "Spirits? Yep. Those particular children?" She shook her head. "Hard to tell. It's like time is fluid for them."

"Fluid?"

"I have no idea if they are the same children at different ages or different children at the same time."

Spencer joined them. "There's my girl." He lifted Ella from Andrea's arms, spun her in a circle, and trotted off.

****

"Are you sure you don't mind?" Catherine asked for the third time, her voice a breathy whisper in the silent house.

Andrea shook her head and took Catherine's hands. "I want to watch the kids and dogs. We'll be fine. Not so sure about you, though. Why so nervous? If you're not ready to sleep with Chance, tell him." She shrugged. "There's no expiration date on his desire that I can see." She settled on the couch.

Catherine plopped in the rocking chair, lifted Ariel in her arms, and stroked her white fur. "I want to be with Chance. But I feel guilty."

"Because of Craig?" Andrea frowned. "You do realize he loved you? He'd want you happy."

"But we were forever. Forever, Craig and me and our children."

"You are forever. It'd be hard not to carry Craig around forever when you're raising a little girl with his beautiful brown eyes surrounded by long black lashes, and her older sister possesses his stubborn chin."

The back door squeaked, footsteps sounded in the hallway. A red head followed by a tall male body ambled into the room. "Hi, Andi." His face lit with a smile. "Ready, Catherine?" He reached out his hand.

Grabbing his hand, Catherine rose. "Ready. Night,

Andi."

Andrea buckled Ella into the stroller just as they entered the living room. "I'll walk you home." Chance grabbed the diaper bag.

"You don't have to."

"I want to." He kissed Catherine on the cheek and they slipped quietly out the front door. The promise of dawn teased the fall sky, black turning to gray. "Thanks again for staying with the girls."

"No problem. Just returning the favor." They walked in companionable silence through the night.

Ella settled in her crib, Andrea climbed between soft sheets and drifted in the place between sleep and wakefulness. Forever. Catherine and Craig promised each other forever. Now Chance wanted to make the same promise. Nikki and Alex promised forever. Why did Andrea waste so much time with Laurence? He never wanted forever. Ahh. But he gave her Ella and her, Andrea couldn't regret. And what about James, Andrea's little girl crush and middle school heartbreak. Time with James couldn't be a waste because they were part of the same tribe. Was history enough foundation to build a lasting love?

Chapter Eighteen

1912

Dear Momma and Daddy,

Happy Statehood Day. Hard to believe our beautiful territory is now a state. George would be celebrating if he were here.

Today, I bought a flower shop. George claimed money needed to work to be of value. I think he'd be impressed by my creative way of putting ours to work. The owner is moving back to Kansas. Rose Adams who lives with us has a true gift for growing and arranging flowers, and the beauty of Eckie House's gardens is mostly her doing. Dottie Mayhew handled her father's books before he died, so she's setting up the books.

I'm excited to start a new adventure and provide a couple of my friends a way to support themselves and their children. This is fun!

~from Beloved Wife, Mother, Sister, and Friend, A Biography of Faith Taylor Eckie by Emaline Eckie Benson

****

"One Less Bell To Answer" chimed through the house. Andrea slipped out the office door and checked the video doorbell app on her phone. She recognized the tall woman immediately from Drew's engagement pictures. Jodi's mom. "Hi, Mrs. Williams, I'm on my way." She grinned at the video camera. Andrea yanked open the heavy door and gazed into brown eyes identical to Jodi's. "Welcome to Eckie House." They strolled down the hallway. "We'll start in the office with Ella. Nikki should be here shortly, and I'll take you on a tour." They stepped through the baby gate. Andrea crouched and Ella took a few steps toward her, collapsed to her bottom, and crawled into Andrea's arms. The kitchen door shut with a thunk, and Nikki's voice rang through the house.

"Sorry I'm late." Michelle in her arms, diaper bag on her shoulder, Nikki dashed into the study. "Hi." She grimaced. "Have you been waiting long?"

Andrea shook her head. "Barely a moment. Nikki, meet Helen Williams, Jodi's mom." Michelle settled in the portable crib and Nikki entertained Ella. Andrea led Helen back into the hallway. "Let's start at the top, okay?" At Helen's nod, Andrea pushed the elevator button. With a whir, the hidden panel door opened. She yanked back the security gate and they rode to the top. Helen's eyes widened as the elevator clanked and whirred its way to the third floor then stopped with a sudden loud click. Andrea tapped in the door code and slid back the gate. The panel door opened into the hallway.

Helen stepped over the threshold. "How old is the elevator?" she asked as the gate clanked shut and the panel door slid closed.

"The first residential one in Creekside, the elevator was installed in 1905." Andrea grinned at Helen's horrified expression. "The mechanics were replaced a couple times. Faith's children replaced them in the 1940s and the last owner replaced them when he remodeled the kitchen."

"Still sounds old."

"My guess is the last owner created the noises on purpose," Andrea admitted. "Wanted to add to the historic building ambience."

They toured the third- and second-floor bedrooms. Downstairs, she led Helen through the kitchen to the dining room, out the French doors, and onto the flagstone patio. "Jodi mentioned wanting an inside ceremony and outside reception." Sunlight danced through the patio's lattice cover, creating an intricate pattern of light and shadow. "Patrick and Scott offered to string solar lights across the patio and through the trees. With candles on the table, there should be enough light."

"It's beautiful. I can see why Jodi wants the wedding here." They wandered inside, finally reaching the front room.

"Ceremony in here." Andi pulled open the panel doors. Light streamed through the lace curtains, creating patterns on the wooden floor. In a shadowy corner, a dozen children sat and sprawled on the floor around a young woman perched in a Morris chair. Her hands held an open book, her voice whispered through the room. Giggles suddenly drifted on the air. They disappeared.

Beside Andi, Helen let her breath out in a quiet whoosh. "Did you see them?"

"Yeah." She gently took Helen's arm and led her down the hall. "We'll have a drink and I'll tell you about Eckie House."

Settled at the kitchen table, plate of cookies nearly demolished, Helen asked, "Do you think they'll be a problem at the wedding? Frighten the guests or something."

Andi shrugged and sipped the tea. "I doubt it. Eckie House hosted a baby shower and a christening party in the last few months. They didn't cause a problem."

"Did anyone see them?" She frowned. "Did they frighten anyone?"

"Nope." Andi shook her head. "They mostly appear when the house is nearly empty." They finished the tea, and Andi walked Helen to the front door. "I'll see you and Jodi tomorrow at three for a final run through."

A small smile crossed Helen's face. "Tomorrow at three. Thank you for the tour." She slowly walked down the front steps. When she reached the front gate, she turned back and gave Andi a brief wave.

Andi stepped over the baby gate and plopped onto the bookroom sofa. Nikki looked up from her finger game with Ella and frowned. "What's wrong?"

"You know how proud I am of the big parlor?"

Nikki nodded. "And you should be. You did an excellent job furnishing the parlor."

"With a flourish, I yanked open the door. So she could get the full effect?"

"And?"

"A circle of children surrounded a young woman who was reading from a book." Andi sighed.

Nikki grinned. "So business as usual in Creekside."

"Of course." Andi shrugged. "But Helen turned parchment paper white. I touched her arm and she was marble cold." She shook her head. "She was scared. Or in shock." Andi rested her head against the sofa back and closed her eyes. "I rushed her to the kitchen and plied her with sweetened tea and cookies."

Nikki nodded. "Excellent treatment for shock."

"She asked if the spirits were likely to appear during the wedding. Do you think she'll convince Jodi to move the wedding?"

"She might try." Nikki frowned. "But where would they go? The wedding's in two weeks."

"Are we the crazy ones, Nik?"

"I'm not sure about you, especially since you're dating my brother." She shook her head. "But I'm absolutely sure I'm not crazy."

Andi raised an eyebrow. "You don't think it's crazy you live in a haunted hotel surrounded by spirits reliving, sort of, their major life moments?"

"Hey. Those spirits kept me company when I was lonely. Victoria and her lover convinced me love, even when it doesn't last, is worth the risk."

"How did we manage before we found this place?" Andrea shook her head. "Where else do spirits take an opportunity to teach us stuff we need to know?"

"Yep. For you and me, Creekside was exactly the right place at the right time."

****

After a horrible restless night, Andrea grimaced at her reflection in the mirror. Dark circles rimmed her eyes; her curly hair lay flat on one side and stuck straight up on top. New lines appeared beside her eyes. Carrie Underwood crooned you can't "Cry Pretty" and Andrea laughed. Apparently she didn't sleep pretty either. Or not sleep. She stepped in the shower and let the hot water caress her tired muscles. Shampoo leaked into one eye, the burn a shock. Water shut off, she stepped out of the shower, wrapped herself in a towel, and hoped today would get better.

At exactly three o'clock, "Up, Up, And Away" chimed through the house. Andrea dashed down the hallway and stopped at the front door. She took a deep breath and plastered a welcoming smile on her face. Breath released in a whoosh, she slowly pulled open the front door. "Welcome back to Eckie House."

"Thank you, thank you for letting us have the wedding here." Jodi grabbed her in a hug and twirled them around. "I'm so excited. It's going to be perfect." Jodi released her and grabbed Helen's hand. "Come in, Mom. There's so much to talk about." They strolled down the hallway. "Where's Ella?"

"Play date." She ushered them into the kitchen where they grabbed drinks and snacks from a selection on the counter and chose chairs around the table. "Okay. Now walk me through the weekend from the moment you leave Colorado Springs."

"I can do better." Jodi pulled a stack of papers from her handbag. "The schedule, this is your copy."

Andrea flipped through the organized packet, which included everything from a timeline to a spreadsheet. "Wow. I'm impressed. We could have used your help planning Nikki's wedding."

"I wish I could take credit, but I can't," Jodi admitted. "The Maid of Honor is an event planner in Lake Havasu City. Heather talked me through the process."

They talked through the schedule, making notes and clarifying details. Up the elevator to the third floor where Jodi wandered in and out of the bedrooms. "Oh, this is perfect for the girls. Are you sure this isn't an inconvenience? We'll try not to make a mess. I know you don't have a housekeeper."

"No housekeeper, but a service," she admitted as they started down the stairs. "They'll be here two days before the wedding and the Monday after." She turned to Helen. "Will you stay here or are you booked into the hotel?"

"The Saint George. We decided to leave The Palace and Eckie House to the young people."

Trailing her hand along the smooth banister, Jodi commented, "This is the perfect staircase for a grand entrance." At the base of the stairs, they turned and faced the first landing. The air stilled. Hanging onto the newel post with two hands a little girl straddled the railing. She pushed up over the post and slid down the railing, her dark braids flying. A boy appeared on the bottom step and plucked her from the banister. Their giggles filled the air and they disappeared. Jodi asked, "Do you suppose they'll show up at the wedding?"

Helen moaned. "I hope not."

Jodi threw her arm around Helen's shoulder and steered her toward the dining room. "Oh, Mom." She winked at Andrea. "What's a couple more kids?"

"I thought the bar could be set up here since you wanted an open bar between the ceremony and dinner." Andrea touched a button on the wall. A lock clicked, and pocket doors slid into the wall revealing a small room dominated by a long bar.

"This place has more nooks and sliding doors than any place I've ever seen." Jodi ran her hand across the polished wood. "Is this original?"

"No. The last owner added the bar. The small room was probably a closet since it's under the stairs." They walked through the dining room, out the French doors onto the patio.

Andrea left Jodi and Helen discussing table arrangements on the grass and dashed into the kitchen. Wine, glasses, water, and small sandwiches arranged artfully on a tray Andrea rejoined Jodi and Helen. Plates and glasses in hand, they settled in lounge chairs. Andrea relaxed against the chair and admired the expanse of grass and the copse of pear and apple trees just starting to turn color. Dancing between shade and sun, appearing beside and disappearing behind the old tree trunks, children played.

"Andi." Jodi's voice startled her. "What do you think?"

"About what?" Andrea asked. "Sorry, I was distracted."

"Do you think the spirit children will join the party?" Jodi set her glass on the tray.

"Hard to say," Andrea answered. "So far, they've avoided my parties. Guess they weren't interested in baby showers and a christening."

"I hope they don't," Helen admitted. "They could frighten someone or cause trouble."

Jodi shook her head. "No, Mom. Creekside spirits are benevolent. Look on the town website." She grinned at Andrea. "Creekside, a town full of friendly people and benevolent spirits."

Helen mumbled, "Yeah. According to the Chamber of Commerce."

****

"One Less Bell To Answer" chimed through the house and Andrea raced to the front door and yanked it open. "Welcome. Come in." She greeted five laughing young women.

Jodi grabbed her in a hug. "We made it." She stepped back. "We left the car out front. I didn't know how to open the gate."

"No problem. Sorry. I forgot you'd have a car." She put out her hand for the key and heard James' footsteps behind her. "The bellhop will take care of your car and luggage.

James kissed her cheek. "Bellhop?" He put out his hand. "Hi, Jodi. Hand me the keys and I'll move your car and bring the bags to third floor." Keys in hand he disappeared through the front door.

"Jodi, when you've settled, there are drinks and snacks waiting in the bookroom." Jodi and the bridesmaids clattered up the stairs. As Andrea strolled down the hallway, their laughter and admiration for the staircase floated in the air. In the bookroom, she poured a glass of wine and moved to the French doors. She pushed them open and muscular arms wrapped around her. Andrea leaned into a familiar firm chest and breathed deeply the scent of aftershave and soap. "You finished in a hurry."

He nuzzled her neck. "Experience." Warm breath tickled her ear. "Not the first time you've elected me bellhop." He rained kisses along her jaw.

Andrea set her wine glass on the desk, turned in his embrace, and wrapped her arms around his neck. His lips found hers and his tongue touched her lips. She opened on a moan. Their tongues played. High heels clattered on the hallway's wood floor. James ended the kiss and stepped back. Andrea lifted her wine glass. "Drink?"

"Yeah. Something cold." He walked to the small

refrigerator and pulled out a beer bottle just as Jodi entered the room.

By the time the bridesmaids held drinks in their hands, the doorbell chimed and James whispered in Andrea's ear, "Bellhop to doorman. I've been promoted?" and he disappeared through the door. The cheerful noise level grew as the room filled with the wedding party and Pastor Tim.

Eventually Pastor Tim herded them into the parlor. Using a hand full of notes, he directed them to specific chairs. "Listen up." The room quieted and Tim grinned. "Wish I could use that on Sunday mornings. Worked like a charm." They laughed. "Jodi and Drew decided their guests could sit anywhere with only a few exceptions. First row on your left is for Jodi's brothers and sisters, leaving room for flower girl and mom and dad closest to the aisle. Drew's family is in the first row on the right including the Bentons and Starks leaving room on the aisle for Andrea and Spencer. When the rest of the family is seated, Colton escorts Andrea with Spencer trailing behind. Then, Rawley, you escort Jodi's mom. That's the signal. Now everybody out to the hallway except Jodi and the bridesmaids. Ladies, you go up to the first landing."

As they stood in line in the hallway, Andrea whispered to Spencer, "Is this normal? Shouldn't I be with the siblings rather than with the parents?"

Spencer kissed her cheek. "You're right where you should be. You've always been a combination sister and parent for Drew." Andrea fought tears.

In a chattering herd, they strolled to The Saint George Hotel for the rehearsal dinner just as the setting sun tinged the sky shades of orange and pink. James' hand a warm presence at the small of her back, Andrea glided through the group. They spent the next few hours laughing and groaning through toasts both silly and sentimental.

Jodi's dad stood and raised his glass. "Thank you all for joining our celebration." Claps and whistles. "Especially thank you, Andrea, for opening your home, hosting the wedding, and making our entire family feel welcome."

Andrea stood, her glass raised. "You're very welcome. It is very much my pleasure to welcome you. And, Jodi, welcome to the family."

Chapter Nineteen

1918

Dear Momma,

Eckie House is full. I believed the house would always feel empty after George died. No more. Today, another widow arrived on the doorstep, an infant in her arms. Her husband lost to the flu stomping through the country. Between the young men lost to war and this horrible flu, are we becoming a world of only women and children? Now the rooms are full. Oh, how I wish there were more rooms, for what will happen to the next desperate woman?

Some of my guests have offered to either share their rooms or move into the barn, leaving the inside rooms for women with very young children. The ladies living in the two houses beyond the orchard offered to share their small homes as well. The owner of The Palace Hotel offered to clear her attic and furnish it with beds if necessary. I hope it doesn't come to that. George shares a room with another boy, and Emaline shares with me. The sounds at night remind me of childhood and sharing a room with sisters. The high-pitched voices of young children blend with their mothers' lower tones in a familiar lullaby.

~from Beloved Wife, Mother, Sister, and Friend, A Biography of Faith Taylor Eckie by Emaline Eckie

Benson

****

"How's it feel watching your chick leave the nest?" James whispered in her ear as they slow danced under the full moon to Keith Urban's "Making Memories of Us."

"I might shed a few tears later, but watching Drew marry is easier than leaving him at the boarding school when he was twelve," she admitted. "Tonight's one more step on a path he chose."

"And he chose you to play the part of mother, including the mother son dance." She felt his deep chuckle. "Loved the choreography. When did you have time to practice?"

"Wasn't easy. Jodi created the dance, taught Drew and sent me a video."

"The three of you made a good team. Can't imagine your mom out there doing high kicks with Drew." He pulled her closer and nuzzled her cheek. "So where is your mother?" He danced her toward the edge of the crowd.

"Bermuda? Paris?" She shrugged and cuddled closer. "She sent her regrets."

Keith's voice faded with the last chord and Ronni touched Andrea's arm. "Cake cutting after the next song." James dropped his arms.

"Thanks, Ronni. I'll scope out a good view." Andrea watched Ronni, camera in hand, stroll toward the dessert table. She lifted her camera and looked through the lens without breaking stride.

James took her hand and tugged Andi around the edge of the dance floor. "How did Ronni end up Jodi's wedding photographer?" "Let's Dance," exclaimed

David Bowie and the floor filled with prancing, shimmying bodies. Andi and James reached the relative quiet of the dessert table and he laid his arm across her shoulder.

"Ronni volunteered when the photographer from Prescott cancelled." Andrea shrugged. "She claims wedding photography paid for her college education." From the other side of the table Ronni lifted her camera and shot their picture. The DJ announced the cake cutting and Nathan appeared beside them, video camera in hand. He winked at Andrea then focused on his camera following Drew and Jodi from the dance floor to the dessert table. Music stopped, and dancers surged forward making a circle around the wedding cake. As the upbeat sound of Fleetwood Mac's "You Make Loving Fun" filled the air, Jodi and Drew clowned for the camera and finally managed to cut the cake. Tiny slice of cake between her fingers, Jodi carefully placed the sweet in Drew's mouth. He lifted an even smaller amount between two fingers and held it against her lips; her tongue darted out and licked the frosting. She opened her mouth and he placed the cake inside, leaned down, and kissed her quickly on the lips. Applause broke out. The DJ flipped the music to "Dancing In The Streets" and the dance floor filled. Andrea felt a warm hand on her shoulder and gazed into familiar eyes.

"Buy you a drink, sister dear?" She nodded and they meandered toward the bar, Drew's arm around her shoulder. "So, you and James Benton?"

"Me and James Benton what?"

"A couple. More than friends?" He signaled the bartender for two glasses of wine and handed her one. They skirted the dance floor.

"Hmm. Before we discuss my personal life, how about sharing all the details of your private life before Jodi?" She grinned at his horrified expression. How could she explain her relationship with James?

"Not going to happen." He guided her away from the dance floor. They sat in chairs at an otherwise empty table. "I really wanted to hurt Laurence."

"But you didn't."

He shrugged. "By the time I could get back to Phoenix, you'd managed your coffee trick, and he was ancient history."

"Coffee trick? One of the most satisfying coffee dates I've ever had. Who knew a little spilled coffee was all I needed to make a point."

"Andi, James is a decent guy you've known forever." Drew took her hand and frowned. "Have you even talked about a future?"

Before she could answer, a bridesmaid dressed in deep teal tapped him on the shoulder. "Jodi needs you now."

Drew stood and kissed Andi's cheek. "Later, sis. Don't think this conversation is over." He dashed away, weaving in and out among the guests.

Grateful for the interruption, Andi picked up her wine and moved farther away from the dance floor. No way to answer Drew's question. She dropped into a chair distant from the dancers. Here, the night air cooled her skin, and a breeze ruffled her hair. Her mind swam with unanswerable questions; she stared unseeing across the shadowy meadow. Clouds drifted and the full moon gradually chased away the shadows. The music changed to Eric Clapton's "Wonderful Tonight," and in the moonlight, a man and woman danced in the meadow. The woman's long skirt drifted in the breeze. A cloud floated in front of the moon; the song ended and the couple disappeared. A warm hand caressed the back of her neck and the familiar scent of expensive aftershave and James surrounded her.

"Taking a break?"

She sighed. "Did you see them?"

"The dancers in the meadow? Yeah." He took her hand. "Dance with me?" She rose and they strolled to the dance floor. Whitney Houston admitted "I Wanna Dance With Somebody" and they joined the laughing, animated, moving bodies.

****

Suitcase wheels on hardwood floors declared the departure of another houseguest. Balancing Ella on her hip, Andrea peeked around the bookroom doorway. "Ready to go, Dad?"

"Ready." He dropped the suitcase and lifted Ella in his arms. "Need one last hug before I start my drive home." Ella grabbed for his glasses and Spencer lifted her over his head. "Oh no you don't. Need those to find my way home." Ella chortled.

Drew ambled toward them from the kitchen. "Hey, Dad. You leaving?"

"Yeah. You about ready?"

"I'm ready." He grinned and took Ella. "My bride's running a little late."

Spencer extended his hand. "Thank you, Drew, and thank Jodi for inviting me."

Drew took the offered hand and shook. "You're welcome. I'm glad you came." He handed Ella to Andi. "I'll walk you out."

Spencer wrapped his arms around Ella and Andi.

"See you in a couple weeks?"

"We'll be waiting." Andi watched Drew grab the suitcase. The two men in her family strolled through the door talking quietly. The elevator's theatric clank and the panel door's whoosh announced Jodi's arrival on the first floor.

"Help? Andi?" Andi sat Ella on the floor, vaulted the baby gate, and dashed to the elevator. Two bags at her feet and a puzzled look on her face, Jodi sported a frown. "Sorry. I can't remember how to open the gate."

"No problem." Andi flipped the old-fashioned lever and the gate opened. "Drew left you to deal with the luggage? Shame on him."

"My fault. He said text him when I was ready." She shrugged. "I figured with the elevator no big deal bringing the bags down." They each grabbed a bag and Jodi looked around. "Where is Drew?"

"On the porch saying goodbye to Dad." Andrea reached for the second bag and nodded. "Go ahead outside and join them." Jodi released the bag and dashed toward the front door. She yanked it open and disappeared outside.

Jodi and Drew stepped inside and suddenly there was a flurry of activity. On the front porch, Andi held her brother close. "Let me know where you are?"

"Of course, sis. Don't I always?" He grinned.

She reached for Jodi. "Please call if you need anything." She wrapped Jodi in a hug. "Make sure he does all the heavy lifting; it's good for him." Andi leaned against the door. Drew threw the bags in the back of the rental, opened Jodi's door, and with a final wave, they disappeared through the gate. Another goodbye.

****

Wrenching sobs pulled Andrea from sleep. Not Ella's angry baby sobs. In a shadowy corner of the bedroom, two women wearing white nightgowns nestled in a flowered loveseat, their arms wrapped around each other. The older woman, her white hair glinting in the moonlight, whispered, "It's okay, baby. It's okay to cry." She stroked the younger woman's hair. "Right now it's so hard, but you're strong and brave." She pulled a white handkerchief from her pocket and folded it into the other woman's hand. The sobs slowed to gasps and hiccups. "You've two beautiful children to raise. Focus on them." She took back the handkerchief and blotted the other woman's tears. "They need you even more now." Ella let out a piercing wail. The women disappeared.

By the time Ella settled again in her crib, sunlight peeked through the shutters. Too late for more sleep. First mug of coffee in hand, Andrea grabbed her tablet and sat on the back porch swing. The scents of fall and bright sunlight dispelled the lingering sadness from the spirits' earlier weeping as Andrea browsed her email. She brought the coffee mug to her lips for a last sip and her cell phone rang. "Hello?"

"Andrea Hamilton?"

"Yes."

"This is Virginia Hennesy, Spencer Hamilton's assistant. Your father is in the hospital." Andrea tried to focus on Virginia's explanation but very little registered. She managed to write down Virginia's phone number and hang up. The monitor crackled and Ella wailed. Punching speed dial for Nikki, Andrea dashed up the stairs.

"My dad's in the hospital. I need to go to Scottsdale."

"I'm on my way." Good as her word, by the time a clean and fed Ella cuddled in Andrea's arms, Nikki wrapped them in a hug, and Patrick leaned against the kitchen counter. Nikki stepped back and took Ella from Andi's arms. "Okay, what's the plan?"

Tears coursed down Andrea's cheeks. She shook her head. "I don't have one."

Nikki nodded. "I can work with that." She grabbed Andi's hand and pulled her toward the stairs. "Patrick, call James and tell him Andrea will be staying with him. Then you can get gas in her car. The keys are there." She pointed toward the hook by the door. Patrick grabbed the keys, pulled out his phone, and dashed out the back door. "So, you're driving to Scottsdale, staying with James."

"What if James doesn't want me there?"

"Why wouldn't he? At the wedding it was obvious you're still an item."

"An item?" Andi pulled an overnight bag from the closet and dropped it on the bed. "I'm not sure what we are." She moved to the dresser.

Nikki stilled Andi's fidgeting hands. "Ask him." Nikki pulled jeans from the drawer. "This one?" Andi nodded. "Anyway, no matter what, you are still my best friend, still part of our tribe, and members get a room at James' condo." She rolled the jeans and stuffed them in the bag. "Next, are you taking Ella with you? If not, she can stay with me." At the sound of her name, Ella crawled to Nikki, grabbed her pant leg, and pulled herself up. "Oh, you heard your name." She picked Ella up, holding her over her head. Ella's giggles filled the room. The sound of feet taking the wooden back stairs two at a time announced Patrick's return.

"Car's gassed up. James says you lucked out. The cleaning service was there today so the condo looks great." Patrick took Ella from Nikki, gave her a smacking kiss, and set her on the floor. "He wants to know if he should grab some groceries or something after work and are you bringing Ella because he can get a porta-crib from one of the associates if you want."

"Andi, decision time. Ella stays with us or goes to Scottsdale?" Nikki pulled a blue sweater out of the drawer; at Andi's nod, she folded the sweater into the suitcase. "She could stay here. Till you know what's going on." She shrugged. "We can drive her down later once you know."

Half an hour later, Patrick tossed Andrea's bag in the SUV, she climbed in the driver's seat, and pulled away. In the rearview mirror, Nikki stood on the back porch, Ella in her arms.

****

Propped up in bed, Spencer smiled when Andrea kissed his cheek. "You didn't have to come."

"Yeah, I did. Only way to find out what's going on."

"Where's Ella?"

"Home with Nikki." Andi pushed a chair beside the bed and sat down. "Tell me what happened."

"Not sure." He pleated the sheet between restless fingers. Andi took his hand, stilled the nervous motion. "I got to the office early. Had a golf game planned and wanted to do a little work before I took off."

"And?"

"I remember standing at the window, watching

traffic stop and start on Scottsdale Road." He sipped water. "Then I woke up. My head pounded. I reached a hand toward my head, looking for the source of the pain." He shrugged. "Virginia appeared beside me. Told me to lie still, paramedics were on the way."

"So, you don't know how you went from staring out the window to staring at the ceiling?"

He shook his head and grimaced. "Virginia says I hit my head on the way down because there's a gash in the back."

Wearing scrubs, a smiling young woman joined them. "Hi, Mr. Hamilton. Time for more tests." She turned to Andrea. "He'll be gone a couple of hours."

Andrea squeezed Spencer's hand and kissed his cheek. "I'll be back."

In the hospital lobby, she checked her messages. There was a text from Nikki with a picture of Ella crawling across the sitting room, and a selfie of Nikki with Michelle in a front pack. —*Fun, Fun, Fun.*— Smiley face attached. —*Keep me posted on Spencer's condition.*—

Text from Patrick, —*Staying at Eckie House just to keep an eye on things. If you need something done, please let me know. (I'm bored already.) Give Spencer my best.*—

—*Hey. Tell me what I can do to help. Condo's ready. How's Spencer?*— from James.

She sent a group text. —*Don't know anything yet. They are doing tests. On my way to the condo then for something to eat before I see Dad again.*—

No answer to her knock at the condo, Andrea punched in the code and pushed open the door. A large male hand grabbed her overnight case, pulled it inside, and strong arms wrapped her in a hug. A familiar scent surrounded her. Tears suddenly coursed down her cheeks.

James lifted her in his arms, walked to the sofa, and settled her on his lap. "Ah, Andi. Not your best day ever, huh?" He rocked her back and forth until the sobs turned to tiny gasps. Andi grabbed a handful of tissues from the box on the end table and wiped her face. "Better?"

She nodded.

He lifted her off his lap and settled her on the end of the sofa. "Be right back." By the time Andi's tears stopped and her face was dry, he returned. He set a tray of sandwiches, chips, bottled water, two wine glasses, and bottle of red wine on the coffee table. "Eat, drink, and take a nap. Don't mean to insult you, but you look exhausted. I'll wake you in a while, and I'll drive you to the hospital."

"You don't have to."

"I want to."

Andrea woke to a low male voice obviously on the phone. "Nik, she's asleep. I'll ask her to call you." He sighed. "Yeah. I'm driving her back to the hospital when she's ready. Yes, I will take excellent care of your best friend. Yeah, love you too." Andrea sat up, looked around for her shoes and overnight bag. Both missing. She found James in the kitchen. He stood when she entered. "Ah. You look better." He handed her a glass of water. "Let me know when you're ready to go."

The hospital corridor rang with sounds of dinner carts on the tile floor. Spencer pushed his dinner tray away when they entered the room. Andrea wrapped him in a hug. "Don't let us interrupt dinner."

He shook his head. "I'm finished."

"How are you feeling, sir?" James shook Spencer's hand.

"Bored, except for when they're prodding, poking, or wheeling me about the hospital." He sighed. "First time I've stayed in the hospital overnight in twenty years. Hope it's another twenty before I return."

The door swung open and a tall, thin man with a close-cropped black beard walked in. "Hi, Mr. Hamilton. You're already looking better." Doctor Hayes introduced himself. "So, do you want me to toss these two out or speak freely, Mr. Hamilton?"

Spencer grumbled. "Go ahead. You probably don't know anything yet anyway."

"There's good news and okay news." He chuckled. "You're right. I don't know why you hit the floor. The good news is no indication of heart damage and the bang on your head caused a little bleeding on the brain. We'll monitor the bleeding but your brain will probably absorb the blood in a few days without damage."

Andrea frowned at Dr. Hayes. "So what's next?"

"More tests."

Spencer groaned.

"They'll be picking you up off and on during the night starting in about an hour." He shrugged. "So, no rest for the injured." Dr. Hayes turned to Andrea. "I'll be back tomorrow about nine for rounds. Might know something by then." He shook hands with Andrea and James, waved to Spencer, and strolled out.

Chapter Twenty

Dear Momma,

Happy New Year 1919. Much to celebrate with the war over and Clay on his way home. Do you know when he will get to Phoenix? A few of the men from Creekside have returned and were welcomed home with a town-wide celebration. Two of my guests are expecting their husbands any day now. They are giddy from expectation and quaking in fear. The news accounts are filled every day with soldiers delayed for some reason as they wait for their entire unit to be released. On the other front, letters to the editor claim returning military cannot find work, the jobs they left have disappeared, filled by those who did not serve. When they leave Eckie House with their husbands and children, where will they go?

~from Beloved Wife, Mother, Sister, and Friend, A Biography of Faith Taylor Eckie by Emaline Eckie Benson

****

Contrast between the mild October temperature and the hospital's artificial chill forced goose bumps on Andrea's skin and made her shiver. Early morning, the corridors filled with a mix of staff and visitors all talking at once. She pushed open her father's door and faced an empty bed. Spencer's laugh carried through the hallway. The door opened. IV pole on one side and nurse on the other, Spencer shuffled into the room and kissed her on the cheek. "Morning, Andi."

"You must be feeling better. Doctor been here yet?"

Nurse assisting, Spencer climbed into bed. "Nope. But they let me up to walk." He sighed. "Had to get out of the bed."

The nurse dashed out and Dr. Hayes ambled in. "Good morning." He pulled a chair near the bed, plopped down and, using diagrams, explained pulmonary embolism. Bottom line, Spencer would spend a few more days in the hospital while they started the treatment plan. With a little care and Spencer's cooperation, eventually he'd recover. The door whooshed shut behind Dr. Hayes and Andrea felt tears slide down her cheeks.

Spencer reached for her hand. "Ah, Andi. What's this? He brought good news."

"Yeah." She nodded. "But I was so scared. I feel like I just found you."

He touched her cheek, brushed a tear away with his thumb. "And I just found myself. Sounds like I've lots more time for you and Ella. I can hardly wait."

The door whooshed open. "Spencer, what did Dr. Hayes say?" Andrea gazed at her father's twinkling eyes. Virginia reached out a hand and stopped dead. "Oh. Sorry, Andrea." She stuttered and blushed. "I didn't mean to interrupt."

Spencer took Virginia's hand. "Andi, you know Virginia."

The connection between her father and his assistant filled the room. More than friends. Andi rose. "See you two later." She strolled from the room.

Under a clear blue sky, she ambled along the sidewalks of Old Town. The scent of grilling burgers drifted in the air and she glided into Rehab Burger. The grilled chicken sandwich filled the plate, skin-on fries nestled around a small cup of marinara. Andrea sipped her iced tea. When the sandwich bore the marks of her sated hunger and one French fry remained, she texted Drew. His immediate response: —*Call me in an hour, please.*—

Fifty-five minutes later, James' overstuffed sofa cradled Andrea, and her bare feet rested on the coffee table. She reached for her phone and nearly dropped it when it played "Up, Up And Away." "You couldn't wait for me to call?" she asked.

"Knew you'd wait till the last second of one hour. I do know you well."

"Well, I hope so."

His voice changed from laughing to serious. She pictured the frown lines on his forehead. "How's Dad."

"Lucky, very lucky." She explained the diagnosis ending with, "He'll be out in a few days and with a little cooperation, his life goes on as before."

"So, when do you go home?"

"Couple days. I want to be sure there's no other problem. Drew, Dad's got a girlfriend or woman friend."

His deep chuckle carried over the phone. "Good for him."

"Yeah. His assistant, Virginia. Did you ever meet her?"

"Once. Thought she was married?"

"Widowed a couple of years ago." Andrea pictured Spencer's smile when Virginia walked into his hospital room. "She makes him happy."

"Good. He could use a little happiness. I'm happy with Jodi. Who knew married life could be this great?"

"It's because Jodi's amazing. Stars must have aligned for you to find her."

"She is amazing." He sighed. "Andi, thanks for teaching me what love meant. I sure didn't learn love or anything good about relationships from our parents." He laughed. "Did Jodi tell you the only reason she agreed to go out with me a second time was because I spent the first date talking about my sister?"

"Oh, Drew." She laughed. "And bragging about your sister convinced Jodi you were worth dating?"

"Yeah. Other guys talked about training, places they'd seen, their career. She asked me about my family, and I started on you and just couldn't stop."

Promising to keep Drew posted, Andi ended the call. She wandered through the condo looking at everything and seeing nothing. If someone asked her about family, she always answered two parents and one brother. Now she'd add Ella and Jodi. If she were honest, she'd include all the Bentons and Benton-Starks. Maybe even Carly Edwards would become family. Only thing missing was a forever partner. The door lock's electronic whir startled Andi from her inner dialog.

"Andi, I'm home. I brought dinner."

The following two days, Andrea divided her time between working and visiting Spencer in the hospital. When night descended, she crawled between the soft sheets of James' bed, curled around him. He rolled to his back and pulled her against the length of his warm body. Each kiss lit a fire, every touch a potent mix of sensual pleasure and comfort. When morning peeked through the shutters, Andi stumbled into the guest bath, showered, and looked into her eyes in the mirror. A worried frown appeared between her brows. Tomorrow she'd go home, back to her baby, back to her regular life. Tomorrow morning she'd ask James where he felt they were headed. Tomorrow.

At the door to Spencer's hospital room Andi listened for Virginia's voice. Only the television's murmur greeted her. She glided quietly into the room, and Spencer grinned at her entrance. "There's my girl. So you're going home tomorrow."

"Yep, and you get out of here the next day and it's all arranged." She grinned. "You're staying with Virginia for a few days."

Red suffused his face. "About that." He looked down. His fingers pleated the white sheet. "Virginia and I are more than friends."

"Yeah. I figured." She sat in the chair beside his bed and took his hand. "Good for you, Dad. Good for you finding someone."

He sighed. "She's amazing."

"So, are you going to live together? Is this a permanent move?"

"No. I'll go back to my apartment in a few days. But I've put an offer on the condo next door to hers."

"Very modern, Dad. You're doing the Live Together Apart thing." She kissed his cheek. "Good for you."

"Don't be too impressed. Living next door was Virginia's idea." He sighed and shook his head. "She says now is the first time she's had a space that was only hers. Decorated for her by her. She's not giving up her space."

Virginia arrived at lunchtime and Andi drifted away. When James pictured the future, what did he see? Live together apart like Virginia and Spencer? Except they'd live an hour and a half apart. Married, planning a life together like Drew and Jodi? Or did he see the limbo of friends with benefits? Their lives apart only together when convenient. Exclusive but not committed. The benefits part ending if one of them found someone else? She sipped her beer. Today alcohol for lunch, not her usual. She crunched the Cantina Taco, letting the mix of mellow cod and spicy salsa distract her. For the moment, she practiced mindful eating, enjoying the sensations of cold, warm, hot, mellow, and spicy. And while she chewed the taco, swallowed, and washed it down with cold beer, she accepted what James saw in his future mattered, but the deciding factor would be Ella's needs. Whatever was best for Ella's future and her own. She remembered thinking her parents were part-time parents, less than part-time for Drew. If she brought a man into Ella's world as father, he needed to be emotionally present full-time.

****

Enticing scents of coffee and bacon woke Andrea. Showered, changed, makeup applied, her steps hesitant, she strolled into the kitchen. James greeted her, "Just in time." He placed two plates of pancakes and bacon plus two mugs of coffee on the table. They dropped into chairs. Andrea sipped her coffee and tried the pancakes. Her throat closed. She set her fork down and watched James consume everything on his plate. He looked up into her eyes and raised his brows. "Don't you like it?"

"Of course I like it. It's my favorite breakfast." She sighed. "James what are we doing?"

"I'm eating breakfast but you're not," he answered. "What's wrong?"

"Dad and Virginia have decided to live together apart."

His face creased in a frown. "What's that mean?"

"He's buying a condo next to hers. They're committed but not sharing space."

"Good for them." His frown cleared. "Like us?"

"Kind of. We're living apart but sometimes together." Andi took a huge breath for courage and gazed directly into his eyes. "But are we committed? And will we ever have a legal commitment?"

"But we're exclusive. That's a commitment."

"Yeah. A commitment there won't be anyone else until one of us wants out." They picked up their plates and scraped them into the disposal, placed the dishes in the dishwasher. They stood side by side at the sink. Andrea felt his warmth all along one side even though an inch separated them. "When I was fresh out of college, all I wanted was someone to have fun with. A traveling companion to the beach, the ski resort, the newest restaurant. An escort always willing to take me home."

"Laurence?"

"Yep. Nothing very intense except his need to always be right." She shrugged. "Sounds pretty shallow but the relationship suited me until it didn't." She took his hands. "I'm thirty-three, a single mother, a homeowner living in a small town."

He wrapped her in his arms. His scent, mixed with lingering smells of coffee and bacon, surrounded her.

"And you need something deeper. You deserve everything, complete commitment." His breath tickled her scalp and pushed her curls around. "Andi, I don't know if I can be what you need."

She blinked, holding back the tears, and gently stepped out of his arms. "You will always be my friend, James."

"But that's not enough, is it? I'm lousy at relationships and have no idea how to be a father. I can't imagine watching you or Ella hurt because of my failures."

She lifted one hand and caressed his cheek. "I love you. Someday I hope you find someone you can love enough to take a chance." He grasped her hand and kissed her palm. "I'm sorry I'm not the one." She turned away.

He carried her bag down the stairs to her car and tossed it in the SUV. Her laptop bag and purse on the passenger seat, she climbed behind the wheel and turned the key before she fastened her seatbelt. He signaled her to roll down the window. He leaned in and softly kissed her lips. "Drive safe. Let me know when you get home." Exactly the same words he said every time.

A few minutes later, she pulled through the drive-through for coffee and moved into a parking space as far from the building as possible. Windows rolled down in the perfect Scottsdale fall weather, Andi laid her forehead against the steering wheel and wept. Her heart hurt, an emotional pain so great the muscles in her chest ached. The tears finally slowed. A gentle knocking on the door startled her.

"You okay? Do you need a doctor?" She looked

up. A gray-haired man wearing a plaid sport shirt and a Yankees baseball cap poked his head in. He blushed. "Oh sorry. Uh, thought you might be sick or passed out or something." He backed up and disappeared between the cars.

Andrea pulled the visor down and grimaced at the vision in the mirror. No wonder he ran away. Best clean up before she scared anyone else.

Two hours later, she pulled through the gate at Eckie House. Car parked, she grabbed her purse and laptop and took the back porch steps two at a time. She pulled open the back door and called, "Honey, I'm home." Laughter floated in the air.

"We're in the bookroom," Nikki's familiar voice called. Suddenly a weight lifted from Andrea's shoulders. Her family. With or without James, she had a family.

Andrea fell asleep on the day bed in Ella's room. She wasn't ready to sleep in her own bed away from Ella and with the specter of James' memory. She woke to the shushing sound of a rocking chair on wood floor. The full moon left a streak of yellow across the nursery rug and pushed shadows into the corners. A woman and little girl gradually took shape in a rocking chair, the girl's bright white nightgown a contrast to the woman's gray gown. "Momma, where's Daddy?" whispered the child.

"In heaven, Emaline. Daddy's in heaven." She kissed the top of the child's head.

"When can we bring him home?"

Tears sparkled on the woman's cheek. "We can't, baby. He has to stay there, and we need to stay here." The rocker slowed. "Someday when we're old we'll see him again. But not for a very long time." With her last word the rocker stopped, the pair dissolved. Andi fell back to sleep with tears in her eyes.

****

Orange and brown leaves crackled as the breeze pushed them along the ground. A puff of air caused a few to dance above the ground. Andrea watched their acrobatics from her chair on the back porch. Giggles floated on the air as Ella toddled from post to post. Wheels crunching on the gravel path added a jarring sound to the mix. Nikki was back. The stroller appeared around the corner at the same time the low growl of a truck engine drowned out the other sounds. Nikki's grin lit her face and she nodded toward the two mugs and teapot sitting on the table. "Were you expecting me or someone else?" She pushed the stroller up the ramp and angled it under the shade of a patio umbrella.

Andrea filled the second mug. "You, of course. You did warn me you'd be back this morning."

"Yeah. I wanted to stay and talk about your trip, but The Palace was calling my name." She took her first sip of tea. Two car doors slammed and the sounds of heavy footsteps on gravel announced visitors. Dressed in identical boots and jeans, Jude and Zack Healy rounded the building and walked toward the porch.

"Good morning." Jude's warm, deep voice rumbled as he stopped at edge of the porch. "Wanted to let you know we're visiting the studio. Ronni and Nathan invited us."

"Yeah. They told me." She pointed toward a fork in the driveway. "If you take the right fork you can park beside the carriage house."

"I know. Nathan told me. Just didn't want you to think some stranger was driving across your property." He nodded and turned away. "Thank you." Two voices, Jude's deep rumble and Zack's high ten-year-old squeak. They disappeared around the corner of the house. Two car doors slammed, the engine growled to life, and Jude's truck rumbled down the driveway toward the carriage house.

"Every time I see Jude I'm surprised." Nikki sipped the last of her tea. "The way he looks we should all be very afraid."

"But no one is. One look in those crystal eyes, a single smile from his bearded face, and you can't be afraid."

"The kindness rolls off him, almost like an invisible wave." Nikki chuckled. "Now we're starting to sound like Ainsley." Ella grabbed Nikki's jean clad leg and laughed. "Oh. You want to play our new game?" She stood Ella on her thighs, holding her around the waist for balance. "Okay. Time for the elliptical." Nikki moved her legs alternately up and down. Ella grabbed Nikki's forearms and giggled. "Enough you rascal," Nikki commented when Ella started bouncing on her legs. She lifted Ella up and swooped her down to the floor. Ella crawled away. Michelle let out a cry. Nikki pulled the stroller over, zipped through a quick change for Michelle's diaper, and cuddled her against her chest. Andrea retrieved a baby bottle of premeasured powder from the diaper bag, added water from a second bottle, and handed the mixture to Nikki.

"She's doing better on the formula?" Andrea plopped back in her chair.

"Yeah. Finally she's filling out." Nikki's mouth turned down. "I wanted to breast feed her but breastfeeding just wasn't working." Bottle empty, Nikki moved Michelle to her shoulder, patting her back. "Enough distraction. Andi, what's wrong?"

"I told James I need more than our casual relationship."

Nikki sighed. "I gather the conversation didn't go well."

"He believes he can't be enough." Andi watched Nikki grimace and roll her eyes. "I know he is enough; he has a lot to give. I'm sorry he can't love me enough to take a chance."

"Sometimes my very intelligent brother is really stupid." Nikki grabbed a handful of tissues from the diaper bag and handed them to Andi. "I hate he hurt you. You do know his problem has nothing to do with you, right? It's all about our dear old dad. If I thought it would help I'd hit him over the head."

Andrea pictured tiny Nikki beating on her very large brother. "Thanks, Nik."

"He's gonna be sorry he hurt you, and I don't think I'll have to do anything to show him the error of his ways." Nikki buckled sleeping Michelle into the stroller. "Stand up and give me a hug, Andi." Wrapped in Nikki's arms, Andi breathed a contented sigh. "Want to come home with me?" Andrea shook her head. "Yeah, if I had this I wouldn't either. Who would trade open space, peace and quiet for three noisy boys, an interfering silent partner, and a house full of paying guests?"

Ten o'clock, Andrea climbed between cool sheets on the daybed in Ella's room. Ella snuffled in her sleep then settled, her breathing even. Andrea focused on her breath. Breathe in, breathe out. Relax toes, ankles, knees. By the time she reached her cheeks she'd drifted into sleep. The sounds of faraway conversation mixed with music startled her awake. She slipped out of bed, into her heavy robe and slippers, and searched for the source. She tiptoed through the hallway and down the front stairs. At the last step she stopped. Animated but indistinct conversation flowed from the main parlor. Men and women dressed in eveningwear from the 1900s lounged on sofas and settees. Glasses and teacups perched on tables or were held in elegant hands. A smiling young woman in deep purple strolled among the groups, her gliding steps in time with the string quartet playing in the corner. Slowly the music faded, the number of people dwindled until only the woman in purple remained. She gazed directly into Andrea's eyes and disappeared.

Chapter Twenty-One

1922

Dear Momma,

Hope you are having a great day. Violet and Richard left this morning for Flagstaff. They decided if I stayed off the main road in Creekside, I drive just well enough not to hurt others or myself. The auto is so much fun! Richard and Violet taught several of the ladies to drive and a few of the older children. Outside of town, the roads are bumpy but mostly clear and barely traveled. I promised not to venture out alone, an easy promise to make since there is always someone at Eckie House interested in a new adventure.

What an exciting week we've had. Victoria Wyatt, who owns The Palace Hotel, hired Adeline O'Brian to care for Victoria's son. We'll miss Addy and Estella but they'll be living only a few blocks away. Victoria offered room, board, a salary, and training in running an inn. It's a great opportunity for Addy to become self-supporting and still be home with Estella.

~from Beloved Wife, Mother, Sister, and Friend, A Biography of Faith Taylor Eckie by Emaline Eckie Benson

****

November first, Andrea turned the page on her desk calendar and stared at a brand new month. Outside the French doors, autumn leaves danced across the veranda, swirling in eddies of a fall breeze. The first notes of "Up, Up and Away" chimed through the room. Andrea checked the image from the video doorbell, lifted a chattering Ella in her arms, and strolled from parlor to the front door. "Welcome to Eckie House, Mrs. Welles." Andrea greeted a white-haired woman with twinkling brown eyes and pulled the door wide.

"Thank you. Please call me Val, everyone does." Val stepped through the door. "Oh my, it's beautiful. I haven't been inside in years." For the next hour Val and Andrea sipped coffee in the parlor while Val explained her request. "We, the Historical Society, lost the venue for our gala. Carmody House had a small fire, no structural damage, but smoke damage." Food, drink, entertainment, and donations for the silent auction all arranged and no venue. Could they rent Eckie House?

Andrea caught Ella in her arms and balanced her on her hip. "Let me give you a tour first. See if you think the space will work." They meandered through the downstairs rooms. Val exclaimed over the large rooms, hallway bar, and finally the commercial kitchen.

"Eckie House is perfect," Val commented when they'd settled in the bookroom. Ella toddled around the room, a teething biscuit grasped in her tiny fingers. "Did you know Faith Eckie often hosted charity events in her large parlor?"

Andrea pictured last night's vision. "Does the Historical Society have much information about Eckie House?"

"Oh yes. *The Creekside Reporter* opened in 1905 and we have many of their issues," Val admitted. "Plus, Emaline Eckie Benson donated a scrapbook full of newspaper articles about Faith and Eckie House. Are you willing to follow in Faith's footsteps? Can we rent Eckie House?"

"You're welcome to use Eckie House, but I'm not comfortable renting it." Andrea shrugged. "I'm not in the business of being a venue, and I'd probably need a permit."

"Would you accept tickets to the event in lieu of rent?" Val asked. "We'll handle any permits, clean up, set up, everything. You'd be there anyway but some of your friends could join you." Andrea agreed and wrote Historical Society on her calendar for the third Saturday in November.

The sun glinted through the French door at a lower angle, sending a shaft of light across the bookroom's wood floor by the time Ella finished lunch and settled down in her crib for an afternoon nap. Andi opened her sleeping laptop and clicked on email. Drew's email, marked with a red flag, caught her attention.

Hi. They're here. The wedding photos. Click on the link below and enjoy the show. Video still a work in process (Nathan claims he's out of practice). Love, Drew and Jodi

Andrea clicked on the link and was suddenly transported back to the wedding. The rehearsal filled with laughter and silliness, pinning a lavender rose on Drew, the bridesmaids' procession, and then Jodi, so beautiful she glowed. The reception, first dance, dance with Drew, the erotic cake cutting. Next, random reception pictures. Alex standing behind Nikki, his arms around her waist. Chance whispering in Catherine's ear, her laughter visible. Ainsley dragging Jude on the dance floor, her red hair a curling waterfall down her back. Patrick dancing with one of the bridesmaids, her lavender dress flowing behind her, a contrast to Patrick's black suit. James, his arm around her waist. Andrea blushed. In the photo, she looked up at James, love obvious in the turn of her body, her smile. Why couldn't he love her back? She pushed through the rest of the photos. In the last one, Faith and George Eckie danced in a shaft of moonlight.

****

Sun glinted through the window and splashed across his mahogany desk. Morning rush hour traffic on Scottsdale Road created a cacophony of growling engines, squealing brakes, and honking horns. His back to the window, James stared at the spreadsheet open on his laptop. His hands rested on the desk, still. Four weeks since Drew's wedding, two weeks since the link for pictures arrived. He couldn't open the link. Not yet. There were probably fifty pictures of Andrea in there. This wasn't getting him anywhere. He accomplished nothing staring at a spreadsheet but seeing only Andrea the morning she drove away. He shut the spreadsheet down and clicked on email. He heard Jen laugh and shook his head. The associates took turns staffing the front desk. Sometimes he even took a turn. But the best was Jen. The clients and the other associates all loved her. The upbeat sound of her voice when she announced a visitor, the laughter when she joked with the clients, everything about her spoke of joy and a zest for living. He recognized the answering voice. His door opened and, a cup of coffee in each hand, Patrick strolled in. He set one cup in front of James and dropped into the client chair. James picked up the coffee and gazed into Patrick's sky-blue eyes.

Patrick sipped the coffee. "You look like shit."

"Thanks. For the coffee," James mumbled. Silence. The challenge they'd created as adolescents. Who would break the silence first? Usually James; Patrick had more patience than a saint.

Jen appeared just inside his door. Patrick nodded at her and she entered, a large manila envelope in hand. Patrick accepted the envelope. "Thanks, Jen." She sauntered away, closing the door silently. Patrick settled back in the chair, set the envelope on the desk, and sipped his coffee.

"Why are you here?"

"Brought you a present." Patrick shrugged and sipped the coffee. "And coffee. And free advice."

"Thought Mom made you promise not to meddle in my life anymore," James mumbled. "Though, I appreciate the coffee." He sipped and set the cup on the desk.

Patrick shook his head. "I don't know, bro. If I don't meddle, you might just end up a lonely old man."

James frowned, gaze locked on his brother's blue eyes. "Whatever you've got to say, say it. I'm busy."

Patrick laughed. "The way you look, you can't be accomplishing anything." He sipped the coffee. "You blew it, bro." He leaned his elbows on the desk. "You had a chance at something most of us would give a right hand for, and you blew it." He unclasped the envelope, set it on the blotter in front of James. "Beautiful woman, kind-hearted, strong, loving, everything any man needs plus the bonus of a super cute baby girl. Andrea loves you, but she's strong enough to move on if necessary."

"Maybe she should move on."

Patrick opened the envelope, pulled out a photo, and dropped it in front of James. "Look at her, the joy in her smile as she leans into you. A woman happy to be in love." Patrick stood and perched on the edge of the desk. "Now look at you." He pointed to James in the picture. "Tell me that's not a man who loves her right back." James stared at the photo. Patrick tossed his empty cup in the trash and shook his head. "You gonna let her get away? Let some other man fill your spot, raise Ella?"

"But what if I screw this up? I don't know anything about being a husband or a father," James admitted.

"That's ridiculous and insulting to our mom, not to mention our sister. We were so lucky with Mom; she could have become a bitter lady when she discovered Dad had a second family. Instead, we had an excellent childhood in a happy home; she set a high bar in the parenting department. Anyway, when it comes to parenting, most of us have no idea what we're doing. The first time I brought Scott home to Mom's, her only advice was to love him and remember I was the adult."

"What about being a partner?"

"Look at Alex and Nikki. I'm no expert, but my guess is beside their obvious love for each other they've found the knack of treating each other with generosity and kindness." Patrick pulled open the door and stepped out. "I thought you were smart, bro. You disappoint me." He disappeared behind the closed door.

Jen poked her head in the door. "I'm going to lunch. Want me to bring you back something?"

James shook his head. "No thanks. Let me know when you get back, okay?" She slipped out the door. He opened the laptop and clicked on Drew's email, then clicked on the link. Pictures of Andrea at the rehearsal, the ceremony, the reception. Andrea laughing with Spencer, dancing with Drew, in Patrick's arms as they glided across the floor. The last picture, Faith and George Eckie dancing in the moonlight. Their faces glowed with a love that lasted more than a hundred years. Their expressions the same as his and Andi's. A man and woman in love forever. He glanced at the calendar. Tomorrow night was the Historical Society party at Eckie House. He didn't have a ticket, but he did have the code to the back door.

Jen peeked her head in the door. "I'm back."

"Please, come in and give me a hand." James picked up two copies of his appointment schedule and Jen plopped down in the client chair. "Please, do you have time to help me reschedule all these or pawn them off on another associate or take some yourself?" He stared at calendar blocks filled with appointments. "I'll be gone next week, maybe longer."

"What should I tell the clients and the associates?" Jen asked.

"Tell the clients family emergency." Jen opened her mouth. "No, the only one with a problem is me. No one's sick or anything. You can tell the associates I'm planning on getting therapy for my lousy mood."

"Well, that's good news." She grabbed the schedule and sauntered out the door. As she disappeared around the corner, her laughter drifted through the door. "Now you owe me, James."

Chapter Twenty-Two

1928

Dear Violet,
I miss her too. My heart hurts and grieves for all of us. No matter we left home so young, you and I, we knew she was always there for us. Standing with Daddy then alone, always available with words of love and wisdom. She let us go because she believed we needed to leave. When George died, she reminded me to focus on remembering the love, and I'm taking her advice again and remembering her love. Although our momma's gone, her love lives forever inside us, warming our hearts and we gift it to our children. When you hold your little girl tonight, gift her our momma's love with yours and mine. Love always, Faith.
~from Beloved Wife, Mother, Sister, and Friend, A Biography of Faith Taylor Eckie by Emaline Eckie Benson

****

Bright sunlight turned the inside of his eyelids red and woke James from a sound sleep. He propped one eye open and knew immediately where he was. The sofa in Patrick's attic apartment. His neck hurt, his legs ached. This one time he should have listened to his older brother and opened the hide-a-bed. The short, narrow sofa left him feeling like someone spent the night hitting him with sticks. By the time he'd driven to Creekside, snuck up two flights of stairs, and yanked off his clothes, he was so tired he couldn't bear to pull open the bed. He stretched and swore every joint creaked. He sat up and grabbed his phone. Nine o'clock. If he didn't hurry, he'd miss breakfast. Instead of rushing around he texted Patrick. —*Please bring me breakfast. Can't let Nik see me. K?*—

Patrick's reply was immediate. —*Right.*—

Fifteen minutes later, he came out of the shower to find a tray on the small table, his brother lounging on the sofa reading the newspaper, and the scent of coffee floating in the air. He spent the day inside working. He answered emails, crafted apologies to clients and associates.

By the time the sun started its descent, James paced the small apartment. What if he was too late? What if Patrick was wrong and Andrea wasn't in love, just a sentimental woman thrilled by her younger brother's wedding? "Stop it." Patrick's voice brought James to a stop. "Whatever you're thinking just stop it." Patrick set his wine glass on the low table in front of the sofa. "We're leaving in ten minutes. You coming with us or planning a grand entrance?"

"Neither. I don't have a ticket so I figured I'd sneak in the back."

"I can fix that." Patrick reached inside the drawer of the coffee table, pulled out a ticket, and flipped it in James' direction. "Compliments of Andrea Hamilton. She thinks I'm bringing a date."

James stuffed the ticket in his shirt pocket. "You were pretty sure I'd show up."

"Nope." Patrick shook his head. "For a smart man,

bro, sometimes you're dumb. I wasn't sure at all. I decided to assume the best, though, after I saw you yesterday. You were a mess."

"What do you think? Should I just go with you guys?" James frowned. "I don't want to cause a scene or anything."

"Up to you but you'd best let Nik know you're here. If she sees you casually stroll into the party, she's likely to beat you about the head." He shook his head. "It wouldn't be pretty." Patrick stood and grabbed his suit jacket from the back of the sofa. "Get your jacket and let's face hurricane Nikki."

When they reached the landing, familiar voices carried from the lobby. Alex, Nikki, Scott, and Casey stood in a cluster by the bar. Eric grinned at Patrick and James. "Hey, guys."

Nikki turned toward James. Her eyes narrowed and lines formed between her brows. She took one step toward James, and Alex wrapped his arms around her from behind. She stopped and leaned against her husband.

James walked within striking distance of Nikki, leaned in, and placed a kiss on her forehead. "I'm gonna fix this, Nik. I promise."

She nodded once. "You'd better."

****

The main parlor filled with the fragrance of expensive perfumes mixed with the enticing scents of warming food. Animated conversation competed with "Blues In The Night," "Sentimental Journey," and "When You Wish Upon A Star" played by the five-piece band occupying a corner of the parlor. Her elbow propped on the foyer bar, Andrea grinned at the young man tending bar. "Is this gig easier or harder than a wedding reception?" He'd been the bartender at Drew's wedding.

Colter picked up a martini glass, wiped it dry, and returned it to the shelf. He shrugged. "Neither, just different."

"Who came up with the list of drinks?" she asked. "I've never heard of most of them." A sandwich board sign in elaborate calligraphy stood on the bar and proclaimed tonight's cocktails: The Sidecar, The Green Dragon, The Dubonnet Cocktail, and The Vesper.

"Aunt Val. She does the research and I practice until she's satisfied. Every year, she finds a few new ones for me to learn."

"So what's your favorite?"

"The Vesper. I've always seen myself as a young James Bond in Casino Royale."

"Then that's what I'll have. Give you a chance to channel 007." Colter started pulling ingredients from behind the bar, and Andrea glanced away to check out the new arrivals. She lifted her hand in a wave. Casey and Scott strolled toward her. Nikki and Alex followed. She saw Patrick behind Nikki, but Alex blocked Patrick's companion. Alex lay his arm across Nikki's shoulder, pulled her slightly to the side, and revealed James. Andrea's stomach clenched, her heart raced, and she felt her smile slip. The band jumped into "Boogie Woogie Bugle Boy" and she stiffened her spine. She could do this. Better they face each other now than over a family Thanksgiving dinner next week. She forced the corners of her lips back up.

"Hey, Aunt Andi, thanks again for the tickets." Scott leaned in and kissed her cheek. "We'll just drop off Casey's coat and browse." They ambled away, disappearing into the crowd.

Nikki stood directly in front of her, blocking James. She whispered, "Be strong. Make him grovel." They disappeared into the crowd. Patrick followed, but not before he placed a warm hand on her shoulder and squeezed. Now James stood directly in front of her.

"Andi, can we talk?" Twin frown lines appeared between his brows. "Please. Somewhere private?"

Before she could answer, a couple approached and asked questions about the house. James stepped aside. Val Welles, with twinkling eyes, strolled up and commented about the Vesper. James moved to her other side. She felt his presence, his warmth, and inhaled his scent. More guests approached with questions, comments, and thanks. Andrea's heart slowed, her gut unclenched. She'd survive the talk, whatever that meant. Maybe due to the alcohol in the Vesper or the approval and interest expressed by the guests, her strength returned. She glanced at the martini glass; only the lemon twist remained. Colter appeared in front of her and offered another drink. She shook her head. James ordered a Sidecar. She turned toward him. "Do you even know what's in it?"

He shrugged. "No idea. Couldn't picture myself drinking a scaly dragon." Andrea chuckled. "Dubonnet sounds girly. At least Sidecar sounded manly."

Colter set the sidecar in front of James. "What can I get you, Andrea?"

"Something without alcohol. Any ideas?"

"I've got just the thing." Colter started mixing something below the bar. He grinned and set a tall glass filled with cola, grenadine, and garnished with a cherry in front of her. "A Roy Rogers." Andi grinned and the band played "Don't Fence Me In." He winked at Andi. "I paid them to do that." He moved down the bar to help another guest.

Between brief conversations with guests, Andrea sipped her drink. She looked at the clock over the bar. "Shoot, look at the time. I have to check the silent auction." James lifted an eyebrow, set his now empty drink on the bar, and followed her. Inside the dining room, guests milled about the displays of goods for auction. Andrea headed for a corner near the door to the kitchen, James a step behind. She stopped in front of a bid sheet, grabbed a pen, and increased the bid by two hundred dollars. "I don't think anyone will go that high." She gazed at the painting propped in the corner.

James looked up at the painting. "Now I understand. It's from Winters' Gallery."

"Yep. The painting belongs in Eckie House because Violet lived in Eckie House." Andrea wove through the tables and stopped to chat with several guests. "I'm going up to check on Ella."

"Okay if I tag along?"

She shrugged and ambled into the kitchen, pulled open the stairway door, and glided up. Andrea carefully opened the nursery door. Stretched out on the daybed, Carly Edwards held a book in her hand. "She fell asleep an hour ago," she whispered and pushed herself to sit cross-legged on the bed.

"Do you need anything? Food or drink? Anything?" Andrea asked as she strolled to the crib. Ella slept sprawled across the mattress.

"Nope." Carly grinned. "This is working out perfectly. I should be able to finish my assigned reading tonight." With thanks for Carly, Andrea strolled out of the nursery. She stepped onto the main staircase and James joined her, matched his pace to hers.

"Carly Edwards babysitter?" James asked.

Andrea shrugged. "She asked to visit this weekend. When I told her about the gala, she volunteered."

As the last notes of "I Don't Want To Set The World On Fire" filled the air, Val Welles picked up a microphone. "Bidding closes in ten minutes. Remember you must increase the last bid by at least ten dollars to count. Good luck." She handed the mic to the bandleader and the upbeat sounds of "Rum And Coca Cola" blended with conversation.

Andrea strode to the silent auction. James kept pace beside her. Guests filled the room making one more bid. Weaving among the tables Andrea reached the painting. James slipped inside the room and waited, leaning against the wall near the door.

Val appeared in the doorway. "Time's up." Volunteers, identifiable by their nametags, grabbed the bid sheets and herded the guests out of the room.

Returned to the bar, Andrea ordered another Vesper and James braved the Dubonnet Cocktail. Andrea sipped her drink. "You've been very patient."

"You're already angry and hurt. Pushing my agenda wasn't going to get you on my side." They sat at the bar and watched a trickle of guests stroll out the front door. Several stopped to say good night.

The band moved into "Don't Get Around Much Anymore." As the final notes drifted away, the drummer raised a mic. "Folks, that's us, we don't get around much and right now we're getting around to our last number." A soft instrumental version of "Thanks

For The Memories" filled the room.

Sounds of music died away and Colter packed his supplies in boxes and carried them away. The vendors folded tables, packed their goods, and disappeared through the kitchen. Val stopped in front of them as they meandered through the house turning off lights in the large and small parlor. "We'll be back tomorrow at ten. I locked the rest of the auction items in the dining room for pick up tomorrow. Anything else I need to do for you before I gather my troops?" Andrea shook her head. Val gave her a quick hug. "Thanks again. You saved the day."

Carly appeared at the bottom of the steps. "I gave Ella a midnight snack, changed her, and she fell right back to sleep. That girl knows how to sleep. A girl after my own heart."

"Thank you for staying with her. You know you're welcome to stay the night."

Carly shook her head. "Nope. Casey invited me tonight. She's expecting me." She gave Andrea an awkward hug. "Thanks for letting me babysit. I'll stop tomorrow morning on my way back to school if it's okay?"

"We'll watch for you," Andrea answered. Carly strolled through the front door. As the door clicked shut Andrea heard a soft rustling sound on the stairs. At the top of the bannister a little girl with long brown braids sat poised. A soft giggle floated on the air and the little girl slid down the railing, disappearing as her hand touched the newel post.

Chapter Twenty-Three

April 10, 1932

Dearest Emmie,

My beautiful daughter, gorgeous bride, and woman in love, today you begin the next chapter. May your days be filled with wonder and gratitude. Though I ache at letting you go, I can hardly wait to see where life takes you, the adventures you have together, the dreams you turn into reality. May you remember the love and laughter of today; hold it inside your heart and let it comfort you when you hit bumps in the road. Wherever you go my heart is with you.

Love, Mom.

~from Beloved Wife, Mother, Sister, and Friend, A Biography of Faith Taylor Eckie by Emaline Eckie Benson

****

Doors locked, the house quiet, Andrea led James to the bookroom. She flipped on the low lights and the gas fireplace and dropped onto the sofa. James lounged at the other end.

James cleared his throat and took her hand. "Andrea, I've watched you for hours and my mind's a blank. Every word I meant to say, every argument I meant to make disappeared."

"Argument?" Andrea raised her eyebrows.

"Yeah. Arguments about why we should be together, why you should give me another chance."

Andrea's blood rushed under her skin, warmed her body, pushed her heart to a faster beat. He wanted her. Pain sliced into her. Wait. The day she walked out of his condo with a broken heart, she knew he wanted her. That was never a question. She pulled her hand away, pushed herself farther into the corner.

James grimaced. "I deserved that." His sigh was loud in the quiet room. "Andi, please. What do you need from me? What can I do or say so you'll love me again?"

She whispered, "I do love you."

The whoosh of his breath was audible in the quiet room. "Did I wait too long? Am I too late to bring us back together?"

"Too late for what?" she asked. "Bring us back together for what?"

He narrowed his eyes and wrinkles appeared between his brows. "Oh, Andi. I'm an idiot." He scooted across the sofa, his arm stretched across the back behind her, his thigh against hers. "Patrick's right. I am stupid." He leaned in, kissed her cheek, and took a deep breath, letting it out in a rush against her cheek. "I love you. Not like a sister. Not like a friend. I love you like forever. I even knew before I saw the picture of us from the wedding."

"Then why did you push me away?" Andrea took his hand and pulled his arm away from the back of the sofa across her shoulder. "You hurt me."

"And I regret hurting you. I regret so much," he admitted. "But I can't guarantee I won't hurt you again. Like Patrick says, for a smart guy sometimes I'm really stupid." His slightly callused fingers stroked her shoulder. "You just tell me I hurt you, and I'll fix it. I mean it. My only excuse is I was stupid and I was scared."

"Scared?"

"Yeah. I never missed anyone the way I missed you. Never needed to hear anyone else's voice before. Never was so desperate for someone else's happiness. One minute you were my little sister's best friend and the next you were everything." He shook his head, pushed their thighs close together. "Took my brain a while to catch up."

She leaned against his chest. The comforting rhythm of his heartbeat echoed in her ear and the scent of James and aftershave surrounded her. "And the next time, James? The next time emotions overwhelm you, are you going to pull away? Because pulling away can't happen. No running."

"I promise. No running away. If you catch me even thinking about running, you grab me tight and remind me I promised." He stroked her hair. "I'll stop. I'll be brave and I'll stay." He pulled her tight against him and whispered, "Please trust me. Give me another chance?"

The crackle of the fireplace, the settling of the old house combined with their quiet breathing. Andrea slowly relaxed her head against his chest. She let her eyes drift shut. James' heartbeat lulled her, his breathing a comforting presence. He claimed to love her. Moonlight glinted through the open shutters and danced across the polished mahogany desk. Beside the shutters, a man with a handlebar mustache embraced a young woman. He held her so close, the only things between them nightclothes and the woman's obviously pregnant belly. He placed his lips on hers. A sigh floated in the air and the couple disappeared.

Andrea untangled herself from James' embrace, stood, took his hand, and urged him to stand. She led him from the bookroom to the front door, clasped his hands, and gazed into his familiar hazel eyes. "Since Nikki brought me home from kindergarten like a lost puppy, I've loved you. First as a big brother, then with an adolescent crush, then as a close friend, member of my extended family. I know you. You're the guy who rescued his sister's friends when their car broke down or the blind date turned creepy. The uncle who gave his four-year-old nephew a bath without getting the cast wet. The godfather who moved his best friend's widow to safety." He opened his mouth; she placed a finger on his lips. "Let me finish, please. But it doesn't really matter what I know, what matters is what you believe about yourself. The last time we talked, you claimed you couldn't be what I need. Before I let you back into my life you need to believe we belong together, a perfect match, and you are enough." She lifted on her toes and gently kissed his lips. Her heart pounded. She'd believed she could move on from him. She could find someone who loved her enough, enough for forever. But, as his scent surrounded her, she accepted there would never be another. She could move on, but she could not love another man the way she loved him. "Go to the hotel, James. Examine your heart. If you believe in us, believe in yourself, come tomorrow evening."

He wrapped her in his arms, returned the gentle kiss, and whispered, "Good night, love. I'll see you tomorrow."

****

The sky boasted the bright colors of sunset and the

frosty air caressed his cheeks as James meandered through Creekside's residential streets. After a full day inside the hotel's library accepting his siblings' unsolicited advice, finally he heard only the voice in his own head and the rhythmic sound of his shoes on the sidewalk. When she wasn't haranguing him for hurting her best friend, Nikki claimed gifts were a good idea and begging a must. Patrick agreed. His right hand clasped Nik's cooler bag filled with food and a bottle of champagne. Yes, he brought gifts. Andrea didn't need gifts or begging. He finally understood she needed him to choose to open his heart and believe in their love forever. Self-fulfilling prophecy if he believed he was enough, loveable enough, kind enough, generous enough he would be filled with enough love to last forever. Enough to parent Ella and build a future including a family

He pulled open the iron gate and strolled between the towering spruces. The muted front porch light pulled him onward, home to Eckie House. Home because Andrea and Ella lived here. He raised his arm to knock and the door swung open. Andrea took his hand and led him to the bookroom. The monitor squawked and Andrea dashed out. James spread the food across the coffee table. Nik packed an excellent party, plates, napkins, wine glasses included. He popped the champagne cork but left the bottle in its ice blanket. He could hear Andi crooning to Ella through the monitor, so he flipped the switch on the gas fireplace and lit a candle on the coffee table. He settled on one end of the sofa and stared at the flames. If she didn't forgive him, if she sent him away again, he'd be back. Patrick was right; he'd be an idiot to give up a chance for a future with a loving woman and a beautiful baby girl, at least this particular woman and child. Life was all about choices. He chose to be a loyal friend, a supportive boss, a caring brother, uncle, and godfather. From this moment, he chose to be a loving partner to Andrea, a loving father to Ella. All he needed now was to convince Andrea.

"That looks excellent," Andrea commented as she dashed into the room. "Your sister packs an awesome picnic."

"How do you know Nik packed it?" He poured them each a glass of champagne. "This might be my packing."

She took the glass and settled on the sofa. "I recognize the candle, wine blanket, glasses, and plates." She sipped. "Looks like one of you ordered everything else from Wellington's."

"Yep. Not only does Nik pack a great picnic, she knows who to call for the food."

They spoke of Nikki and Patrick, the upcoming holiday, and the spirits who responded to Ella's cries before Andrea could. When only the partially empty champagne bottle and two glasses remained on the table, James took her hand. "You were right, Andi. I've spent my life afraid I wasn't enough. I love you, Andi, you, and Ella. For you I choose to be enough, to be what you need and want. Please, accept me; accept my love. I believe in us. I believe we are a perfect match. Whatever you want or need from me, I'm committed."

"Let me show you exactly what I want." She took his hand and led him in front of the mantel, flipped a switch beside the fireplace, and a tiny spotlight suddenly glowed on an immense painting. She pulled him back a couple steps and he moved behind her, wrapped his arms around her waist. She leaned her head against his shoulder. "Can we be that, James? Our love so strong it's forever."

"Forever," he whispered. "It's what I want too. Sometime beyond this life, that's where we'll be. Dancing in the moonlight. While our children and grandchildren live and love, you and I will be dancing in the moonlight." He turned her in his arms, leaned in, and placed a gentle kiss on her lips. Tiny kisses followed on her cheeks, behind her ear. He nuzzled her neck. His hands stroked her back, caressed the nape of her neck. Her heart beat hard behind her ribs; her blood heated, flushing her skin. "Somehow I'll make it up to you, Andi. Somehow I'll heal your hurt."

She pushed up on tiptoe, wrapped her arms around his waist, and placed her lips on his, touching gently. He followed her lead, kissed her back. She licked the seam of his lips, he opened, their tongues played, and passion heated the room.

He gentled the kiss, ending with tiny kisses at the edge of her lips. "May I stay with you? Not just for tonight but forever? Will you trust me to love you and Ella, build a life with you?"

"And will you trust us enough to stay even when loving isn't easy?" She touched his cheek, now scratchy from hours without a shave. "Because if you stay tonight, then you're committed. All in. No backing out."

"So was that a yes? Because I can't wait for the rest of our life to begin." He waltzed her across the room, dodging the desk. He twirled her in a circle, lifted her in his arms. She grabbed his shoulders for balance and laughed.

"Yes to everything. Yes to the rest of our life together." He slid her slowly down his body, placing her feet on the floor. He wrapped his arms around her, leaned in, and kissed her. She felt his passion, and this time she felt his commitment, his love.

She gentled the kiss and took his hand. She turned off the fireplace and lights and led him to the door. They both glanced back at the picture over the mantel. Through the window, moonlight glinted across the room, lighting the lovers forever dancing in the meadow.

Chapter Twenty-Four

From The Creekside Reporter. Obituary. May 2, 1953:

Today Creekside grieves the loss of a generous, compassionate, beloved member of our community. Surrounded by family Faith Elizabeth Taylor Eckie slipped into eternal rest last evening.

Born February 4, 1888, to Glen and Olivia Taylor of Phoenix, Faith married George Wyatt Eckie in 1905 and moved to Eckie House with her new husband. After the sudden passing of her husband in 1910, Faith opened Eckie House to women and children, providing shelter and hope. In a 1929 interview, the editor of The Creekside Reporter asked Faith what prompted her to offer Eckie House as a refuge. She smiled her infectious smile. "George built Eckie House because we meant to surround ourselves with the laughter of children. That's all I tried to do, fill the house with children's laughter."

She is survived by sisters Violet Tuley and Priscila Finch; brothers Douglas, Emory, and Clay; children Emaline Benson and George Eckie Jr.; four grandchildren, six great-grandchildren and a multitude of nieces, nephews, and friends.

Celebration of Life is scheduled for Saturday, May 7 at 11 o'clock in the morning at Emanuel Lutheran Church. In lieu of flowers, the family requests donations to Creekside Family Support Center, Foster

Family Support of Creekside or Emanuel Lutheran Church pre-school Scholarship Foundation. A reception at Eckie House will follow the Celebration of Life.

~from *Beloved Wife, Mother, Sister, and Friend, A Biography of Faith Taylor Eckie* by Emaline Eckie Benson.

****

The rumble of a familiar deep male voice counterpointed with baby giggles woke Andrea from a deep, but too short, sleep. Light peeked through the shutters. The clock's red numbers showed six-thirty. She threw back the covers. When her skin sprouted goose bumps, she realized she wore nothing. A winter nightgown decorated the footboard and she dropped the gown over her head. Stealthily, she glided from her room to the nursery door. Ella lay on the changing table, her chubby legs kicking in the air. One hand on her belly, James used the other to snap on the diaper.

"There you go, little lady. That was the heaviest diaper I've ever seen." He lifted her into his arms and buzzed her cheek. Ella giggled.

Andrea smiled at the picture they made, the very large man and tiny girl.

"Morning, Andi." He strolled toward her and kissed her cheek. "I think this one's ready for breakfast."

The next few hours flew by as they ate breakfast, showered, and changed. By nine o'clock, Ella played in the playpen in the kitchen while James and Andi worked together on the Thanksgiving turkey and stuffing.

As she chopped the apples, Andi felt the

engagement ring suspended on a chain bounce against her chest. Her face heated remembering their lack of clothing when James proposed. Definitely no engagement photos and not a story she'd tell their children. Memories of the passion when she agreed heated her blood.

James' hands moved confidently as he sliced celery and carried on a one-sided conversation with Ella. The scent of frying sage sausage combined with onion filled the kitchen. The sound of "Up, Up And Away" echoed through the house. Side dishes covered the stainless steel counter. A ham warmed in the oven. Salads and desserts filled the commercial refrigerator. The kitchen rang with voices and laughter.

In the main parlor, children played, laughed, toddled around holding onto the furniture. Older siblings and cousins supervised, moving breakables out of harm's way and distracting little hands from being too rough. Seated on the floor, Ella climbing on one leg and Michelle plopped on the other, Spencer laughed at their antics. James dropped down beside him, and Michelle crawled on his lap. "May I talk to you for a minute?" James asked.

Spencer grinned. "Sure." Virginia grabbed Ella, and Casey lifted Michelle. James and Spencer strolled onto the front porch.

"I've asked Andrea to marry me," James blurted. "She agreed."

"Of course she did." Spencer cuffed James on the shoulder. "She's a grown woman and her answer's the only one that matters." He chuckled. "Of course if you hurt her again, I'll hunt you down."

"Thank you, sir. I'll do my best not to hurt her."

"I know." Spencer wandered back inside, James on his heels.

Dinner was announced and the room filled with the sound of footsteps and children's piping voices. Parents herded children to the dining room. They assembled, standing around the table; Andrea took James' hand on her right side and Drew's on the left. The others followed suit until the circle was complete. Nearly thirty friends and family surrounded a table groaning with the weight of a feast.

Andrea said, "Let us pray. Dear Heavenly Father, thank you for friends and family gathered here. Surround those who are missing in your loving arms. Bless this house and our celebration of Thanksgiving. Amen."

A chorus of "Amen" filled the room. The scraping of chairs on the wood floor, the passing of platters and bowls of food joined the animated conversations.

Eventually, plates emptied and guests lounged back in their chairs. James rose and tapped his wine glass. He blushed. "We've an announcement. She said yes." Cheers and congratulations filled the air. Andrea slipped the diamond ring off her chain and onto her finger.

Spencer rose and lifted his wine glass. The room quieted. "To family and friends. To Love."

****

A final note from Emaline Eckie Benson:

Family and friends filled Emanuel Lutheran Church, spilled into the Narthex and onto the steps on May 7. During the reception at Eckie House, the hum of conversation soared through the rooms, joined by the joyous sound of children's laughter. Exactly as my

mother dreamed, exactly as my father promised.
   ~from *Beloved Wife, Mother, Sister, and Friend, A Biography of Faith Taylor Eckie* by Emaline Eckie Benson.

A word about the author...

An Arizona native, I spent my childhood visiting small towns and campgrounds all over the state and entertained myself on long car trips writing stories. Married and living in Scottsdale, I still imagine every new acquaintance's story and spend my free time traveling, reading, walking my tiny dog, and practicing yoga.

http://stellajaynephillips.com

Thank you for purchasing
this publication of The Wild Rose Press, Inc.

For questions or more information
contact us at
info@thewildrosepress.com.

The Wild Rose Press, Inc.
www.thewildrosepress.com